Aunt Dimity
Digs In

Aunt Dimity
Digs In

Nancy Atherton

VIKING

VIKING
Published by the Penguin Group
Penguin Putnam Inc., 375 Hudson Street,
New York, New York 10014, U.S.A.
Penguin Books Ltd, 27 Wrights Lane,
London W8 5TZ, England
Penguin Books Australia Ltd, Ringwood,
Victoria, Australia
Penguin Books Canada Ltd, 10 Alcorn Avenue,
Toronto, Ontario, Canada M4V 3B2
Penguin Books (N.Z.) Ltd, 182–190 Wairau Road,
Auckland 10, New Zealand

Penguin Books Ltd, Registered Offices:
Harmondsworth, Middlesex, England

First published in 1998 by Viking Penguin,
a member of Penguin Putnam Inc.

PUBLISHER'S NOTE
This is a work of fiction. Names, characters, places,
and incidents either are the product of the author's imagination or
are used fictitiously, and any resemblance to actual persons, living
or dead, events, or locales is entirely coincidental.

ISBN 0-670-87061-7

Printed in the United States of America

For the Bubble Brigade,
friends indeed

Aunt Dimity
Digs In

1.

I had two infants at home and I was drinking heavily: two pots of tea before noon and another pot before nap time. For some reason, I was having trouble sleeping.

It wasn't the caffeine—as a nursing mom, I stuck to herbal tea—and it wasn't the twins' fault, either. After three grueling months of round-the-clock feeding, Will and Rob had discovered the joys of sleeping through the night—and given their parents a chance to rediscover those same joys. My husband and I now had a full six hours of blessed silence in which to recover from the rigors of the day.

But while Bill used those golden hours to full advantage, dropping off still fully clothed and usually on the sofa, I catnapped restlessly, listening with a mother's ears for the softest cry, the tiniest cough or gurgle.

It wasn't new-mother jitters alone that kept me awake all night. Will and Rob had been born too soon, in March instead of April, and they'd spent their first full week on earth entombed in incubators. At four months they were strong as bulls—with the lung power of pearl divers—but the fears attending those first uncertain days had never truly left me.

The world, which for the most part had treated me with kindness, now seemed a treacherous, threatening place in which every corner of every coffee table had been fashioned solely for the purpose of battering my boys' brains out. It was up to Bill and me to protect our sons from lurking coffee tables, and we took our responsibilities very seriously.

We fled Bill's family mansion back in noisy, bustling Boston and brought the boys to England, to a honey-colored cottage in a tranquil rural corner of the Cotswolds. The cottage had been left to me by my late mother's closest friend, a woman named Dimity Westwood, and I could think of no more perfect place in which to raise a family.

Bill bicycled each day to Finch, the nearest village, to an office on the square where, via fax, modem, and telephone, he conducted business for his family's law firm. He traveled to London once a month, and farther when necessary, but for the most part he was home for lunch and rarely late for dinner.

It wasn't the food that drew him. Meals at home hadn't amounted to much since the early days of my pregnancy, when I'd brought my culinary skills to bear on the creation of wholesome baby foods. Bill had grown accustomed to mealtimes spent taste testing samples of mystery mush.

William Willis, Jr.—my own sweet Bill—was the kind of husband every woman dreams of, the kind of father every child deserves. He changed diapers, gave baths, sang lullabies, and heroically rode out hormonal tidal waves of the postpartum variety that had me wobbling unpredictably between laughter and tears. He shared my absorption in our sons and seemed to understand my need to envelop them in a danger-free environment. He said nothing as I swaddled each piece of furniture in cotton batting, and didn't utter a word of protest when I secured the kitchen cabinets with latches so complex that neither he nor I could open them for days.

But when Bill came into the master bedroom one evening in early July to find the boys watching from their bouncy chairs as I wrestled with the mattress on our football field–sized bed, he must have thought I'd well and truly lost it.

"Lori," he said softly, standing in the bedroom doorway, "what are you doing?"

"Taking the mattress off the frame," I grunted, tugging ineffectually at a recalcitrant corner.

"Why?" Bill asked, very gently.

I rolled my eyes at him, as though the answer were self-evident. "What if Will and Rob crawl under the bed and it collapses on top of them? Much safer to have the mattress on the floor."

Bill surveyed four dimpled knees and tiny waving hands that had yet to touch the carpet, and said, "I see."

Something in his tone of voice made me pause. I stared down at the mattress, glanced over at the boys, then recoiled from the bedding, as though it had burst into flame. "Bill," I whispered, shaken, "what *am* I doing?"

"It's more what you're *not* doing." Bill took me by the hand and pulled me over to the armchair by the dresser. He nudged the mattress back into its frame, squatted for a moment to gobble Will's belly and snuffle Rob's chin, then sat on the footstool at my knee. "You're not sleeping," he elaborated. "You're not eating right. You're not getting enough fresh air and exercise." He looked pointedly at the mattress. "It's no wonder you're going overboard."

I whimpered. "B-but the boys—"

"The boys are fit as fleas," Bill broke in. He swung around to make a face at his bright-eyed, drooling sons. "Look at them. Dr. Hawkings said he's never seen preemies rally so well. You've done a magnificent job, Lori."

I smiled weakly. "*We've* done a magnificent job."

"I've done what I can," Bill acknowledged, turning back to me, "but I'm not here all day, the way you are. Taking care of one child is enough to run a full-time mom ragged, and you've got two. Let's face it, love—you're outnumbered."

I sank back in the chair and nodded miserably. "I have been more tired than usual lately."

"And more strung out," Bill asserted. "Now that we've gotten the boys up to speed and started on solid foods, it's time for you to take a break."

"*Leave* my babies?" I gasped, horrified.

"Of course not," Bill said hastily. "But I've talked things over with Dimity—"

"When?" I demanded. "When did you talk things over with Dimity?"

"Last week, when you padlocked the medicine cabinet and hid the key so the boys wouldn't find it," Bill replied. "Have you remembered where you hid it yet?"

"Er . . ."

"Never mind." Bill pulled my feet into his lap and began kneading them gently. "The point is that Dimity thinks it'd be a good idea to hire someone to help you with Rob and Will. And I agree."

I blinked at him, incredulous. "You can't be serious. I'd never let a stranger take care of my boys."

"Then she can help with the laundry and the cooking and all the other housework," Bill said reasonably. "Anything to give you a breather. Lori," he added, grasping my toes firmly, "Aunt Dimity says that you have to start taking care of yourself or you'll be no good at all to our sons."

Bill had spoken the magic words, and wisely refrained from saying more while he waited for them to take effect. He knew that I never quarreled with what Aunt Dimity said—rather, with what she wrote, since her conversation was confined to sentences written in a small blue leatherbound book, which we kept in the study. I'd been too busy to consult with Aunt Dimity since the boys had arrived, but she'd apparently been keeping watch over me—and worrying about what she saw.

Had I really given her cause for alarm? I closed my weary eyes and thought back over the past three months. A few scenes stood out with pristine clarity: Bill and his father changing diapers side by side during one of Willis, Sr.'s frequent visits; the boys' first splashy bath in the padded bassinet; a hushed, golden morning with Bill rocking Rob while I nursed Will, both of us pajama-clad and drowsy and besotted by the bundles in our arms. Most of my memories were blurred, though, one day running into the next without shape or distinction, like a watercolor left out in the rain. It was not how I wanted to remember my sons' childhood.

"Maybe you and Dimity are right," I conceded at last. "Maybe I have been overdoing it."

Bill choked back a snort of exasperated laughter and pulled the rest of me into his lap. "Have you ever done anything *without* overdoing it?" he asked, nuzzling my dark curls.

I smiled sheepishly. "Okay. I admit it. I could use some help around here." I pushed away from him to ask, "But how do we find the right person? I don't know anyone in the village."

Although we'd been living at the cottage for nearly a

year, Finch was about as familiar to me as the far side of the moon. I'd spent my entire pregnancy memorizing child-rearing manuals, knitting oddly shaped booties, and turning every available scrap of food into nutritious goo. My social calendar had been left to gather dust.

"There's Emma and Derek," I said, "but they've already got full-time jobs." Emma and Derek Harris lived up the road from us in a fourteenth-century manor house they'd refurbished. Emma was a computer engineer and master gardener; Derek, a building contractor who specialized in restoration work. They were our closest friends in England, but I somehow doubted that they'd jump at the chance to mop floors or launder loads of diapers.

"There's Ruth and Louise, of course," I continued thoughtfully, "but I don't think they'd have the stamina." Ruth and Louise Pym were identical twin sisters who shared a house just outside of Finch. No one knew how old they were, but the fact that their memories of the First and Second World Wars were equally vivid suggested that they weren't spring chickens.

"And Sally Pyne . . ." I was on my feet now, ticking off the short list of locals with whom I was personally acquainted. Sally Pyne was the cherubic, white-haired widow who ran the tearoom next door to Bill's office. She was good-natured and energetic, ". . . but Emma told me that Sally's granddaughter is staying with her this summer, so I imagine she has her hands full. So who . . . ?" I turned to Bill and saw that he was examining his fingernails, a smug smile plastered across his face. "Don't tell me you've already found someone!"

"Okay. I won't." Bill nodded agreeably and leaned over to lift a cooing Rob from his bouncy chair. "Let's get these poor mites fed and ready for bed."

I spent the remainder of the evening trying doggedly to

worm additional information out of my insufferably self-satisfied husband—and Dimity—but the only detail I was able to nail down was that "someone suitable" would be arriving shortly.

I wasn't taken completely by surprise, therefore, when the Pym sisters fluttered up my flagstone walk on Monday morning with a calm and competent-looking dark-haired woman in their wake.

It was the other woman, the one who showed up screaming, who surprised me.

2.

I answered the front doorbell slightly flustered, with Will on one shoulder, Rob on the other, and a generous helping of hideous green glop smeared across my canvas apron.

Ruth and Louise Pym, by contrast, looked as though they were on their way to an Edwardian garden party. They were, as always, dressed identically, in dove-gray gowns with lace collars and tiny pearl-shaped buttons. They wore matching gray-and-cream cameos at their matching throats, sprigs of lavender pinned to their diminutive bosoms, and crocheted ivory gloves on their dainty but capable hands.

The third woman towered above the Pyms like an exotic hothouse bloom above a pair of Michaelmas daisies. She was a stranger to me, tall, broad-shouldered, and voluptuously curved, with an olive tint to her complexion, full lips, and almond-shaped eyes so dark they were almost black. Her auburn hair was drawn back from a high forehead and braided in an intricate coil at the nape of her neck. She wore a severely plain white shirtdress and comfortable-looking beige flats. The open collar of her dress revealed a slender leather thong from which hung a curious bronze-colored medallion.

I detected a look of swift appraisal in her dark eyes and blushed self-consciously as I greeted the Pyms. Even on my better days I looked like a scrub beside them, and this was not one of my better days.

"My dear Lori," said Ruth. Ruth always spoke first. It was the only way I could tell the two sisters apart. "You look the very picture of . . ."

". . . industry," Louise continued. Watching the Pym sisters converse was like watching a Ping-Pong match. "We do hope we haven't come . . ."

". . . at an inconvenient time. We would have rung first . . ."

". . . but Bill urged us to drive over straightaway."

The Pyms' car, an ancient vehicle with a wooden dash, quilted upholstery, and running boards, was parked on the graveled drive beside my black Morris Mini and the Mercedes Bill drove on rainy days.

"You know I'm always glad to see you," I assured them, wishing I'd taken a minute to sluice the boys down before answering the door.

"And how are our . . ."

". . . sweet angels today?"

"Fine, just fine," I managed. Will and Rob had by now recognized the Pyms' familiar voices and were squirming to get a look at the only other pair of identical twins they'd ever met. As Bill had pointed out the night before, I was outnumbered, and when the dark-eyed woman reached for Will, I handed him over with a wholly unanticipated sense of relief.

"Thanks," I said. I shifted Rob so he could see where his brother had gone, and felt a perverse twinge of dismay. Will was taking the handover much too cheerfully. He dribbled happily on the dark-eyed woman's shirtdress and showed more interest in flirting with Ruth than in fussing about who was holding him.

Ruth was not immune to Will's charms, but as she leaned in to rub noses with him she said, in a puzzled voice, "Lori, are you certain that our darling Will . . ."

". . . is feeling quite himself today?" Louise's bright eyes had also fastened on my son.

"I think so," I said, my pulse quickening. "Why? What's wrong?"

Ruth's brow wrinkled. "He seems to have come out . . ."

". . . in little green spots. As has his darling brother." Louise was now peering closely at a wriggling Rob. "I've seen red spots before, and pink ones . . ."

". . . but never green ones," said Ruth. "I do hope it's nothing . . ."

". . . tropical."

My heart unclenched. "It's not a rare disease," I told them. "It's avocados. I forgot to put the lid on the blender." I stood aside. "Please, come in. The cottage is a bit of a mess, but—"

"Tut," said Ruth, as she stepped over the threshold. "I'm certain you've had far more important things on your mind recently . . ."

". . . than housekeeping," Louise finished cheerfully, following me up the hall and into the living room. "And rightly so. What could be more important than . . ." The Pyms' dueling dialogue trailed off into a politely discomfited silence.

I was almost as nonplussed as Louise. I distinctly remembered the living room as one of the most inviting rooms in the cottage, but at the moment it looked as though a gang of tramps had been camping out in it. Yards of cotton batting dangled from the coffee and end tables, an overflowing basket of laundry obscured the fireplace, parenting magazines spilled from the cushioned window seat to the floor, and a chaotic tangle of toys, stuffed animals, and oddly shaped booties littered the overstuffed armchairs and sofa.

The dark-eyed woman picked her way down a narrow path leading from the doorway to the playpen, but I had to kick aside a set of building blocks, a sock puppet, and a whole circus of plastic animals to enable Ruth and Louise to reach the sofa.

"Sorry about the mess," I mumbled, scooting ahead to clear the sofa's cushions by shoving an army of stuffed animals onto the floor. "I guess things have gotten a little out of hand."

"That's why we've come," said Ruth. "That's why we've brought you . . ."

". . . an extra pair of hands," Louise went on. "Please allow us to introduce . . ."

". . . our very dear friend . . ."

". . . Francesca Angelica Sciaparelli."

The dark-eyed woman straightened from the playpen, where she'd carefully deposited a gurgling Will. "How d'you do?" she said.

As if in answer, Rob threw up on my shoulder.

"Come, give him to me." The woman crossed to where I stood, and held out her arms. "I'll give him a wash while you get yourself a fresh blouse."

I don't know why I handed Rob over to her so readily. It may have been because I trusted the Pyms' judgment. It may have been because of her willingness to take charge of a pukey, avocado-stained four-month-old, or because of my acute awareness of the aroma rising from what was already my second blouse of the day. But I think it was the smile in her eyes that did the trick, the understated gleam of understanding.

"It'll save time if you call me Francesca," she added in a soft, west-country burr that seemed at odds with her distinctly un-west-country name. "Sciaparelli is too much of a mouthful for every day."

"I'm Lori," I told her.

"I know." Francesca turned slowly to survey the room. "I've always been fond of this place."

"You've been here before?" I asked.

"Many times," said Francesca. "Miss Westwood moved to London after the war, but she kept the cottage, as a kind of retreat. My father looked after it for her when she was away. Miss Westwood was always a good friend to my family."

"She was a good friend to me, too," I said.

"I'm sure she was." Francesca closed her eyes and inhaled deeply. "Lilacs. Such a pretty scent. Lilacs were Miss Westwood's favorite flower. Funny how scents can bring back memories. If I didn't know better, I'd swear Miss Westwood was somewhere about the place."

"It's because I haven't changed anything," I said quickly. "The cottage is pretty much as Dimity left it—except for the mess."

I steeled myself for the moment of separation, then told myself firmly not to be such a ninny. If Dimity had decided to lay down a lilac-scented welcome mat for Francesca Sciaparelli, I had nothing to worry about.

"I guess I'll . . . I'll be right back." I kissed Rob's foot and, for the first time since the twins had been born, climbed the stairs alone.

Panic assailed me the moment I reached the bedroom.

I peeled off my soiled apron and blouse, flung them in the general direction of the hamper, and grabbed a fresh blouse from a pile in the closet. I was dashing out of the bedroom, still doing up my buttons, when a glance in the full-length mirror stopped me cold.

Who was that wretched wraith staring back at me?

Her short dark curls were dappled with dried avocado, her brown eyes smudged with bruises of fatigue, and although her blouse stretched tightly across unusually full breasts, her jeans hung from her hips as though she were a scarecrow. I stretched a hand out toward the mirror and realized, with a shudder, that I was staring at a sickly pale imitation of *me*.

"Good grief," I murmured dazedly. "I'm in worse shape than the living room. Why hasn't Bill—"

I left the foolish question hanging fire. Bill could've shot off flares and sent up fireworks and it wouldn't have made any difference. For the past four months I'd put myself on hold for the twins' sake, and no amount of nagging, pleading, or reasonable argument would have persuaded me to alter my priorities.

But things were different now. As Bill had said, the boys were fit as fleas. They'd not only caught up with their peers, they'd outpaced every growth chart Dr. Hawkings could produce. The boys' doctor couldn't explain it, but maybe Bill had hit the nail on the head: Maybe I *had* done a magnificent job.

I began to preen proudly in front of the mirror, but the reflected image was so pathetic that I wound up cringing. Maternal boot camp had definitely taken its toll.

"Ruth?" I called, moving toward the top of the stairs. "Louise? Will you be okay without me for a few more minutes?"

"Take your time," Ruth warbled. "We're getting along . . ."

". . . famously."

I hesitated, then turned and marched resolutely into the bathroom for a shower and shampoo. It was the height of luxury to wash my hair in the middle of the morning, even though I had to clear the tub of squeaky toys and sailboats. I felt almost sinful as I changed into a completely fresh set of clothes and descended to the ground floor smelling of soap instead of baby.

I felt irredeemably sinful when I saw what had happened to the living room. Toys had been piled in one corner, stuffed animals in another, and the dangling yards of cotton batting had been folded into soft bumpers that fit each table snugly. The laundry basket, along with assorted booties, had been whisked out of sight, and my parenting magazines, standing in ranks beneath the window seat, no longer blocked the sunlight streaming through the diamond-paned bow window. Ruth and Louise stood over my sons, who were not only green-spot-less but contentedly blowing spit-bubbles in the playpen.

I tiptoed toward the kitchen, drawn by the sound of sloshing water, and stood in the doorway, blinking dazedly. Francesca was mopping the floor, having already removed the spattered evidence of the blender incident from the cabinet doors and countertops, and put the dirty dishes in the dishwasher. Overwhelmed by the sight of a gleaming floor and an empty sink, I leaned against the door frame and began to blubber.

"What's all this, then?" Francesca said, setting the mop aside.

"It's . . . just . . . so . . ." I covered my face with my hands and hiccupped helplessly.

"A breath of fresh air . . ."

". . . will soon put you right, my dear."

Ruth and Louise swept up the hall to take me by the elbows and steer me out into the back garden. Ruth used her cambric handkerchief to dust off the stone bench beneath the apple tree, and Louise handed her own embroidered hankie to me.

I blotted my tears as I sat down, bracketed by solicitous Pyms. "You must think I'm a terrible mother," I sniffled.

"We think nothing of the sort," Ruth declared. "You're simply . . ."

". . . a *new* mother," said Louise. "And no amount of studying can possibly prepare a woman . . ."

". . . for the demands of motherhood." Ruth nodded. "We've seen it . . ."

". . . all too often. Why, when Mrs. Farnham, the greengrocer's wife, had her three delightful daughters . . ."

". . . Mr. Farnham's shop was at sixes and sevens for months!" Ruth smiled fondly at the memory. "Damsons with the onions, sultanas with the almonds . . ."

". . . and cabbages everywhere!" Louise's identical smile appeared. "It's only to be expected. A truly good mother . . ."

". . . always puts her children before her cabbages."

I looked from one pair of bright eyes to the other. "Is that what I've done?"

"Of course it is!" Ruth exclaimed. "That's why we've brought Francesca to you. While you look after the boys . . ."

". . . she'll keep your cabbages in order." Louise clasped her gloved hands together excitedly. "She cooks, cleans, sews . . ."

". . . and she's perfectly magical with children," Ruth informed me.

"But who is she?" I asked. "Is she from Finch?"

"Francesca was born and raised on her father's farm . . ."

". . . not far from the village," said Louise. "She lives there now with her eldest brother and his wife . . ."

". . . and their eight children."

"Eight children . . . ?" I nearly swooned.

"Yes, the Sciaparelli farm is quite a lively place. Francesca's had . . ."

". . . bags of experience with babies." Louise exchanged a hesitant glance with her sister before adding, delicately, "We'd rather hoped, however, that you might have room for her . . ."

". . . here at the cottage," said Ruth. "Francesca's thirty-seven years old, you know. She's spent all of her adult life nursing her sick parents and looking after her brother's children. She needs a change of scene . . ."

". . . as much as you do, Lori. Would it be too great an imposition?"

Images of sparkling kitchens and clutterless living rooms danced in my bedazzled brain. "Well," I said slowly, "there's the guest room. It's right next to the nursery, so—"

"Perfect!" Ruth got to her feet. "We'll retrieve Francesca's things from our motor . . ."

". . . and tell her the happy news." Louise had also risen. "You rest quietly in the shade awhile, Lori . . ."

". . . while we help Francesca settle in." Ruth linked arms with her sister, and they fluttered back into the solarium.

Rest quietly, while a stranger moved into my cottage? Panic bubbled ominously, but I clamped a lid on it. I needed help, I reminded myself, and I was getting it from the most exclusive employment agency in the British Isles.

Pyms, Extremely Ltd., was as reliable as April rain, and Dimity had already signaled her lilac-scented approval.

A warm breeze drifted through my damp curls and I drifted with it, soothed by the sounds of high summer. We'd had a dry start to the season, and were in the midst of a hot, muggy spell reminiscent of the sticky Chicago summers of my childhood.

Still, the apple tree's shade was delicious, and the light breeze helped cool the humid air. I might, with a little practice, grow accustomed to resting quietly. A robin whistled in the leafy branches above my head, bumblebees hummed among the daisies and delphiniums, and a pair of sparrows splashed in the rose-wreathed reflecting pool. I gazed from one tranquil tableau to the next with growing anxiety and muttered dismally, "Emma will *kill* me."

My best friend and next-door neighbor, Emma Harris, had designed, built, and painstakingly planted my back garden. Spring was Emma's favorite season, but it had come and gone without my noticing. I'd missed the lilacs and tulips, the bluebells and daffodils, the redbuds flowering down by the brook. I glanced guiltily at the leaves overhead, knowing I'd missed the apple blossoms, too.

Emma Harris was an artist. Her greatest reward was a quiet sigh of admiration, but I hadn't managed so much as a grunt this year. I'd spent Emma's favorite season holed up inside the cottage, scarcely conscious of the marvels she'd wrought with hoe and spade. I felt like an ungrateful worm.

"I'll make it up to her," I vowed. And I'd start right now, by making the most of this opportunity to savor the peaceful haven she'd created. I leaned back against the apple tree, tried fully to appreciate each trembling leaf, each glorious blossom, and failed. My eyelids were too heavy, nature's music too hypnotic. I tuned in to the bumble-bees . . . dozed . . . and was rudely awakened.

"Lori Shepherd!" a voice thundered, sending birds and bees scrambling for cover. "That man must be stopped or there'll be *bloodshed!*"

3.

"Wh-what?" I blinked the apparition into focus and felt my blood run cold.

Peggy Kitchen was standing in my garden.

Peggy Kitchen—shopkeeper, postmistress, and undisputed empress of Finch—had not only talked me into donating an irreplaceable heirloom afghan to the Saint George's church-fund auction, she'd also convinced my semisedentary and wholly unmusical husband to strap on bells and dance at dawn on May Day with Finch's geriatric troupe of morris dancers. Bill bought back the afghan—for the price of a year's beeswax candles—but he could do nothing to keep Peggy from plastering her shop with incriminating photographs of him waving a white hankie while prancing dementedly on the village green.

Peggy Kitchen was an extremely dangerous woman.

Pointy glasses dotted with rhinestones, graying hair in an obligatory bun at the back of her head, flowery dress cloaking a mature figure—her disguise would have been perfect but for the lunatic glitter in her pale blue eyes. Peggy Kitchen was on the warpath—again—and I'd somehow ended up in her line of fire.

"Hi, Peggy," I croaked.

"Would've rung first," Peggy barked, "but Bill agreed that this matter was *far too pressing* to be discussed over the telephone." I flinched as she smacked fist against palm for emphasis.

"I'm sure he's right," I said gravely, wondering how many more unannounced callers Bill planned to send my way before lunchtime.

"He is!" Peggy roared. "If *that man*"—*smack, smack*—"isn't gone by the seventeenth of August, I won't be responsible for my actions!"

"Er," I began, but relapsed into silence when Francesca's statuesque figure appeared in the solarium's doorway.

"Morning, Mrs. Kitchen." Francesca squared her shoulders and folded her strong arms. "Fine day, isn't it? All this peace and quiet—just the ticket for a pair of babes like the two I'm looking after." The faintest hint of steel entered her purr. "You'll keep the noise down, for their sake, won't you, Mrs. Kitchen."

It was not a question, and Francesca didn't wait for a reply. She simply turned on her heel and disappeared into the cottage, leaving me alone with a ticking Peggy Kitchen. I held my breath, awaiting the explosion.

"Humph," said Peggy. She stared daggers at Francesca's retreating back, sat beside me on the bench, and murmured, "You're letting *that woman* look after your cubs? After what her father did?"

"What did her father—"

"I've no time for gossip," Peggy interrupted, glancing nervously at the cottage. "I've a crisis on my hands and I need your help."

"What crisis?" I asked.

"It's *that man!*" Peggy repeated in a furious whisper.

"That specky professor who digs things up. If he wants to muck about in Scrag End, that's his affair, but I won't have him mucking up my festival!"

"The festival . . ." I clung to those words as to a slender reed of sense in a rushing river of babble. *That specky professor* and *Scrag End* meant nothing to me, but even I, in my self-imposed isolation, had heard about Peggy's festival. I doubted that there was a kayaking Inuit or a Sherpa climbing Everest who hadn't received one of her harvest-gold flyers. My cottage had been bombarded by no fewer than seven.

> *Come One, Come All*
> *to the*
> *Harvest Festival!*
> *Saturday, August 17—10:00 A.M.*
> *Exhibitions! Competitions!*
> *Demonstrations of Arts & Crafts!*
> *Traditional Music & Dance!*
> *Refreshments at Peacock's Pub*
> *Organ Recital*
> *and*
> *Blessing of the Beasts*
> *at*
> *Saint George's Church—9:00 A.M.*
> *£2 General Admission Pets and Under 5's Free!*

"Is there a problem with the Harvest Festival?" I asked timorously.

"Is there a *problem?*" Peggy snorted. "I've been stabbed in the back, *that's* the problem!"

"By the specky professor?" I hazarded.

"No," Peggy said with exaggerated patience. "By the vicar, of course."

"What's the vicar done?" I was unable to conceive of a less likely backstabber than the mild-mannered man who'd performed my marriage ceremony and christened my children.

"He's only gone and given over the schoolhouse to that specky chap. Don't know what he was thinking, handing it over without asking me first. How am I to run the Harvest Festival without the schoolhouse?"

"Well . . ." I fell silent as Peggy leapt to her feet and began listing what I assumed to be contest categories.

"There's the Shepherd's Crooks, the Local Vegetables, the Best Floral Arrangement in a Gravy Boat!" she fretted. "There's the Photography, the Hand-Spun Fleece, the Wines and Beer! Not to mention the Sponge Fruit Flans and Lemon Bars! Where are we to put 'em all, if we don't have the schoolhouse?"

"Tables in the school yard?" I ventured meekly.

"No room!" Peggy exclaimed. She glanced over her shoulder before continuing, in a strangled murmur, "Not with the poultry, rabbits, goats, sheep, and ponies. And don't bother mentioning the square because the Merry Morrismen and the Finch Minstrels'll be there." She flung her hands into the air and sagged onto the bench.

"I see your point," I said, and I meant it. I'd envisioned the Harvest Festival as a sort of al fresco picnic on the square, but Peggy's plans were more complex than that. The vicar had to have been in a fugue state when he'd snatched the schoolhouse from her—if, in fact, he had. Peggy had a habit of overdramatizing events, but if she'd truly lost the schoolhouse, she had a right to be miffed. Apart from the church it was the largest building in Finch, and the only one suited to the kind of pageant Peggy had in mind.

"Can the vicar give the schoolhouse away, just like that?" I asked.

"It belongs to the church," Peggy informed me. "Most village schools do. It hasn't been a proper school for donkey's years, but it's still church property. But it's not whether he *can*," she huffed indignantly, "it's whether he *should*. He's no right to fill my schoolhouse with Scrag End rubbish less than two months before the Harvest Festival. Especially since—" She broke off and gave me a sidelong look. "I'll tell you something, Lori, and it's not something I've told very many people. As soon as the Harvest Festival is over, I'm leaving Finch. For good."

I gaped at her in disbelief. "You're leaving Finch?"

"Don't try to talk me out of it," said Peggy. "My old friend Mr. Taxman tried that already, and I'll tell you what I told him: I've done what I set out to do in Finch. I've livened the place up a bit, set a good example for the villagers, and now it's time for me to move on."

"Where will you go?" I asked.

"There's a village up in Yorkshire called Little Stubbing. Mr. Taxman and I passed through it on a driving holiday last year. It reminded me of the way Finch was before I took it in hand. Little Stubbing needs me, Lori." She clutched her hands together in her lap. "But I won't be driven from Finch by *that man*. He must go!"

I shook my head doubtfully. "I think you'll have a hard time getting rid of the vic—"

"Not the vicar!" Peggy cried. "*That man!* The specky chap! Says he's from Oxford, but I don't care if he's from Windsor. He's not going to interfere with my festival." She turned her glittering eyes on me. "And you're going to see to it that he doesn't."

I gulped.

"You're going to persuade the vicar to turn him out," Peggy continued, with terrifying composure.

"I don't suppose you've talked things over with the vicar," I said, with wan hope.

Peggy sniffed. "The Reverend Theodore Bunting and I are not, at present, on speaking terms. And if he thinks I'm going to special-order his finicking tinned prawns after he's ridden roughshod over a time-honored tradition like the Harvest Festival"—she paused for a breath—"he's very much mistaken."

I began backpedaling for dear life. "I'm honored by your faith in me, Peggy, but honestly, I don't know the first thing about the Harvest Festival. I've been kind of busy lately, what with the boys and all, and—"

"That's exactly what I said to Bill," Peggy broke in. " 'Bill,' I said, 'Lori's the only person in the village who isn't involved in the festival.' "

"You've been talking with Bill?" I asked, catching a faint whiff of rat in the air.

"I have, and he pointed out that you're just the person I've been looking for. What did he call you?" Peggy peered upward, squinting slightly through her pointy glasses. "An independent witness. An unbiased observer. An impartial third party."

"Bill said all that, did he?" I pursed my lips and contemplated life as a single parent.

"I had my doubts," Peggy assured me, "but Bill laid them to rest. You've been on the sidelines, he said, you've got no ax to grind. The vicar's bound to listen to you." She got to her feet and looked down at me, her mad gaze pinning me to the tree. "So you just trot over to the vicarage and tell Mr. Bunting that unless he wants to special-order his own tinned prawns for the rest of his natural life, he'd best give that specky chap the boot. And I'd thank you not to tell anyone that I intend to leave Finch. I plan to announce my departure at the end of the Harvest Festival." Peggy nodded affably and left the garden by the side path, puffing like a granny on a rampage.

"That rat," I muttered between gritted teeth. "That low-down, conniving, flea-bitten—" I spotted two pairs of bright eyes peering at me from the solarium and ceased murmuring sweet nothings about my lord and master.

"You can come out," I said, beckoning to the Pyms. "She's gone."

Ruth emerged first, carrying a cup of tea. "It seemed such an urgent interview . . ."

". . . we didn't like to intrude." Louise came to stand beside her sister. "But we thought you might need a little pick-me-up . . ."

". . . after your visit with Peggy." Ruth eyed me sympathetically. "One usually does."

"Thanks," I said, accepting the proffered cup. "If I weren't breast-feeding the boys, I'd ask for something stronger. Like strychnine."

Ruth tittered. "Now, Lori, I'm sure it will all . . ."

". . . work out for the best," Louise finished.

"Ha." I slumped against the tree. "Didn't you hear? I'm an impartial observer. That's another way of saying 'innocent bystander,' and we all know what happens to them."

Ruth laid a gloved hand on my shoulder. "I have no doubt that you'll rise to the occasion. I'm afraid, however, that we must . . ."

". . . leave you to it," said Louise. "Do feel free to call on us . . ."

". . . should you need our help. We wouldn't want to keep Mrs. Kitchen from her new life in Little Stubbing." Ruth turned to go.

"Wait!" I cried, nearly spilling my tea. "Do you know

anything about this specky—" I was interrupted by the sound of a telephone ringing inside the cottage. A moment later Francesca came out to hand the cordless phone to me.

"It's the vicar," she said.

"Oh, Lord . . ." I groaned.

Francesca went back into the cottage, and the Pyms gave me a synchronized finger-flutter before tiptoeing stealthily out of the garden.

"Hullo?" a voice piped in my ear. "Lori Shepherd? Are you there?"

"I'm here, Vicar." I paused to listen to the familiar cough of the Pyms' ancient automobile as it putt-putted out of my driveway. Cowards, I thought bitterly. "What's up?"

"I hardly know how to answer that question." The vicar sounded a bit dazed. "Would it be at all possible for you to come round to the vicarage? Something's happened, you see, of a confidential nature. I'd feel much more comfortable in my mind if you were on hand, as it were, to view the scene of the . . . ahem . . ."

The word *crime* hovered, unspoken, in the air and I sat up straighter, intrigued. "Can you give me a hint?" I coaxed.

There was a pause. "Dear me," the vicar said, "I don't wish to alarm you unduly, but . . . there's been a burglary at the vicarage!"

4.

There are few more rigorous tests of teamwork than feeding, bathing, and bedding down a pair of active four-month-olds. Francesca and I demonstrated the axiom that four hands are better than two when dealing with twins.

We had novelty going for us, of course. The excitement of having a new grown-up in their lives—one who dispensed with training spoons and dipped their fists right into the farina!—wore the boys out so completely that, once bathed, powdered, and freshly diapered, they required a minimal amount of rocking to send them off to dreamland.

Before I left my babies alone with a relative stranger, however, there was something I needed to clear up. While Francesca loaded the dishwasher with still more dirty dishes, I went quietly into the study, closed the door behind me, and pulled the blue journal from its place on the bookshelves. Then I switched on the mantelshelf lamps and curled up in one of the pair of tall leather armchairs that sat before the hearth.

"Dimity?" I said, opening the journal. "There's something I'd like to ask you."

I spoke in a barely audible undertone because I didn't want Francesca to come in and find me talking to a book. Bill knew about the blue journal, as did Emma and Derek Harris, but I'd so far resisted the temptation to announce its function to the populace at large. I didn't relish the notion of being dubbed the village nutcase.

I could scarcely believe it myself, much less explain how it worked, or why Dimity's spirit lingered in the cottage long after her mortal remains had departed this earth—but I couldn't deny the evidence of my own eyes. The skeptic within me fell silent each time Aunt Dimity's words appeared, written in royal-blue ink in her fine copperplate, on the blue journal's blank, unlined pages.

"Aunt Dimity?" I repeated. "Can you hear me?"

Not very well.

I glanced nervously toward the door as the looping letters scrolled across the page.

I take it that you do not wish Francesca to overhear?

"I think it might give her the wrong impression of her new employer," I whispered.

Does Francesca meet with your approval?

"She's fantastic," I acknowledged. "The boys took to her right off the bat, and she handles them like a pro."

But?

I sighed. "It's something Peggy Kitchen said."

In that case, I suspect it is sheer nonsense. What did she say?

"Nothing specific. But she implied that Francesca's father had done something—"

Ignore Peggy Kitchen. She's quite incapable of judging Francesca fairly. Small minds and unforgiving hearts are the bane of village life.

I looked at the door again, listened intently for a moment, then returned my attention to the journal. "Why can't she judge Francesca fairly?"

Because she hated Francesca's father. Piero Sciaparelli was a prisoner of war, you see. He was captured in North Africa in 1942, worked as a farm laborer for old Mr. Hodge until VE day, and a year or two later married a local girl. Piero and his wife raised six children, all of them as English as crumpets, save for their extraordinary names. Still, some people have never ceased to regard men like Piero as the enemy. As I said, small minds . . .

". . . and unforgiving hearts," I finished for her. "I should've known. Sorry to bother you, Dimity. I won't worry about the boys now."

You most certainly will, my dear. But with Francesca at hand, you needn't worry quite so much.

I closed the journal and caressed its smooth cover with my fingertips. Dimity never ceased to amaze me. Her fiancé had been killed in the Second World War. His death had hung over her soul like a shadow. She'd never married, never had children of her own, yet she bore no grudge against an enemy soldier who'd found the kind of happiness she'd lost. I doubted that I'd have been as generous, had a foreign bullet taken Bill from me, and wondered briefly if some part of Peggy Kitchen's heart lay buried beneath shifting North African sands.

The mantelpiece clock chimed the half hour, and I put the journal back on the shelf. It was half past noon. I could drive over to the vicarage, view the scene of the *ahem,* and be back in plenty of time for the boy's three-thirty snack. I switched off the lights and went to the kitchen, where Francesca had just finished wiping the table.

"Will you be all right on your own for an hour or so?" I asked. "I promised the vicar that I'd come over this afternoon."

"I should be able to manage," said Francesca.

"The phone number for the vicarage is—"

"On the notepad in the hall." Francesca dried her hands on a clean towel. "Along with the numbers of your husband's office, the Harris manor, and both car phones."

"Right." I headed for the front door, and Francesca followed me. "If the boys wake up before I'm back . . ." I bit my lip and scolded myself silently for being an over-protective mother.

"If there's a peep out of 'em I'll ring you straightaway," Francesca assured me.

"I won't be long," I told her, opening the door. "Oh, and Francesca . . ." I turned to her and stuck a hand out awkwardly. "Welcome to the cottage."

Francesca's dark eyes lit with amusement, but she gave my hand a firm shake. "Glad to be back," she said.

I shot a last anxious glance toward the stairs, then left the cottage and climbed into the Mini.

I wasn't sure what puzzled me more—that a burglary had taken place in Finch, or that the vicar thought I could do something about it. Since Finch's crime rate was virtually nonexistent, I thought it likely that the vicar's summons would turn out to be nothing more than Phase Two of Bill's Fresh-Air Campaign.

I didn't mind. Despite an occasional geyser from my guilt glands, it felt good to be out and about. I cruised past Emma's curving drive, waved to the Pyms, who were busily filling the birdbath in their front yard, and called a blessing down upon the Mini as I negotiated the sharp turn just beyond their house.

I'd bought the tiny black car secondhand, though it had clearly passed through more than two before reaching mine. Bill called it a clattering rattletrap, too slow to

take me anywhere in a hurry and too small to accommodate the twins' safety seats, but that was why I liked it.
The Mini was mechanically incapable of responding to
my lead foot, and its diminutive proportions made the
narrow lanes surrounding Finch seem spacious.

Besides, a shiny new car would have seemed out of
place in Finch, where nothing was shiny or new. As I
bumped over the humpbacked stone bridge and entered
the square, I was struck once again by the thought that
Finch, unlike so many Cotswolds villages, would never
win a berth in a Best-of-Britain calendar.

No one could fault the setting. Finch nestled in the
broad bend of a rushing stream that flowed so clearly, an-
glers could count the speckles on the trout. The surrounding countryside was an undulating mosaic of meadow,
cropland, and forest. The lanes were lined with fluttering hedgerows and bedecked with wildflowers. It seemed
a shame to desecrate such an idyllic landscape with a
grubby outpost of civilization like Finch.

Finch abounded in unrealized potential. It would have
been a gem, had anyone taken the time to polish it. Instead, it clustered, unkempt and neglected, around an
irregular oblong of semiarid lawn fringed by a ribbon
of weed-sprouting cobbles. The glow of the Cotswolds
stonework was muted by grayish grime, the green was be-
set by bald spots, and the dignified Celtic cross memorial-
izing Finch's Fallen had been swallowed by a tangle of
untamed willows.

There were no sidewalks on the square. A mutually
agreed upon no-wheel zone extended three to twelve feet
from the shop fronts, a distance that varied with passing traffic, of which there was very little. Finch's main
road merited a blue line in the atlas, as it had been paved

sometime in the early 1960s, but it hadn't been touched since, and few casual travelers were willing to risk their axles on it.

The village's one glory lay beyond the square, a hundred yards or so up Saint George's Lane, in the midst of a walled graveyard shaded by cedars of Lebanon and dotted with mossy headstones. Saint George's Church had the usual mixed pedigree—a Saxon crypt, a Norman tower—and a pleasantly plain face, but it was blessed with an interior feature that lifted it above the commonplace.

Saint George's possessed a set of five medieval wall paintings, most notably an imposing figure of Saint George battling a snaky-looking dragon. The paintings had once been hidden by layers of plaster, but Derek Harris had skillfully uncovered and restored them. I found the primitive images vaguely creepy, but scholars had been known to come from overseas to view them.

As I drove into the square, I noted Bill's bicycle—an old-fashioned black three-speed with upright handlebars—leaning beside the door of Wysteria Lodge, the vine-covered building that served as his office. Few passersby would suspect that the high-powered Boston law firm of Willis & Willis had as its overseas headquarters a modest stone house half hidden by purple wysteria—unless they peeked inside.

Bill's father had equipped the place with every electronic office device known to man, which meant that Bill could travel from Hamburg to Padua without ever leaving Finch. I considered stopping in to have a word with him— I still owed him big-time for siccing Peggy Kitchen on me—but decided to wait until after I'd spoken with the vicar.

The village school occupied the northeast corner of the square, and as I rolled past the disputed territory, I noted signs of occupation. A young man was handing boxes from a paneled van to a young woman, who carted them into the school. They wore khaki shorts, colorful T-shirts, and hiking boots, and their shouts of laughter could easily be heard in Kitchen's Emporium. God help them, I thought, turning into Saint George's Lane and pulling up, at last, to the vicarage.

Bill and I had held our wedding reception in the vicarage, and fond memories tripped through my mind whenever I came to call. Still, I had to admit that the rambling, two-story house had the same down-at-heels air about it as the rest of Finch, as though it had, like my Mini, passed through a number of neglectful hands. The surrounding garden was little more than a jungle. Lilian Bunting couldn't be bothered with it—she had a bookish turn of mind—and the vicar believed in leaving nature to God's mercy.

Lilian Bunting met me at the door. The vicar's wife was a slender woman in her mid-fifties who favored tweeds and twin sets in winter, linen suits in summer, and sensible shoes all year round. She greeted me with a smile.

"Lori, my dear, do come in. Teddy's got himself into the most frightful pickle, and I'm counting on you to get him out."

"What's going on?" I asked.

Lilian laughed. "That's what I hope you'll discover. But I'll let Teddy tell you his part in it. He's been longing to confess his sins to someone."

Lilian led me to the library, a book-lined room at the rear of the vicarage that stretched the full width of the house. Its mullioned windows and French doors overlooked a broad meadow that sloped sharply down to the tree-lined riverbank. The vicar's mahogany desk sat before the French doors, but his desk chair faced into the room, as though he found the sight of books more pleasurable than any natural vista. The view through the French doors was obscured, in any case, by a dense growth of rhododendrons.

The Reverend Theodore Bunting sat slumped in a worn armchair near the hearth. He was a tall man, with short iron-gray hair, a beak of a nose, and a look of perpetual mourning in his gray eyes. He wore a navy-blue cardigan over his clerical collar and shirt, and a pair of scuffed wing-tip shoes on his rather large feet. When I entered the room, he was staring disconsolately at the French doors, but the moment he became aware of my presence, he sprang from his chair and strode over to greet me.

"Lori, how good of you to come," he said, a note of desperation in his voice. "I'm at my wit's end. If you can't help, I don't know what I'm going to do."

Lilian motioned for me to sit on the green velvet couch opposite the vicar's armchair, then turned to address her husband. "First," she instructed him, "you're going to explain the situation to Lori. She doesn't have the faintest idea why she's here, Teddy."

"Of course," said the vicar.

"You get started," said Lilian. "I'll be back shortly." She gave her husband's shoulder an encouraging squeeze and left the library.

The vicar heaved a forlorn sigh as he returned to his chair. "Lilian's too good to say it, but it's all my fault. I'm so dreadfully absentminded." He sighed again. "It all began when Adrian Culver came up from Oxford to see me last November." The vicar gave me an inquiring look. "Have you met Dr. Culver?"

"Not yet," I said, "but I'll bet he wears glasses."

"Half glasses, to be precise," said the vicar. "How did you know—"

"I'll tell you later," I broke in. "Please, go on."

"Dr. Culver is a university lecturer and a well-known archaeologist," the vicar informed me. "Last autumn, his nineteen-year-old niece embarked upon a solitary walking tour of the Cotswolds. She paused one afternoon to take her lunch in Scrag End field—"

"Scrag End field?" I said.

The vicar nodded. "It lies alongside Hodge Farm," he explained, "just beyond the copse of woods at the north end of the village. Scrag End is glebe land, though it's never brought a groat into the church's coffers. It's useless for cultivation. Hence its unflattering name."

"Right," I said. "So Adrian Culver's niece had just stopped in Scrag End field to have a picnic lunch, when . . . ?"

"She found herself sitting on the business end of a fifth-century Roman spearhead!" the vicar exclaimed.

"Golly," I said. "That must have come as a surprise."

"Indeed," said the vicar. "Naturally, she reported her discovery to her uncle, who lost no time in returning to Scrag End. While there, he turned up a number of potsherds, coins, and a small head of Minerva, all Roman, ranging in date from the second to the fifth century."

"Sounds like quite a find," I said.

"Adrian was beside himself," the vicar confirmed. "Scrag End was, he told me, exactly what he'd been looking for. He hoped to conduct a preliminary survey of it this summer. Adrian's a very persuasive fellow, and when he asked if he might use the schoolhouse as a temporary storeroom and laboratory, I'm afraid I . . ." The vicar leaned back in his chair and moaned.

"How could you possibly forget about the Harvest Festival?" I asked, genuinely curious. "Peggy's worked on it for years and—"

"No, she hasn't." Lilian Bunting had reentered the library, carrying a round tray with two teapots, and a selection of pastries and sandwiches. "Finch hasn't held a Harvest Festival since September 1913. The Great War put an end to that tradition, as it put an end to so much else."

"Peggy Kitchen said—" I began, but Lilian shook her head authoritatively.

"Mrs. Kitchen is painfully enthusiastic about reestablishing village traditions." Lilian placed the tea tray on the table at my knees and sat beside me on the couch. "She has been, ever since she moved here."

"Moved here?" I said. "I thought she was born here."

The vicar grunted. "She's no more Finch-born than we are."

"*You* aren't from Finch, either?" I said, taken aback.

The vicar and his wife looked at each other and smiled.

"We are now," said Lilian, "but we've been here less than a decade. We came to Finch from London. Teddy's previous parish had become a bit too . . . urban . . . for his nerves, and when a friend offered him this living, he snapped it up."

"Out of the frying pan . . ." muttered the vicar.

"Now, Teddy," chided Lilian, "you can't accuse Finch of being too lively."

"Dull as ditchwater," said the vicar, sighing. "Or it was, until Mrs. Kitchen arrived from Birmingham. She bought up old Harmer's shop and turned it into Kitchen's Emporium. Then she got herself appointed postmistress. Then she started in on her village-tradition scheme."

"Garden fetes, morris dancing, sheepdog trials," said Lilian. "She's even revived the Women's Institute. Tea, Lori? There's chamomile for you and a stronger brew for

Teddy. Please, help yourself to a little something while I pour. I've made my lemon bars."

I wasn't hungry—Francesca had managed to whip up an omelette for me in the midst of the boys' feeding frenzy—but Lilian's lemon bars were legendary. While she coaxed her distraught husband into choking down a cheese-and-tomato sandwich, I sampled one of the sweet, tangy treats, and wondered if they would have any competition at the Harvest Festival—assuming the festival took place.

"The thing is," the vicar said, gazing gloomily into his teacup, "I've never been entirely convinced that Finch *needs* a Harvest Festival."

"It's the blessing of the beasts," Lilian put in. "Teddy isn't sure who'll clean the church afterward."

"I suppose that's why I forgot about the festival," the vicar went on. "Wishful thinking. Besides, Adrian swore that he'd be here no longer than three weeks. Yet, not an hour ago, I learned from an Oxford colleague of mine that Adrian is applying for funds to extend the project. If he gets them, he may be here forever!"

At that moment I was glad I hadn't mentioned Peggy's plans to move to Little Stubbing. The vicar would resign his post if he knew he was responsible for prolonging Mrs. Kitchen's reign of terror in Finch.

"You could ask him to leave," I suggested.

"Out of the question," said the vicar. "Adrian came here in good faith. I can't evict a man of his stature because of my own abysmal stupidity."

"Stupidity?" Lilian clucked her tongue. "You can't be blamed for wanting to bring something of lasting value to the village."

"Vanity," the vicar murmured. "All is vanity."

"Sit up and drink your tea, Teddy. You'll feel much better." Lilian took a sip from her own cup before continuing. "Teddy thought that Dr. Culver's excavation might put Finch on the map. It seemed to be the most exciting thing to happen here since 1642."

"That's when the Royalists rode through on their way to Warwick Castle," the vicar intoned. "Nothing's happened here since."

"Unfortunately, Teddy forgot to mention Dr. Culver's plans to me," Lilian went on.

"November's such a hectic month," the vicar murmured.

"It completely slipped Teddy's mind," said Lilian. "Most unfortunate, since I so easily could have spared us all a great deal of unpleasantness."

"How?" I asked, reaching for another lemon bar.

The vicar got up and walked behind his desk to toy with the handles on the French doors. "Lilian's been writing a history of Saint George's parish," he said over his shoulder. "She was going through the old books here in the library last year when she came upon a curiously pertinent pamphlet."

"It was written by the Reverend Cornelius Gladwell, one of Teddy's Victorian predecessors," Lilian explained. "Mr. Gladwell was an amateur—a frustrated amateur, I fear. But he dreamt of becoming a famous archaeologist. He spent years combing the hills around Finch but was poorly rewarded for his troubles."

"Meanwhile," said the vicar, "his friends in other parts of the country were uprooting Roman gewgaws right and left. They'd post a piece to him now and then, as a sort of consolation prize."

"He regarded the gifts as gestures of contempt," Lilian

stated firmly. "In a fit of pique, he buried them, along with pieces he'd purchased, in Scrag End field, hoping to impose his own frustration on some future archaeologist."

"Cornelius did not possess a charitable nature," the vicar observed.

"But he did possess a printing press," said Lilian. "Another of his hobbies. He wrote an account of his prank, printed ten numbered pamphlets, and sent nine of them . . ." She looked toward her husband. "Well, we're not sure where he sent them, are we, Teddy? Or even *if* he sent them."

"Might have burnt them, for all we know," said the vicar.

"We do know that he kept the tenth copy for himself," said Lilian, "because I read it last year, while I was doing research for my little history. When Dr. Culver and his team arrived in Finch yesterday morning, I showed the pamphlet to Teddy."

"It seemed unkind to dash the man's dreams on a Sunday," said the vicar, "but I intended to bring the pamphlet round to the schoolhouse first thing this morning." He turned to point accusingly at his blotter. "I left it there, in the center of my desk, so I wouldn't forget to bring it with me."

"I saw him put it there," Lilian added.

"But when I came in after breakfast, the pamphlet had vanished. Lilian hadn't touched it, nor had I. Annie, our charlady, stopped by for her wages on Sunday, but she wasn't here above five minutes. We can only assume, therefore . . ." The vicar rattled the door handles again. "They must've got in through here. We never lock these doors. Leave 'em open most days when the weather's fine. Never thought twice about it. It's never been necessary."

I was staring at the vicar's back in amazement. "Do you mean to tell me that you had proof that Dr. Culver's big find is a hoax?"

"Printed proof," Lilian confirmed. "The pity of it is that if Dr. Culver knew that he was the victim of a practical joke, I think he would just pack up and go home."

"And you think someone stole Cornelius Gladwell's pamphlet?" I said.

"There's no other explanation," the vicar replied. "Though I can't comprehend why anyone would be willing to risk his immortal soul by thieving on the Lord's Day."

I drained my cup and wished for the second time in as many hours for something more bracing than herbal tea. "Incredible," I said. "A burglary at the vicarage *and* an archaeological swindle, right here in Finch. Do you want me to find out who took the pamphlet?"

The vicar staggered as though someone had shoved him. "Good heavens, no!" he cried. "Anything but that!"

5.

Was it my imagination, or had Adrian Culver un-
earthed an ancient virus that was making everyone in
Finch hysterical? I looked uncertainly at Lilian, who'd led
her husband back to his armchair and was fanning him
with a sheaf of Harvest Festival flyers.

"Don't you want to know who robbed you?" I asked.

"I don't want it known that we've *been* robbed!" the
vicar exclaimed.

Lilian placed the flyers on the mantelshelf. "The village is already divided into warring factions because of
the schoolhouse. One camp is foursquare behind the excavation, the other is rooting for the festival. It's Dr.
Culver versus Mrs. Kitchen, I'm sad to say, and Teddy
doesn't wish to intensify the acrimony by sowing seeds of
suspicion."

I was still at sea. "Do you want me to tell Dr. Culver
about the pamphlet?"

Lilian shook her head. "We've tried that."

"He didn't believe us," the vicar said. "He'd had a run-
in with Mrs. Kitchen, you see, and thought we'd invented
the story to appease her. 'I understand, Padre' were his

precise words. Then he winked at me." The vicar wrung his hands. "Padre and winks, that's what it's come to."

"Then what, exactly, do you want me to do?" I looked expectantly from the vicar to his wife.

Lilian refilled my cup. "Do you remember telling us about the fascinating work you used to do for Dr. Finderman?"

I nodded. Dr. Stanford J. Finderman was the curator of the rare book collection at my alma mater back in Boston. I'd scouted books for him in England for a couple of years before the boys were born.

"We wondered if, perhaps, with your connections—and your expertise—you might be able to locate another copy of Mr. Gladwell's pamphlet," said Lilian. "Once Dr. Culver has read the pamphlet, I'm certain he'll . . ." Lilian's words trailed off as she caught sight of the expression on my face.

I opened and closed my mouth once or twice before managing, in as level a voice as I could muster: "You want me to find one of nine privately printed copies of an obscure piece of Victorian archaeological ephemera?"

"That's right," said Lilian.

I gave a weak laugh. "It's a tall order."

"All things are possible," the vicar reminded me.

"Oh, I agree with you, Vicar. Amoebas can turn into apes, given a few million years. But we have less than six weeks." I ran a hand through my hair. "I'll do what I can, but—"

"Splendid," said Lilian. "I've jotted down everything Teddy and I can remember about the pamphlet to aid you in your search." She went to the desk, withdrew a red spiral-bound notebook from the center drawer, and held it out to me. "If we think of anything else, we'll ring you immediately."

"Okay," I said, crossing to take possession of the note-book. "But try not to expect instant results. This kind of search can take . . ." I looked into the vicar's woebegone eyes and finished less than accurately, "a bit longer than six weeks."

"It mustn't," the vicar urged. "Civil war will have bro-ken out by then. And I shall be held responsible."

Lilian rolled her eyes heavenward and took me by the arm. "I'm sure we've kept you from your sons long enough," she said. "Shall we go out the back way?"

Our exit through the French doors was as unexpected as it was inconvenient. Lilian and I had to descend the short flight of weed-grown stairs in an awkward half crouch to avoid losing an eye to the encroaching rhodo-dendrons. The lawn at the bottom of the stairs was equally treacherous. A dense matting of brambles plucked at my socks and concealed ankle-threatening humps and rabbit holes.

Once we escaped the overgrown shrubbery, though, the view was exceptionally serene. Cloud shadows raced across the open meadow, and the waist-high wild grasses rippled sinuously in the passing breeze.

"How lovely," I murmured.

"How damp," Lilian corrected. "Even in the midst of a drought like the one we're having now, the mist rises like an army of wraiths at night, and the river floods the meadow every spring." She shook her head at nature's im-providence, then turned to face me. "About Mr. Glad-well's pamphlet . . . I wouldn't dream of calling in the police against Teddy's wishes, but I'd very much like to learn the identity of our uninvited guest. Would you . . . ?"

I sighed. "Just tell me one thing. Were the French doors open when you were discussing the Gladwell pamphlet?"

Lilian nodded guiltily. "It was such a warm day. It was

just before the morning service, as well. Anyone pausing in the lane on their way to church might have overheard us."

My laughter held a touch of hysteria. "So anyone could
have known about the pamphlet, and anyone could have
stolen it, since you never lock the French doors."

Lilian frowned pensively. "I suppose that leaves you
with a rather broad field of suspects."

I pointed toward the river. "Broader than the meadow."

"Well," she said briskly, "if I hear anything, I'll let you
know."

"Fine," I said, "but in the meantime . . ." I turned to
face the library steps and drew a hand through the air.
"Have someone take a machete to this mess. Think of it as
camouflage—and get rid of it."

Lilian pursed her lips. "Point taken."

As we picked our way carefully toward the front of the
vicarage, Lilian reverted to her scholarly persona. "You
know," she said, "Finch isn't quite as boring as Teddy
makes out. The village has its share of interesting quirks.
The war memorial, for example, is unique."

"In what way?" I asked.

"It honors not only the dead," she replied, "but all
those who served, man or woman, in any capacity during either or both of the great world wars. And that . . ."
Lilian drew my attention to the house next door, a humble, one-story dwelling built of golden stone and set well
back from the lane. "That was the schoolmaster's house,
when Finch had a schoolmaster. The last man to occupy
the post was a bit of a lad. If the church records are to be
trusted, he fathered half the pupils in his classroom. He
was, unfortunately, a bachelor."

"Wow," I said. "The PTA meetings must've been—"

I broke off and stared in the direction of the square. "What's that noise? It sounds like . . ."

Lilian Bunting's eyes met mine as we chorused: "Peggy Kitchen."

"You stay here," I said. "I'll go and see what's happening."

"Are you certain you want to get involved?" Lilian asked.

"Don't worry about me," I told her, with a wry smile. "I'm an impartial observer."

Peggy Kitchen's ceaseless roar guided me toward the schoolhouse, where I paused to reconnoiter before advancing. Peering cautiously around the corner, I saw Peggy standing, arms akimbo, behind the paneled van, haranguing the two young people I'd seen earlier.

I studied the young couple closely. They appeared to be no more than twenty. The girl was on the chunky side, with a spiky crop of sun-blond hair and wide-set blue eyes. The boy was taller, leaner, and brown-eyed, with light-brown tresses caught in a ponytail that hung halfway down his back. They stood with folded arms, observing Peggy with expressions that hovered dangerously between incredulity and mirth.

". . . I'll have the law on you!" Peggy thundered. "You're ruining my trade, you are! Your infernal racket is frightening my customers!"

"Mrs. Kitchen!" I shouted, abandoning my secure position. "I've got important information for you! It's about that matter we discussed this morning!"

Like a maddened bull distracted by a fly, Peggy stopped her forward charge and looked in all directions before finally focusing in on me. "Well?" she snapped.

I threw caution to the wind and took her by the elbow.

"I've figured out a way to handle the situation. Come with me." I shot a meaningful glance over my shoulder as I guided Peggy toward her shop, and the two young people retreated meekly into the schoolhouse.

Peggy was still breathing hard, but the red glow in her eyes had diminished by the time we stopped to talk. "What's the plan?" she demanded, coming to a halt in the middle of the balding green.

"I can't discuss the details yet," I told her, improvising like mad. "I have to consult my husband first."

"Aha," said Peggy, brightening. "A *legal* solution. When can we expect results?"

"In plenty of time for the festival," I assured her. "Until then, it's imperative that you stay away from the schoolhouse. Otherwise . . ." I had no idea what to say next, but it didn't seem to matter.

"I knew I could depend on you, Lori," said Peggy. She tapped the side of her nose, gave me a knowing nod, and made a stately procession back to her shop.

I wilted with relief, then retraced my steps to the schoolhouse. The door had been left open, and I stepped into the cloakroom, a long, narrow foyer with rows of hooks affixed to the walls at child height.

As Peggy had said, the village school hadn't been used as a school for ages. It had once contained two classrooms, but the dividing wall had been removed to create a single open space that served as an all-purpose meeting place. Bill and his fellow Merry Morrismen practiced there on inclement days, Lilian Bunting held church jumble sales under the peaked roof, and Peggy Kitchen chaired Women's Institute meetings from the raised platform at the far end, where the teachers' desks had once stood.

The young man and woman were hovering over the boxes they'd unloaded from the paneled van, and a daunting array of archaeological equipment—black-and-white measuring sticks, high-powered lamps, dental picks, tarpaulins, spades—lay strewn across folding tables or stacked in the cupboards lining the schoolhouse walls. The vicar's fears, it seemed, had been well-founded. It looked as though Adrian Culver was preparing for an extended stay.

"Hello," I said, from the inner doorway. "My name's Lori Shepherd. I'm the local UN peacekeeper, and I hereby declare these premises to be a safe haven."

The boy grinned, set aside an armful of rope, and came over to shake my hand. "Simon Blakely and Katrina Graham," he said, beckoning to the stocky girl. "We're working with Dr. Culver on the dig. Thanks awfully for helping us out. We'd no idea we were making such a nuisance of ourselves."

"That woman is more of a nuisance than we are, Simon," said Katrina, coming to join us. "She made the same sort of scene when we arrived. At seven o'clock on a Sunday morning! Frightened the poor vicar half to death. Is she mad?"

It was a debatable point, but I let it slide, choosing instead to spell out Peggy's concerns about the festival.

"That explains the camp bed," said Simon, pointing to a folding cot in the corner. "We couldn't understand why Dr. Culver decided to sleep here for the duration, but if the natives are restless . . ."

Katrina nodded. "He won't want to leave our gear unprotected."

"Where is he now?" I asked.

"Staking a grid at Scrag End," Simon answered. "He's

eager to get the project under way." Simon glanced again at Katrina. "It's a pity about the festival, but we've scarcely begun the preliminary survey. We're here to help Dr. Culver set up, but there'll be ten more students joining us next week."

"And we must have a local building for storage and analysis," Katrina chimed in, gesturing toward the boxes. "My word, can you imagine carting this lot back and forth from Oxford every day?"

"I suppose not." I gazed at the boxes, disheartened. I'd nursed a faint hope of convincing the two sides to share the schoolhouse, but realized now that my simple solution wouldn't fly—the schoolroom just wasn't big enough for both of them.

"We're sorry," Simon said. "Honestly, we didn't know about the festival. If we had—"

"It wouldn't have mattered," said Katrina, with a ruthless glint in her eye. "Any fool can see that Dr. Culver's discovery takes precedence over a local fair."

Simon flushed. "You'll have to forgive my colleague," he said. "She's caught a bad case of academic zeal."

"I understand," I said, smiling. "But I'd suggest that you keep your zeal under wraps while you're here. A low profile will go a long way toward appeasing the natives."

"We'll do our best," said Simon. "No more loud laughter on the square."

The pair returned to their unpacking while I headed for Bill's office. I had half a mind to let the air out of his bicycle tires. The three-mile walk to the cottage would give my husband ample time to reflect on the evils of plunging his devoted spouse into the middle of a civil war.

Seething with righteous indignation, I let myself into the office, faced Bill's desk squarely, and was on the verge of firing a stream of well-chosen words into his much-loved face when a voice behind me asked, "Can you stand on your head?"

I froze, openmouthed, then pivoted slowly until I beheld a pair of grubby pink sneakers, a bruised shin, and a bandaged knee waving unsteadily in the air. They belonged to a little girl who was going beet-red in the face as she demonstrated her own gymnastic prowess.

"I'm Rainey Dawson," she added, bouncing to her feet. "I'm staying with Gran while Mum gets used to Jack. Jack's my new baby brother and he doesn't half make a row, so Mum sent me to stay with Gran until he's more grown-up, and Gran said I could visit Bill this afternoon while she has a lie-down, and I'm having a *splendid* time."

Rainey Dawson's auburn hair hung down her back in two bedraggled braids and across her forehead in an uneven, flyaway fringe. Her long nose and narrow face were smudged with dirt, as were her formerly pink T-shirt and checked shorts.

"I'm going to be nine this coming Sunday," she announced, jiggling from foot to foot. "Do you live in Finch? Will you come to my party? Bill's going to sit with me and Gran, and help me cut the cake." She leaned against Bill's desk and fluttered her eyelashes worshipfully. "I adore Bill. He lets me push the buttons on the fax machine."

My adorable husband was sitting with his eyes shut and his head in his hands. I looked down at the little chatterbox and beamed. I couldn't have invented a better form of revenge. An afternoon with Rainey Dawson was surely equal to twenty minutes with Peggy Kitchen.

"I'd love to come to your party, Rainey," I said. "Thank you very much for inviting me."

"Gran said I could invite anyone I liked," Rainey informed me. "She has the tearoom next door and—"

Rainey broke off abruptly and stared hard at my chest. "*You've* got a baby," she said.

I folded my arms self-consciously. "What makes you say that?"

Rainey pointed at my folded arms. "You've got spots on your blouse, just like Mum."

"Spots on my . . ." I glanced down and saw a pair of telltale damp patches on the front of my hitherto clean blouse. "Ack!" I cried. "I'm late! The boys'll be starving! And it's all your fault!" I shook a fist at Bill as I sprinted for the door, and hollered over my shoulder, "Keep talking, Rainey!"

6.

I gunned the Mini all the way home and skidded into the driveway with such reckless abandon that I came within inches of hitting the horse.

"Sorry, Rosie!" I cried, as the poor creature shied. "But I'm late!"

The chestnut mare's presence on my front lawn meant that Emma Harris had come to call. Rocinante belonged to Nell, Emma's thirteen-year-old stepdaughter, but since Nell was spending the summer in Paris with her paternal grandfather, Rosie's daily regimen of training and exercise had become Emma's responsibility. "It's the least I can do," Emma had told me, "considering Rosie's voluminous contributions to my garden."

I scrambled out of the Mini, gave Rosie's nose an apologetic rub, and hastened into the cottage, ears cocked for the piteous wailing of my neglected infants.

Silence greeted me.

I dashed into the living room, saw that the playpen was empty, and darted upstairs to check the nursery.

No sign of life.

"Francesca?" I called, flying back downstairs. "Emma?" No answer.

I ran into the kitchen only to be waylaid by a cloud of delectable aromas emanating from a stockpot that had been left simmering on the stove. I crept over to lift the lid and stood inhaling the heady fragrance of garlic, onions, herbs, and fresh tomatoes until, faint above the sauce's bubbling, I caught the sound of Rob's raspy laughter.

The sound was coming from the back garden. I dropped the lid onto the pot, flew through the solarium to the back door, and was brought up short once again.

Francesca and Emma were sitting in two wicker arm-chairs in the shade of the apple tree. Emma had pulled her gray-blond hair back into a single thick braid that hung past her waist, and placed her black velvet riding helmet on the stone bench. She wore black riding boots and fawn breeches, but had dispensed with her fitted jacket in favor of a short-sleeved cotton top that was better suited to the heat of the day. She was cradling Will in her arms and feeding him with a bottle.

The sight of Emma Harris playing nursemaid was enough to make my jaw drop. Emma had about as much maternal instinct as a frying pan. She'd stumbled into stepmotherhood by marrying a widower who had a son and daughter already in place. No one could deny that she'd made a go of it—her stepchildren adored her—but she was the first to admit that her success with Peter and Nell owed far more to their patient coaching than to her natural aptitude.

Yet there she sat, with my son in her arms, looking for all the world as though she knew what she was doing. Stranger still, Will seemed to think so, too.

He sucked industriously at his bottle, while his brother lay on a blanket at Francesca's feet, kicking and grabbing

at an array of circus animals that hung from strings tied to
the apple tree's lower branches. Each time he made contact, the elephants, monkeys, and zebras would bounce
and sway and Rob would give a triumphant giggle.

I took in the homely scene and felt bereft, so superflu-
ous and inconsequential that if Rob hadn't caught sight of
me and promptly let out a piteous wail, I might have
beaten him to it.

"My poor little angel," I crooned, scooping Rob up
from the blanket and cuddling him to within an inch of
his life. "I'm so sorry I was late." The moment I spoke,
Will pulled away from his bottle and set up a racket that
sparked panic in Emma's eyes. Francesca quickly motioned for me to take her place in the armchair, and deposited Will alongside Rob as soon as I was seated.

"Good grief," said Emma, mopping her brow, "what
was that all about? One minute they were fine and the
next . . ." She handed the half-empty bottle to Francesca.

"They're letting Lori know they missed her, is all. You
wait and see. They'll settle down in two ticks." Francesca
tucked the bottle into the pocket of the apron she'd tied
over her shirtdress. The apron, I noted in passing, was
spotless.

Two ticks later, the boys had finished offloading their
grievances and were competing to see who could wriggle
out of my arms first. Francesca returned Rob to the blanket, where he resumed his game with the dangling circus
animals, while I took up the task of feeding Will.

"Sorry I'm late," I told Francesca.

"No trouble," she said. "I spotted the bottles you'd left
in the fridge—"

"Did you use the right ones?" I asked anxiously.

"Would the ones labeled *My Milk* be the right ones?"
Francesca asked.

I blushed. "Yes, well . . . Bill sort of mixed them up a few weeks ago and—"

"Stop!" Emma clapped her hands over her ears and shuddered. "Remind me to thank Derek for presenting me with two children who were already weaned and potty-trained."

Francesca smiled. "Rob's finished his supper," she informed me, "so I'll pop inside and get on with ours. I hope you don't mind, but I used the tomatoes and such Mrs. Harris brought over from her garden. I'll manage better once I've learnt the trick of opening the kitchen cupboards."

"I don't mind at all," I assured her, and as Francesca went back into the cottage, I made a mental note to take a screwdriver to the cupboards' safety catches first thing in the morning. If my new nanny could whip up a sauce like that from a bag of miscellaneous veg, there was no telling what she might do with a fully stocked kitchen at her fingertips.

"Thanks for the fresh produce," I said, turning to Emma.

"I can't guarantee the quality. This drought is wreaking havoc on my garden. I shudder to think what the farmers are going through." She leaned forward to straighten Rob's blanket. "When did you decide to hire live-in help?"

"I didn't," I told her. "I'm the victim of a conspiracy." I gave Emma a quick rundown of my action-packed day, then sat back with Will and waited patiently while she laughed herself hoarse. "Go ahead, yuck it up," I said darkly.

"Sorry," Emma said, wiping her eyes. "But wait till you see *this.*" Chuckles continued to percolate from her as she reached over to her riding helmet and pulled a familiar-looking sheet of harvest-gold paper out from under it. "I found it in my mailbox this afternoon. It's the reason I came over in the first place." She cleared her throat and declaimed, with appropriate emphasis:

S!O!F!
Save Our Finch!!!
Do you want YOUR village ruled by OUTSIDERS?
Do you want STRANGERS knocking down YOUR door?
Stop them NOW!!
PETITION the BISHOP to STOP the INVASION!!
Signers welcome, night and day,
at Kitchen's Emporium.
But if any provide not for his own,
and specially for those of his own house,
he hath denied the faith,
and is worse than an infidel.
—*I Timothy 5:8*

"Take that, Vicar!" Emma peeked at me over the flyer and came perilously close to losing her tenuous grip on sobriety. She was saved by the sound of two hands clapping.

"Bravo," called Bill. My husband had come up the side path and stood at the rear corner of the cottage, grinning broadly as he applauded Emma's performance. He'd exchanged his workaday suit and tie for sneakers, shorts, and an old Harvard sweatshirt. Thanks to the bicycle, his legs were shaping up nicely, his face was ruddy with good health, and he was beginning to lose the broker's bulge he'd brought with him from Boston. Some men went to seed under the burden of fatherhood, but my Bill was blossoming. "No need to ask who composed that call to arms. Will your name be on the petition, Emma?"

"Absolutely not," she declared. "After what Lori's told me, I'm going to stay as far away from Peggy's shop as possible. Are you going to sign the petition, Lori?"

"I have to," I replied gloomily, "or Peggy'll be out here with a bullhorn. I can't wait until she moves to Little Stubbing."

"I pity the poor people of Little Stubbing. They don't know what's about to hit them." Emma reached for her riding helmet and got to her feet. "Let me know if there's anything I can do to help. My computer skills are, as always, at your service."

"What's all this about Little Stubbing?" Bill asked as he bent to examine Rob's bouncing menagerie.

"I'll tell you after dinner." Will had long since finished his afternoon meal, so I handed him to his father and buttoned my blouse. "You're home early. Rainey wore you out, did she?" I expected a bantering reply, but Bill answered seriously.

"To tell you the truth, I feel sorry for her," he said. "She doesn't have anyone her own age to play with."

"No one?" I said.

Bill raised Will to his shoulder and gently patted his back. "When Sally Pyne came by to fetch Rainey, we got to talking, and she told me that there aren't any children in Finch. A few kids out on the farms, yes, but none in the village." He rubbed his cheek against Will's fuzzy head. "It's going to be a long summer for that little girl."

"Poor kid," I said. "We'll have to come up with an extra-special birthday present for her."

Bill's nose wrinkled suddenly and he leaned closer to Rob. "Right now I think our boy has a present for us. Here, you take Will and I'll change Rob while you start in on dinner."

I stretched out my arms for Will and smiled as I recalled

the stockpot simmering on the stove. "Have I got news for you. . . ."

Francesca not only prepared our dinner, she served it to us in the dining room, on real plates, and cleaned up the mess afterward. It was a revelation to me, to relax and enjoy a meal with my husband after four months of snatching mouthfuls on the run.

"She did the laundry, put the linen closet in order, and got dinner ready while I was in town," I told Bill as we lingered over the raspberries and cream. "And she never gets her apron dirty."

"She's beginning to sound vaguely supernatural," Bill commented.

"Now that you mention it . . ." I lowered my voice, feeling for the first time like a chatelaine with servants to consider. "When she arrived, the cottage was filled with the scent of lilacs."

Bill's eyes widened. "No chill in the air? No smoke?" He was referring to tricks Dimity had once used to rid the cottage of an unwelcome visitor.

"Just lilacs," I replied.

Bill sat back and rubbed his jaw. "I guess Ruth and Louise picked the right nanny." He pushed himself away from the table. "It's still light out. How about a walk? If I'm not careful, Francesca's cooking will ruin my girlish figure."

We put Will and Rob in their all-terrain strollers, advised Francesca of our plans, and set off down the path through the oak grove that separated the Harrises' property from mine.

The grove was a tranquil oasis. Leaf-filtered sunlight patterned the path with quivering shadows, squirrels chittered in the branches overhead, and sparrows flitted from bower to bough. For a moment, walking at my husband's side and watching my sons absorb a world of wonder, I felt so lighthearted that if I'd let go of Rob's stroller, I'd have floated.

Then Bill asked how my day had gone.

I told him. In great detail. With many gestures. I think I may have frightened the squirrels.

"Now Peggy's petitioning the bishop. God knows what she'll do next. And unless you want your sons to grow up fatherless," I concluded testily, "you'll wipe that smirk off of your face this instant!"

"I'm sorry." Bill wrapped his arms around me and kissed the top of my head—a diversionary tactic, I was certain. "I was only trying to get you out of the house. If I'd known the Gladwell pamphlet would do the trick, I wouldn't have sent Hurricane Peggy in your direction."

"Well . . ." I allowed grudgingly, "you sent Francesca in my direction, too, so I guess we can call it a wash."

Bill reached for Will's stroller and we resumed our walk. "Do you think we'll have to catch the thief," he asked, "or will it be enough if we can persuade Adrian Culver to leave the schoolhouse?"

"They're not separate issues," I replied. "We have to find the thief in order to find the stolen pamphlet. And we have to find the stolen pamphlet in order to prove to Adrian Culver that his big find is a bad joke. That's the only way we'll get him to vacate the schoolhouse in time for the Harvest Festival. And that's the only way we'll get Peggy Kitchen out of the vicar's hair and into Little Stubbing's."

"Wait." Bill stopped in his tracks. "Haven't you skipped a step? What about asking Stan to find another copy of the Gladwell pamphlet?"

"I'll ask him," I said, "but, frankly, his chances of tracking down another copy are as remote as . . . as the chances of Peggy Kitchen making a huge donation to Saint George's this coming Sunday."

"No hope?" said Bill.

I held my thumb and forefinger a hairsbreadth apart. "About this much. There's a reason documents like the Gladwell pamphlet are called ephemera. Brochures, broadsheets, posters—they're not made to last. If they do survive, they're usually buried in the bowels of a poorly indexed collection. It could be years before Stan gets lucky."

"Then we'll simply have to keep our eyes and ears open," said Bill, stepping off briskly. "Someone must have seen something, and they're bound to talk. You'll be surprised at how quickly news spreads in a place like Finch." The twins chirped with delight as we steered the strollers around a dip in the path. "The village grapevine is the most effective means of communication known to man. It makes the Internet look like a pair of Dixie cups on a string."

"So all I'll have to do is make myself available? Bill," I added, pausing to catch my breath, "could we slow down? I'm getting winded and you're going to bounce Will right out of his stroller."

"Sorry." Bill adjusted his stride and tried, halfheartedly, to suppress a self-satisfied grin. "Shall we call it a day?"

I squirmed at the thought of Bill taking pity on me— Bill! The man who'd scarcely been able to climb Pouter's Hill without collapsing!—but I nodded. Four months of diaper-changing were no match for four months of bicycle-riding.

"Peggy's petition won't help me find the burglar," I said as we turned the strollers around. "Everyone in the village will sign it, including the thief. No one in his right mind is going to defy Peggy Kitchen openly."

Bill stooped to rescue a tiny sock that was in danger of escaping from Will's flailing foot. "You know how I hate to contradict you, my love, especially in front of the children, but Sally Pyne's defied Peggy already."

"To her face?" I said, astonished.

"More or less," said Bill. "Sally offered room and board to the two young people Dr. Culver brought with him."

"Simon and Katrina," I said. "Did they accept?"

"They moved in Sunday afternoon." Bill straightened. "Sally Pyne is clearly a Culverite."

I picked a long blade of grass from the edge of the path and twirled it slowly between my fingers. "An archaeological site might pull in tourists," I reasoned, "and tourists would boost business at Sally's tearoom. I suppose Sally might've burgled the vicarage."

"Fat Sally?" Bill lifted an eyebrow. "It's hard to imagine a woman of Sally's proportions managing stealthy footsteps, but it's possible."

"Too much is possible," I grumbled. "The only villagers I can scratch off the list of suspects are the Buntings and Peggy Kitchen."

"And Jasper Taxman," Bill put in. "According to Sally Pyne, Mr. Taxman is courting Peggy Kitchen."

I whistled softly between my teeth. "Brave man."

"He's a retired accountant," Bill explained. "Perhaps he craves excitement in his golden years."

"Perhaps," I said doubtfully. I crossed Jasper Taxman's name off of my mental list, then frowned. "What if all of the villagers decide to keep their mouths shut?"

Bill patted my hand. "It'll never happen. Gossip is a competitive sport in Finch. As you said before, all you have to do is make yourself available."

"I'll have tea tomorrow, at Sally Pyne's," I said, warming to the idea, "and you'll eat lunch and dinner at the pub for the next few days."

Bill sighed mournfully. "I feel compelled to point out that we'll be forsaking the delights of Francesca's cooking. Are we willing to make such a sacrifice for the Buntings' sake?"

I paused, remembering the vicar's troubled face and the undercurrent of concern in Lilian's voice. I owed an awful lot to those two kindly souls. I'd given up on religion when my mother had died, but the twins had made me reach for it again. Delivery rooms, like foxholes, make believers of us all, and when I'd first entered Saint George's, furtively and by a side door, too embarrassed to admit how lost I felt, the Buntings had welcomed me as though I'd never strayed.

Bill had turned to look back at me. The playful note was gone from his voice when he said, "I know. It's the least we can do."

I hugged him, then pushed away. "Hey, Mr. Big Shot Boston lawyer—how did you get to be such an expert on small towns?" I'd intended to lighten the mood, but Bill's face remained somber.

"Finch reminds me of my prep school," he said, "which means that we'd better catch our thief quickly. When people in a close-knit community start taking sides in a dispute, things can turn ugly overnight."

7.

"Shepherd! How the hell are you? Up to your armpits in crappy nappies?"

Dr. Stanford J. "Call me Stan" Finderman wasn't your standard academic. My old boss looked more like a long-shoreman than a scholar, with a bristly crew cut, a barrel chest, and hands that could wring the neck of a rhinoceros. His forthright manner and colorful vocabulary were legacies of a stint in the navy.

"Brats off the tit yet?" Stan continued. "Or d'you plan to go to college with 'em?"

"The boys are fine, Stan," I replied. It was nine o'clock in the morning and I felt like a million bucks. I'd slept like a rock for six hours, fed the boys, then rolled over for another luxurious half hour while Francesca got them bathed and dressed. My sterling nanny had baked croissants for breakfast—after I showed her how to open the kitchen cabinets—and Bill had pedaled off to work whistling blithely, while I retreated to the study to make my call to Stan. "Can you spare a minute? I need your help."

"Anytime, anyplace, Shepherd." Stan's sense of loyalty was another legacy of his stint in the navy.

"I'm trying to do a favor for some friends," I explained. "Do we know anyone who collects obscure Victorian archaeological ephemera?"

"To buy or to borrow?" he asked.

"A loan would suffice," I replied.

"Tried the British Library?" It was a logical suggestion. A three-hundred-year-old law required British publishers to send a copy of every book to the British Library, free of charge.

"Don't think it'll help in this case," I said. "I'm looking for a privately printed pamphlet, written and published by a hobbyist named Cornelius Gladwell. He was a C of E vicar, an amateur archaeologist, and a vindictive son of a gun. I don't think he'd've bothered with the niceties of publishing laws."

"My kind of guy," said Stan. "Tell me more, Shepherd."

Stan chortled gleefully while I recounted Mr. Gladwell's uncharitable scheme to defraud posterity—Stan had always had a soft spot for scoundrels—but he settled down when I got to Lilian Bunting's description of the missing pamphlet.

"I'm afraid there's not much to go on," I said, consulting the red spiral-bound notebook. "My friends describe the pamphlet as 'small, mouse-colored, and flimsy.' "

"That's a big help," Stan said sarcastically. "Has it got a title?"

"It's called *Disappointments in Delving*," I told him, "and we know that Mr. Gladwell printed ten numbered copies."

"Ten copies!" Stan exclaimed.

"That's right," I said. "And we need to find one ASAP."

Stan grunted and fell silent. I could almost see him leaning back in his office chair, his shirtsleeves rolled up, his collar undone, his red face pointed ceilingward as he scanned his enormous memory bank of names, faces, and book-collecting habits.

"I'm drawing a blank," he grumbled at last, "but don't get your knickers in a twist. I'll throw out the nets and see what I can haul in."

"Great," I said. "Thanks, Stan."

"Stow it," he replied. "Taught your brats to read yet?"

I spent the rest of the morning on the phone, explaining my plight to friends at museums and libraries in Great Britain and the United States. Gradually, by working the network of experts I'd come to know over the years, I managed to connect with about a dozen antiquities scholars who promised to search their respective collections for me.

Finally, I called Emma and asked her to run a computer search of on-line catalogs. I also pleaded with her to see what she could do about taming the Buntings' jungle. She agreed to undertake both assignments, but I suspected that the latter would receive priority treatment.

"I'm an old hand at reviving neglected gardens," she assured me, "and I've been dying to yank out all of those weeds. I swear there's a *Rosa hemisphaerica* buried in there somewhere, and the *Clematis cirrhosa* would be glorious if it were given room to breathe. And the *Cotinus coggygria!* Can you picture it against the wall?"

I let her burble on, though I couldn't understand one word in twenty. By the time she'd finished, the boys were ready for lunch and I was ready to toss the telephone out of the window.

"Watch your step," Francesca cautioned as I entered the kitchen, rubbing my phone-sore ear.

Will and Rob were waving furiously at me from their bouncy chairs, as though trying to draw my attention to

Francesca's latest stroke of genius. I looked down and saw that she'd tied a long cord to their chairs, so she could give them a reassuring jiggle from across the room. She was, at that moment, standing at the stove, stirring yet another aromatic stockpot.

"Francesca, this is brilliant," I said, stepping carefully over the cord. "Just like the circus animals in the tree yesterday." I crossed to breathe in a bouquet of mouth-watering scents. "Lunch, I hope?"

"Tomato-and-basil soup," Francesca replied. "I thought it'd go well with the croissants left over from breakfast." As she reached for the wooden spoon, her bronze medallion swung forward.

"That's a striking piece of jewelry," I said. The medallion featured a raised, cherubic face surrounded by a halo of curly hair—not unlike my own—with a pair of tiny wings protruding from the temples. "Is that supposed to be Mercury?"

"It's Mercury's winged head." Francesca touched the bronze disk. "It's called a *phalera*. It's a military decoration Roman soldiers used to wear. My father gave it to me, to remind me of where he came from." She lifted the wooden spoon to her lips and switched off the stove. "Finito. D'you want to take care of the bambinos before or after we eat?" She used the Italian words offhandedly, and without a trace of an accent, apart from her west-country burr. I wondered if she was testing the waters to see if the cottage had been infiltrated by the prejudices her father had encountered.

"Bambinos first, is my motto," I said, and was rewarded with an amused flicker from the corner of her eye.

Francesca had already prepared bowls of pureed chick peas and rice, and we spent a splendidly messy half hour helping Will and Rob vector in on the glide path between bowl and mouth. My little aces hit the target so often that they barely had room for milk afterward, and were willing to doze, full-bellied as Buddhas, while Francesca and I sat down to eat.

Between spoonfuls of savory soup and bites of buttery croissant, I told Francesca my plans for the afternoon. "I'm not sure how long I'll be, and I don't want to be late for the boys' next meal the way I was yesterday, so . . . Would you mind coming along? I know it'll be a lot of trouble, loading Will and Rob into the car and all, but . . ."

Francesca's dark eyes gleamed. "I've run eight kiddies to the Sleepy Hollow Farm Park and back any number of times. I think I'll be able to manage a pair of lamb chops like Rob and Will."

I looked down at my empty bowl, remembering the agonized hours I'd spent preparing for the six-mile (roundtrip) journey from the cottage to Saint George's for the boys' christening. I felt limp with inadequacy.

"I'd just as soon not bring the boys into the tearoom, though," Francesca added. "Wouldn't want to bother Mrs. Pyne's other customers. I'll sit with 'em up at Saint George's churchyard, if you like. You could meet us there when you've finished."

I nodded my agreement. None of the churchyard's customers would complain if the boys decided to exercise their right to free speech. "I'll get the keys to the Mercedes. The Mini's backseat isn't big enough for—"

"You've reminded me . . ." Francesca interrupted. She reached into her apron pocket. "I found this in a ratty old plimsoll at the back of the linen cupboard. Thought you might've misplaced it. D'you know what it's for?"

I gazed at the key resting in Francesca's palm and

blushed to my roots. "Yes," I admitted. "It unlocks the padlock on the, um, bathroom cabinet."

"Clever of you to hide it," Francesca commented. "Can't be too careful where little ones and medicine chests are concerned. I could tell you stories. . . ." She gazed at my bambinos and pocketed the key. "I'll put it right back where I found it."

I nearly wept into my soup. At last! I'd done something right!

Francesca took the wheel of the Mercedes while I kept an eye on the boys in the backseat. They dozed as soon as the engine started, and were fast asleep by the time we reached the humpbacked bridge.

It was another warm and sunny day, without a breath of wind to stir the willows on the green, but the square was—by Finch's standards—a beehive of activity. Christine and Dick Peacock were hosing down the pub's windows. Able Farnham, the aged greengrocer, was restocking his outdoor bins. Mr. Barlow, who garaged my cars when I was back in the States, was out walking Buster, his yappy terrier.

Bill's bicycle was propped in its customary place among the wysteria, and the paneled van was parked in front of the village school. The schoolhouse doors were firmly shut, however. Katrina and Simon were apparently heeding my advice and keeping a low profile.

Peggy Kitchen, on the other hand, had decided to make a statement. An array of Union Jacks had sprouted overnight from the front of her shop, and the display window, which usually featured a humble pyramid of baked-bean cans, now trumpeted an urgent call to arms. A hand-lettered sign placed strategically above a portrait of the queen shouted: SHE WANTS YOU TO SIGN THE PETITION! But only a tourist would think that *she* referred to Elizabeth II.

"Good grief," I said, dazzled by the display.

"Stupid woman," said Francesca. "Everyone knows the bishop won't heed her silly petition."

"Why not?" I asked.

"The bishop's daft about Roman ruins," Francesca replied. "Everyone knows that."

"Peggy doesn't," I pointed out.

Francesca tossed her head dismissively. "You could fill a barn with what Mrs. Kitchen doesn't know about Finch." Her gaze drifted away from Peggy's declaration of war, and her eyes narrowed slightly. "Now there's something *I* didn't know about."

I followed her gaze and saw, to my dismay, that the tearoom was closed. The door was shut, the windows were shrouded in bedsheets, and the freestanding slate sandwich-board that served as both sign and daily menu wasn't teetering in its usual spot on the cobbles.

"Tearoom's closed for renovation," Mr. Barlow called from across the square.

Francesca frowned. "Why's Mrs. Pyne bothering with that? I liked the tearoom as it was."

I, too, had been fond of the tearoom's disarming flea-market decor—the mismatched chairs, the rickety tables, the astonishing variety of chipped china. I wondered what would replace it.

"No point in it," Francesca went on sourly. "She only set up shop three years ago. No need for her to be re-arranging things now."

I blinked. "Sally Pyne's not from Finch?"

"Lord no. She came here from Plymouth, to be nearer

her son and daughter-in-law." Francesca glanced at the boys, who were still snoozing in their car seats, lulled by the idling engine. "Back to the cottage?"

"No . . ." I hated the thought of going home empty-handed. Bill would return from the pub, great with gossip, and I wouldn't have a crumb to contribute. "I think I'll stop by the Emporium. Want to come along?"

"And disturb the bambinos?" Francesca shook her head. "I'd sooner wait for you in the churchyard. See you in"—she checked her watch—"one hour?"

"I'll be there." I waved Francesca off, then squatted to greet Buster, who, unleashed by Mr. Barlow, had raced over to sniff at my sneakers.

"Mornin', Lori." Mr. Barlow coiled Buster's leash around his hand as he approached. "Nothing wrong with the Mini, I hope."

Mr. Barlow was a retired mechanic who'd come to regard my Mini as a dependable pension supplement. He never failed to ask after its health.

"The Mini's fine," I assured him. I picked up the rubber ball Buster had dropped at my feet and nodded toward the pub. "The Peacocks are industrious this morning. I don't think I've ever seen them hosing down the pub before."

"They're not just cleaning it," Mr. Barlow informed me. "They're renaming it and putting up a new sign."

"Foolish nonsense." Old Mr. Farnham had joined us, teetering precariously across the cobbles from his greengrocer's shop. "Pub doesn't need a sign. Everyone knows it's Peacock's pub."

"It's that wife of Dick's," Mr. Barlow explained. "She's full of queer ideas." He leaned toward me. "She reads science fiction, you know."

"There's nothing wrong with reading science fiction," I protested.

"Not when you know it's fiction," retorted Mr. Barlow. "Christine Peacock thinks it's all true!"

"Too bad that son of hers joined the army instead of the space program," said Mr. Farnham. "He could've given his mum a lift in his rocket ship."

I smiled thinly at the mean-spirited little joke, then tossed Buster's rubber ball in the direction of the tearoom. "What do you suppose Sally Pyne is up to?"

"Turning the tearoom into a juice bar, probably," said Mr. Farnham. "You know Sally—always trying to lose weight. Fat lot of good it's ever done her."

"I heard she's doing it up Roman," said Mr. Barlow, "on account of that chap at Scrag End field. Sally thinks his dig'll pull in tourists."

"Delusions of grandeur," Mr. Farnham scoffed. "There's never been tourists in Finch and there'll never be tourists in Finch."

Mr. Barlow nodded his agreement. "Folks may come here to live, but they don't come just for visits."

I turned to Mr. Barlow. "Did you move here from somewhere else?"

He nodded again. "Came from Bristol, same as Jasper Taxman. Why do you ask?"

"I was just wondering." I was wondering if *anyone* had been born and raised in Finch. The Buntings were from London, Sally Pyne was from Plymouth, Mr. Barlow and Mr. Taxman were from Bristol. Even Peggy Kitchen, the empress herself, had moved to Finch from Birmingham.

Mr. Barlow eyed the tearoom reflectively. "It may be that Sally's just trying to get up Peg Kitchen's nose. Never been the best of friends, those two. Ancient history, of course, but they do say history has a way of catching us up."

I glanced down at Buster, who'd returned, rubber ball clamped securely between his jaws. "Did Sally and Peggy know each other before they came to Finch?"

"No." Mr. Barlow shook his head decisively. "Their quarrel started right here. No telling where it'll end." He squinted over his shoulder at Kitchen's Emporium. "Planning to sign the petition?"

I shrugged. "I'm not sure. I've heard that the bishop's not likely to pay attention to it."

"Bishop doesn't run the shop, does he?" said Mr. Farnham. "If Her Majesty wants us to sign the petition, I reckon we'd best sign the petition, eh, Mr. Barlow?"

Mr. Barlow nodded sagely, then bent to snap the leash on Buster's collar.

"I'd better sign it, then," I said, "before Her Majesty comes gunning for me. Here, Mr. Farnham, let me walk with you."

I took Mr. Farnham by the arm and steered him back to his shop. Finch's greengrocer was in his seventies and painfully thin—if he stumbled on the cobbles, he'd shatter. The day's warmth inspired me to buy a bag of lemons at his shop, for lemonade, before heading for Kitchen's Emporium.

Peggy's shop sat unobtrusively in the center of the row of buildings that made up the west side of the square. Apart from the display in the window, it looked very much like its neighbors: a two-story building of Cotswolds stone, with a gabled roof and dormer windows above, a white-painted door, and a large white-framed window below.

The interior of Kitchen's Emporium featured a long

wooden counter running from front to back, with an ancient cash register at the end nearest the entrance. A grilled window at the far end denoted the post office. Rows of shelves and racks opposite the counter held the usual assortment of groceries.

Behind a small brown door at the rear of the shop, however, lay a realm so vast and wondrous that Bill had dubbed it Xanadu. Few travelers had roamed its byways and lived to tell the tale, but Peggy seemed to have a map tattooed upon her wrist. From its depths she'd extracted, on demand: sun hats, gumboots, strange elixirs to ward off colds, fishing poles, freckle cream, cricket bats, puce-colored thread, and the vicar's favorite brand of tinned prawns. The merest glimpse of Xanadu's shadowed aisles had convinced me that Peggy's shop was very much like Peggy: a facade of normalcy concealing the unfathomable.

Sleigh bells jingled as the shop door opened and a straggle of villagers emerged, murmuring quietly among themselves. The empress of Finch was no doubt holding court behind the counter, extending credit to the favored, withholding mail from the damned.

I pushed the door open, silently cursed the sleigh bells, and paused in the doorway to scan the aisles. Peggy Kitchen was nowhere in sight. Instead, an oddly silent Rainey Dawson sat cross-legged on the counter, her elbows on her knees, her pointed chin cupped in her grubby palms, staring fixedly at a man who stood in Peggy's place behind the cash register.

As I closed the door, Rainey's eyes slewed toward me and she hissed, in a whisper that could be heard in twenty counties, *"Say something to him."*

I smiled awkwardly at the man behind the counter. He was middle-aged, of middling height, with brown hair going gray at the temples. His brown tie matched a plain brown suit that in turn matched a pair of brown eyes peering out from behind brown-framed glasses. He was nondescript to the point of invisibility, but he held himself erect and seemed unflustered by Rainey's penetrating whisper.

"Mr. Taxman?" I guessed. "I'm Lori Shepherd, Bill Willis's wife. How do you do?"

"Very well, thank you," said Mr. Taxman. "And you?"

"Fine, just fine," I said, taking stock of Peggy Kitchen's alleged boyfriend. "Are you looking after the shop for Mrs. Kitchen?"

"I am," said Mr. Taxman.

"It's a nice day to be out and about," I commented. "A bit warm, of course."

"It is," Mr. Taxman agreed.

"Good window-washing weather, though," I prompted. Mr. Taxman nodded.

I put my sack of lemons on the counter and tried again. "The spring-cleaning bug seems to have bitten everyone lately. Sally Pyne, for instance . . ." I paused, but Mr. Taxman was evidently impervious to cues. "And the Peacocks," I continued doggedly. "Must be a bit of a nuisance for you. Hard to avoid tripping over all of those buckets and rags and . . . and puddles," I finished lamely.

The Great Stone Face registered no opinion.

Rainey leaned toward me to confide, in a stentorian murmur, *"He hardly ever talks."*

"Rainey," I scolded, "this isn't a zoo and Mr. Taxman isn't a caged animal, so stop treating him like one."

Rainey fixed her eyes virtuously on the ceiling. "I'm sorry, Mr. Taxman," she said. "I don't think you're one bit like a monkey *or* an elephant. They're *much* noisier."

A shy smile touched Mr. Taxman's lips. "Apology accepted," he said, then turned to me. "May I help you?"

"The petition," I said. "I'd like to sign it."

"Of course." As Mr. Taxman reached below the counter, a jangle of sleigh bells announced the arrival of Adrian Culver's young assistants.

Simon Blakely and Katrina Graham looked as bedraggled as Rainey. Their shorts were filthy, their T-shirts drenched in sweat. Simon was pulling bits of debris from his ponytail, and Katrina was massaging her biceps. Simon said hello to Rainey, then slumped against the counter, but Katrina used the counter as a barre, bending and flexing like a ballerina.

"Hard day at the dig?" I asked.

Simon gave a dispirited laugh. "We haven't even been to the dig. Katrina, queen of the Amazons, brought ten tons of the wrong equipment, so we've spent the entire morning repacking the van."

"Stop whining, Simon." Katrina rose from a deep knee bend. "You wouldn't be so tired if you took care of yourself."

"If you think I'm working out with you tonight, after what you've put me through this morning, you've got another think coming." Simon slouched over to grab a bottle of soda from a shelf. "You're a fitness freak."

"Dr. Culver expects us to be fit and healthy," Katrina retorted. "And I thought he'd want to use the equipment I brought. I don't know how we're going to do a proper job of soil analysis, chromatography, or spectrographic scans without it."

"This is a preliminary survey," Simon reminded her, "not the dig at Herculaneum." He unscrewed the cap on the bottle and gulped the soda noisily.

Katrina eyed the soda with disgust and selected a bottle of springwater from a shelf at Simon's elbow. "We'll take a case of these, if you have one, Mr. Taxman."

"I'll bring it over when Mrs. Kitchen returns. No need

to pay now," he added, waving off Katrina's cash. "I'll put
it on your account."

Simon choked on his soda. "Mrs. Kitchen extended
credit to *us?*" he sputtered.

"To your project," Mr. Taxman replied.

Katrina frowned. "Why would Mrs. Kitchen—"

Simon nudged her toward the front door. "Don't ar-
gue," he muttered. "See you at supper, Rainey."

Katrina tried to stand her ground, but as Simon
hustled her out into the square, her question remained
unanswered.

Why would Peggy Kitchen extend credit to the very
people she was trying to evict? I looked at Mr. Taxman,
who was conscientiously recording the pair's purchases in
the shop's ledger. If he knew what Peggy was up to—and I
was sure that she was up to something—he would no
doubt keep it to himself. I was beginning to get the hang
of his courtship strategy.

Mr. Taxman closed the ledger and pulled a clipboard
from beneath the counter. "The petition," he announced,
placing the clipboard, and a pen, in the space between
Rainey and the cash register.

The petition was, predictably, printed on harvest-gold
paper. A paragraph at the top of the first page stated
Peggy's version of the case—with yet another biblical
verse thrown in, excoriating "spiritual wickedness in high
places"—and demanded that the bishop exert his moral,
legal, and ecclesiastical authority in restoring control of
the schoolhouse to local hands. The numbered lines below
the paragraph were already filled with signatures, as were
three-quarters of the lines on the following page.

My eyebrows rose when I saw Emma's hasty scrawl
near the top of the second page. "Rainey," I said, "were
you here when Mrs. Harris stopped by today?"

Mr. Taxman might be able to hold his peace, but Rainey was reliably irrepressible. "Mrs. Harris's little girl is in France," she replied, "and her little boy is in New Guinea, but she told me that's not where guinea pigs come from so I asked her, if she wasn't sending lettuce leaves to feed the pigs, what was in the package? And she said it was photographs Nell wanted her to post to Peter, her little boy."

Smiling smugly, I picked up the pen, bent to add my name to the list, and caught sight of a signature that drove all thoughts of Emma's surrender from my mind. "Is that . . ." I pointed to a bold, barely legible line of script halfway down the page. "Does that say *Dr. Adrian Culver?*"

"Yes," said Mr. Taxman, a muted note of triumph in his voice.

His effusiveness caught my attention.

"Odd, isn't it?" I commented. "That Dr. Culver should sign a piece of paper that could put him out of the schoolhouse?"

"Indeed," Mr. Taxman replied.

A brick wall would have been easier to read. I scribbled my name on the page, wondering how Adrian Culver had managed to hold a pen with Peggy Kitchen twisting his arm.

"I'd like to make a copy of the petition before Mrs. Kitchen sends it to the bishop," I said.

"We have no photocopier," Mr. Taxman pointed out.

"My husband has one," I told him. "It won't take him more than a minute to make a copy. Please tell Mrs. Kitchen that a . . . a historic document like this should be preserved for posterity."

"I will." Mr. Taxman slid the clipboard beneath the counter.

Rainey's foot began to jiggle and I turned my attention to her. She had no business sitting indoors on such a beautiful day. At her age, I'd spent the summer months climbing trees, hopping fences, and racing through alleys from dawn to dusk. But then, I'd had a gang of neighbor children to play with, whereas Rainey, according to Bill, had no one. On impulse, I said, "I'm going for a walk, Rainey. Want to come along?"

Rainey sprang from the counter in such a tangle of arms and legs that she would have broken a dozen bottles of vinegar, as well as her neck, if I hadn't caught her in midair.

"Yes, please," she piped as I set her firmly on her sneakered feet.

"You'll have to get your gran's permis—" A cacophony of sleigh bells cut me off as Rainey tumbled headlong out of the shop.

Mr. Taxman gazed after her. "How kind of you to invite her to accompany you on your expedition," he said softly. "Such a quiet little mouse. I'd half forgotten she was here."

8.

Rainey Dawson didn't walk. She bounced, skittered, twirled, and all but took to the air in flight as we made our way across the square. The oppressive heat had no effect on her, and her prodigal expenditure of energy contributed nothing to our progress.

She was infinitely distractable. She dropped onto the cobbles to pry a thumbtack from the sole of her left sneaker, ran to the war memorial to retrieve a willow wand, paused for a refreshing splash in the Peacocks' puddles, and scampered over to Bill's office to admire—and "accidentally" break off—a pendant of wysteria, which she presented to me as a token of affection.

It wore me out to watch her, but I made no move to check her. The boys wouldn't require my presence in the churchyard for another twenty minutes, and Rainey clearly needed to blow off a little steam. I let her stretch her legs at random for a few minutes more before I finally lassoed her with a question.

"Did your grandmother send you over to the Emporium," I asked, as she whizzed by, "so she could concentrate on the tearoom?"

"Sort of." Rainey skidded to a halt, then launched into a word-flurry that would have taxed Peggy Kitchen's well-developed lungs. "Gran and Mrs. Kitchen aren't speaking to each other because Gran said Mrs. Kitchen's petition should be used to line the cat's box, and Mrs. Kitchen called Gran a greedy old cow, but Gran needed a pound of butter for the Pompeii puffs so she sent me to fetch it."

"Pompeii puffs?" I said, with a twitch of foreboding. "Is that something new?"

"It's cream puffs with a new name," Rainey informed me, trotting beside me into Saint George's Lane. "Gran and Katrina've made up all sorts of new names for Gran's goodies. Chariot wheels is doughnuts, and Hadrian cakes are the ones with jam in the middle, but Gran won't eat any because she's slimming again. And Gran's tearoom isn't Gran's tearoom, it's the *Empire* tearoom, with a capital *E* and a helmet sort of thing next to it. Gran says Bath's made a packet off the Romans, so why shouldn't we?"

I quaked as my little oracle bubbled over with fresh portents of madness in Finch. We'd come abreast of the vicarage, and while Rainey put her willow wand to use, beheading thistles, I gazed worriedly at the overgrown shrubs.

The long-running feud Mr. Barlow had mentioned seemed to be heating up. Sally Pyne was clearly in open rebellion against Peggy Kitchen, and she was using Dr. Culver as a weapon. First, she'd taken his assistants in as lodgers. Then she'd refused to sign the petition demanding his departure. Now she was transforming the tearoom into a little corner of ancient Rome. She seemed bound and determined to get up Peggy's nose in every way imaginable. It wasn't difficult to conceive of her going one step further, and stealing the Gladwell pamphlet in pursuit of her vendetta.

When I informed Rainey that the twins were waiting for us in the churchyard, she flung her willow wand into the air—narrowly missing my eye—and rocketed up the lane to get a firsthand look at "WillanRob."

I picked up my own pace, pausing at the Mercedes to exchange the bag of lemons for a bottle of My Milk from the ice chest. The sprig of wysteria I kept with me, to place on a headstone in the churchyard.

Because Saint George's was the focal point of Finch's tourist trickle, the churchyard was kept in better order than the vicarage garden. The lych-gate's shingled roof didn't leak, and the sword-shaped weather vane atop the church didn't squeak. Weeds were not allowed to choke the roses twining on the low stone wall, nor were they permitted to stem the fall of ivy clinging to the moss-topped sundial. The headstones might be crooked and the tombs defaced by weathering, but they rose from a cool green pool of cropped lawn, among graveled walks that were raked smooth once a week.

A pair of graceful cedars of Lebanon grew within the churchyard walls; the taller sheltered a stone bench with a well-worn seat and backrest. The twins' toy and diaper bags sat on either end of the bench, and a blanket covered the thick, soft bed of needles in front of it. Will and Rob lay on the blanket, and Rainey knelt between them, talking a mile a minute. I could tell by my sons' vigorous kicks that they were doing their level best to keep up their end of the conversation.

Francesca stood nearby, half in and out of shade, gazing northward, toward the belt of woodland that curved along the riverbank. The vicar had said that Scrag End field lay beyond the woodland, alongside Hodge Farm. Was Francesca worried about Adrian Culver's dig? Her dark eyes were grave, her lips tightly set, as though she sensed danger lurking in the shadows. I was about to call her name when she turned, and I caught my breath. Francesca, silhouetted against the cedar's deep-green boughs, with dappled sunlight striking coppery sparks from her auburn hair, was more than handsome. She was resplendent, an olive-skinned goddess in a glowing white shirt-dress and grass-stained flats.

The church bells—automated since the early seventies, according to Lilian—tolled the hour and Francesca's pensive expression vanished. "You're right on time," she said. "Here, give me the bottle and I'll get Will started."

Francesca and I lifted the boys into our arms, sat on the bench, and got snack time under way. Rainey watched in silence for a moment, then flopped onto her back, declaring listlessly, "Just like Mummy."

So much for nature's miracles, I thought. I felt like a magician whose best trick had fallen flat. Hoping to redeem myself, I cradled Rob in one arm and groped through the toy bag until my fingers touched a familiar cottontail.

"Rainey," I said, "I've got someone here I'd like you to meet. He used to live on a shelf in my cottage, but these days he prefers to be with the boys."

With a wizardly flourish, I produced a rabbit from the toy bag. Not a lettuce-nibbling rabbit, but a small pink-flannel bunny with black button eyes, hand-stitched whiskers, and a grape-juice stain on his snout that brought to mind a little girl who'd been every bit as rambunctious as Rainey.

"His name is Reginald," I continued, "and as you can see, he doesn't have anyone to play with."

"I'll play with him!" Rainey scrambled to her knees and reached for my pink bunny. "Reginald," she began, "my name is . . ." She hesitated, gazed intently at Reginald's face, then looked up at me, round-eyed with astonishment. "He already knows my name. And he wants to show me where the hedgehog lives."

"Hedgehog?" said Francesca.

"Reginald says there's a hedgehog family living in the wall, round back of the church. He says I simply *must* see them." Rainey jumped to her feet and galloped away, Reginald flopping and braids flying as she dodged between headstones. I looked deeply into Rob's eyes and hoped that Reg would one day fire my son's imagination as vividly as he was firing Rainey Dawson's.

"Did you tell Rainey about the hedgehog?" Francesca asked.

I looked at her uncertainly. "There's a hedgehog?"

Francesca nodded. "My brothers found the burrow years ago. It's right where Reg—where *Rainey* said it'd be, in the wall, round back of the church."

"Is that right?" I shouldn't have been surprised. Aunt Dimity had made Reginald for me, and I had reason to believe that she'd put something besides strong cotton into her needlework. It would have been easier to explain to Rainey than to Francesca that Reg wasn't your average pink-flannel bunny, however, so I feigned nonchalance. "Maybe the vicar told Rainey about the hedgehog."

Francesca rolled her eyes. "The vicar knows as much about hedgehogs as I know about his evensongs."

"You don't go to Saint George's?" I said.

"My family's Roman Catholic," she replied. "But my father and brothers used to mow the grass and rake the paths here." She nodded toward the low wall. "My father planted the roses."

"They're gorgeous," I said. "The parishioners must have been delighted."

"Some were." Francesca shifted Will in her arms. "You sign Mrs. Kitchen's petition?"

"Yes," I admitted. I would have said more, but Hurricane Rainey had returned.

"Lori! Francesca! Look who I found!"

I looked up, fully expecting to see Rainey juggling a pair of hapless hedgehogs. Instead, she was bobbing cheerfully in the wake of a tall, not unattractive man.

He was slender and deeply tanned, dressed in khaki shorts, a short-sleeved blue shirt, and a crumpled, battered digger hat that looked as though it had been through several wars. His face was long and narrow, the skin drawn tightly across high cheekbones and a wide, thin-lipped mouth. He wore hiking boots and carried a small khaki rucksack on his back. A pair of half glasses dangled from a lanyard around his neck.

"He was looking at the wall paintings," Rainey shouted breathlessly, "because Katrina and Simon made a muddle of the schoolhouse, so he couldn't spend the whole day at Scrag End field, and he didn't want to meet the hedgehog, but he wanted to meet you."

"Thank you, Rainey." The man's resonant voice was like a cello accompaniment to Rainey's trumpeting. "You've explained the situation admirably."

He ducked under the cedar's drooping branches, blinked at the sudden change from light to shade, caught sight of my exposed breast, and flushed crimson.

"I do apologize." As his head snapped to one side, his eyes met Francesca's, and the flood of color drained from his face. He froze in place and at the same time seemed to melt, swaying slightly as a soft, involuntary moan escaped his lips.

"Dr. Culver," said Rainey. "Why are you staring at Francesca?"

"*Francesca,*" whispered Dr. Culver.

9.

Rainey peered up at the tall archaeologist with a look of helpful concern. "I thought you wanted to meet Lori."

The crimson tide returned to Adrian Culver's face. He averted his gaze from Francesca, found himself staring once more at my maternal splendor, and was finally reduced to examining a buckle on his rucksack. My heart went out to him. Bill's father was similarly ill at ease when he inadvertently caught sight of one of his grandsons dining au naturel.

"Are you sick, Dr. Culver?" Rainey asked, hugging Reginald to her chest.

"Rainey . . ." I reached for the sprig of wysteria she'd liberated from the vine on Bill's office, and pointed to a headstone that was awash in a fragrant froth of climbing roses. "Would you please put the wysteria on that headstone?"

Rainey turned to see where I was pointing. "But it's got flowers already," she objected. "Why do you want me to—" She broke off to listen to Reginald, then took the wysteria from my hand and without another word trotted off.

"Take your time," I called after her. "Reginald likes to visit that grave."

"I know," she called back.

Adrian Culver watched Rainey's departure, then fixed his gaze at a neutral point halfway up the cedar's trunk. "Ms. Shepherd . . ." he began.

"Please, call me Lori," I said. Most of the time it was easier to use my first name than to explain that I hadn't taken Bill's last name when we'd married. "And allow me to introduce my friend, Francesca Sciaparelli."

"Afternoon, Dr. Culver." Francesca's greeting was cool enough to chill lava.

"Please, you must call me Adrian. Both of you." The poor man must have felt faintly ridiculous proclaiming his identity to the sky, because he dragged his digger cap from his head and cautiously lowered his gaze.

Abruptly, Francesca hefted Will to her diaper-draped shoulder and got to her feet. "I'll pay my respects to Miss Westwood, as long as I'm here. I don't want Rainey trampling the roses. My father planted 'em special." She patted Will's back and swept past Adrian Culver, without so much as a "Nice to have met you."

Adrian stared after her, nonplussed. I, too, was taken aback by her bluntness, but I had no time to stare. The twins had, as always, finished their meals simultaneously, so I shifted Rob to my lap and closed down the mess hall. Adrian ventured a hesitant glance in our direction.

"Miss Sciaparelli wouldn't by any chance be related to Mrs. Kitchen, would she?" he inquired politely.

"They can't stand the sight of each other," I replied.

Adrian slung his rucksack onto the ground and sank onto the bench. "Did I somehow offend Miss Sciaparelli? Or is she always so . . . formal with strangers?"

His choice of words hinted at a gallant nature. I'd have described Francesca's behavior as downright rude.

"She may be tired," I said. "She's been stuck here for an hour with my twins. Francesca's been helping me look after them."

"I'm amazed to hear that you require her assistance," Adrian said. His wide mouth turned upward in a smile. "Simon and Katrina led me to believe that you're indefatiguable. They've come to regard you as our guardian angel."

"That's because they're laboring under a grave misapprehension," I informed him.

Adrian's high forehead wrinkled. "It was you who chased Mrs. Kitchen from our door yesterday, wasn't it?"

"It was," I acknowledged.

"And Mrs. Kitchen was affability itself when I stopped by the Emporium yesterday evening. I thought you were responsible for her change of heart. Naturally, when she suggested that I sign—"

"What did you sign?" I interrupted.

"Her list of creditors. At least, that's what she—" Adrian's eyes narrowed suspiciously as he studied the expression on my face. "What have I done? Signed a confession to some unspeakable crime?"

I patted his arm. "Let's just say that, if I were you, I'd think twice about signing anything Peggy Kitchen put in front of me. This time it was only a petition calling for the bishop to evict you from the schoolhouse, but next time—"

Adrian's bark of laughter made Rob jump. "I should have known!" he exclaimed, slapping the digger hat against his thigh. "That woman is a national treasure. She'll be prime minister before she's through." He shook his head ruefully. "I shan't hear the end of it from the bishop."

"You know him?" I said.

"He and I share a common interest in antiquities." Adrian cocked his head to one side. "Do you know, someone else asked me about the bishop today—a chap I met at the pub. Bill Willis, his name was. Some sort of expat Yank barrister. Do you know him?"

"He's my husband," I said, but Adrian's attention had wandered. He leapt to his feet as Francesca returned, and stood, cap in hand, to offer her his seat. She passed him by without a second glance.

"Time Rainey was off home," she said as the little girl came trailing up behind her. "Shall I give her a lift?"

Adrian immediately volunteered to walk with Rainey. "I should be getting back in any case. My assistant's brought rather more equipment than we need, and I've had the devil's own time sorting the essentials from the extraneous."

"Really?" I said. "I was under the impression that you'd hoped to extend your stay in Finch."

Adrian risked a furtive glance at Francesca's face. "One may hope, of course, but in fact it's far too early to make long-range plans. I thought I'd explained that to Katrina and Simon, but I must not have made myself clear." He bent to pick up his rucksack. "They brought enough gear to see us through until spring."

Adrian slipped the rucksack onto one shoulder and extended his hand. "It's been a great pleasure to finally meet you, Lori. You must come to Scrag End for a tour. And you, Miss Sciaparelli, if you're not too busy—"

"I've no time for tours," Francesca snapped, ignoring his proffered hand.

"Why are you cross with Dr. Culver, Francesca?" Rainey asked. "Gran says he's going to make Finch famous."

"Will he, now?" Francesca said witheringly.

Adrian opened his mouth to speak, but words seemed to fail him. He stood there, love-stunned and mute, turning and twisting his hat in his hands, trying not to stare at Francesca's sumptuous curves and failing miserably.

Rainey tugged on his shirt. "*I'm* not cross with you, Dr. Culver," she said consolingly. "And Gran thinks the world of you."

"Thank you, Rainey," said Adrian. "Perhaps I'll take your grandmother up on her kind invitation this evening." He bowed graciously, first to me, then to Francesca. "Do stop by the dig, Lori. And don't hesitate to bring your sons. I'm extremely fond of children. Good day, ladies."

I smiled as he strode off. I knew full well that his eagerness to play host to my sons had less to do with his affinity for children than with his affinity for my nanny. I couldn't blame him. He was enamored of antiquities, after all, and Francesca was a dead ringer for Venus.

It didn't take a psych degree to figure out what had happened to Dr. Culver—I could hear Cupid chortling as he restrung his bow—but Francesca's harsh reaction seemed inexplicable. I didn't believe for a minute that Will or Rob had worn her out. She hadn't been peevish with me or Rainey. Her surliness had been directed like a laser beam at Adrian Culver, and I was itching to find out why.

"We'd best be off, too," she remarked. "Time I was getting supper ready. Poached salmon suit you?"

"Sounds great." I said nothing more until we were seated in the Mercedes and ready to go. Then I commented casually, "Adrian seems like a nice guy."

"He's a puffed-up popinjay," Francesca snapped. "What's more, he's a liar." She started the engine and began turning the car around.

Her vehemence startled me. "What makes you say that?"

"Promised the vicar he'd be in and out, no trouble," Francesca replied. "Forgot to mention his plans to build his own museum, here, in Finch. Calling it after himself, too. The Culver Institute."

My eyebrows rose. "Who told you about the museum?"

"Mrs. Pyne found a stack of letters when she was tidying Katrina's room," Francesca said.

"Sally Pyne read Katrina Graham's private mail?" I exclaimed, appalled.

"They were right next to her computer," Francesca declared, "where anyone could see 'em. And they were all about raising money for the Culver Institute." She tossed her head. "That's why Sally Pyne's tarting up the tearoom and the Peacocks are cleaning up the pub. They think the Culver Institute'll be *good* for Finch."

"Won't it?" I asked.

"We don't need any more outsiders coming in here," Francesca stated firmly. "There's enough of them running round the village as it is."

"Gee, thanks," I said.

Francesca blushed. "I don't mean you or the Buntings or such. Your kind don't interfere. But Dr. Culver'll interfere, right enough. He'll be as bad as Mrs. Kitchen. Besides," she continued, "I don't hold with putting dead folks' belongings in museums. It's not right."

"Didn't your medallion come from a museum?" I asked.

"It did not," she declared. "My father made the *phalera* with his own two hands. He'd never go poking and prying into dead folks' things. Which is more than can be said for a puffed-up popinjay like Dr. Culver."

Francesca's burst of fury abated as she guided the car toward the square. "Bill rang," she said, making conversation. "Said he and Derek Harris'd have supper at the pub tonight."

I felt a stab of disappointment. I'd been looking forward to swapping gossip with my husband, and Francesca's late addition was pure gold. If Adrian Culver really was planning to build a museum in Finch, Sally Pyne would have two extremely good reasons to steal the Gladwell pamphlet. An antiquities museum would help her business and at the same time serve as a perpetual irritant to her old foe, Peggy Kitchen.

The more I thought about it, the more excited I became. Sally Pyne wasn't the only one who'd benefit from having a museum in Finch. Christine Peacock's pub would prosper. Katrina Graham would have a proper laboratory in which to conduct the experiments she'd cataloged to Simon in Peggy's shop. And no self-respecting archaeologist would throw away a chance to name a museum after himself. If Adrian, Katrina, or Christine had gotten wind of the Gladwell pamphlet on Sunday night, they'd each have a good reason to make sure it never saw the light of day.

As the Mercedes rumbled through the square, I gazed at Bill's bicycle and sighed. I couldn't fault my husband for following my instructions, but I hoped he wouldn't dawdle at the pub. I was champing at the bit to hear what Adrian had told him about the bishop—and to share with him my burgeoning suspicions.

Dinner had been marvelous: chilled cucumber soup, poached salmon with salad, and homemade lemon sorbet for dessert. I felt a pang of pity for Bill, who'd missed out on the feast, glanced at the clock for the hundredth time, and folded my hands to keep myself from fidgeting.

After supper, I'd taken the boys for a walk, bathed

them, and put them to bed. I'd spent an hour or so in the kitchen with Francesca, discussing her terms of employment, a discussion that had consisted mostly of Francesca calmly stating her requirements and me saying okay.

Having dispensed with my duties as chatelaine, I'd stretched out on the couch in the living room to record the day's events in Lilian Bunting's red notebook. I wanted to be armed and ready when Bill came through the door.

Francesca sat in the chintz-covered armchair, hemming a skirt. When she glanced up, I nodded and smiled and silently ordered myself not to worry. Bill hadn't told me when to expect him back from the pub, so he wasn't late, exactly. His bicycle was equipped with lights and bristling with reflectors, so he'd be safe on the road after dark. There was no cause to—

A car's headlights illuminated the bay window and I leapt to my feet. Francesca gave me an odd look as I dashed into the hallway, but I was past caring. It was too late in the evening for casual callers, but policemen bearing bad news—and mangled bicycles—might turn up at any time. Dreading dire revelations, I opened the front door and nearly fainted with relief when I saw Adrian Culver striding up the flagstone path.

"Sorry to bother you at this hour," he said, "but I didn't want you to lose sleep over Reginald."

"Reginald?" I said stupidly.

He held my rabbit out for me to see. "Rainey pleads guilty to rabbit-napping. She asked me to return him to you. Unfortunately, I was detained—first by Mrs. Pyne, then by Mrs. Bunting, and finally, by Mrs. Kitchen."

For a moment I forgot my own distress. "Sounds like you've been through the wringer," I said, taking custody of my pink bunny. "Can I offer you a cup of tea?"

"It's awfully late," he said, hanging back.

"Don't be silly," I told him. "Francesca's just brewed a fresh—" I broke off as understanding belatedly dawned. It would have dawned much sooner had I bothered to take note of Adrian's appearance. He'd left his crumpled hat and rucksack at the schoolhouse and replaced his work-clothes with a pair of gray dress slacks, polished shoes, and an immaculate, though silently rumpled white shirt. If Reginald had been a wrist corsage, I'd have sworn it was prom night.

"Come in," I said unsteadily. I put Reg on the hall table and ushered Adrian into the living room. "Francesca, look who's here."

"Evening, Dr. Culver." Francesca picked up her sewing basket and got to her feet. "It's late. I think I'll go up."

Adrian wilted visibly as Francesca strode past us, but perked up again when she stopped short.

"You've a button missing," she said to him. She made it sound like an accusation.

"Have I?" Adrian peered down at his shirt, dismayed.

Francesca was not the sort of woman who could let an empty buttonhole stay empty. She heaved an exasperated sigh and began to rummage through her sewing basket. She retrieved a threaded needle and a white button, then turned to Adrian. The reproachful look she gave him was exactly what she'd use on Rob or Will in the future, if they ever returned home from the playground without their sneakers. "Hold still," she ordered.

I'm convinced that Adrian Culver held his breath, though his heart must have been thundering. With a twist of her wrist, Francesca slipped the fingers of her left hand inside his shirt to hold the button in place while her right hand plied the needle back and forth. Her movements were brisk and businesslike, but her head was bent low, her coil of dark hair mere inches from Adrian's lips.

Adrian peered down at her woozily. "I can't help but admire your . . . medallion," he said. "It's a miniature *phalera,* isn't it?"

"Never mind about my *phalera.*" Francesca snipped the thread short. "You just keep track of your buttons."

"Th-thank you, Miss Sciaparelli." Adrian fumbled with his shirtfront as she gathered up her basket and stalked out of the room.

I waited for the fumes of unrequited passion to dissipate, then gently guided Adrian to the couch. I poured a cup of tea and wrapped his hands around it, but the warmth failed to recall him from the land of the lovesick. He was, in my judgment, ripe for interrogation.

"It was kind of you to return Reg to me this evening," I began, "especially when you have so much else on your mind—organizing the schoolhouse, excavating Scrag End field, planning your museum . . ."

"Yes," he agreed, nodding vaguely. "There's quite a lot to do, but—" He straightened abruptly. "Museum? What museum?"

"The Culver Institute," I said helpfully.

"The . . . the *Culver Institute?*" Incomprehension gave way to sudden laughter. "Oh, dear," he said, placing his teacup on the end table, "how flattering. I presume you've been speaking with Rainey's grandmother."

"Indirectly," I said. "She seems to have gotten the impression that you're planning to build a museum in Finch."

"I may have mentioned it in passing," Adrian admitted candidly, "as a very long-range, very remote possibility—a dream, if you like. As I told you this afternoon, however, it's far too soon to plan anything of that magnitude. We've scarcely begun to explore Scrag End. Apart from that, I'd

never name a museum after—" He broke off as another
set of headlights flared across the bow windows. "Is that
a car?"

I was already halfway to the door. I flung it open just in
time to see Derek Harris, all six foot four of him, trying to
keep my husband from toppling into the lilac bushes.

"Evening, Lori," Derek called, leaning Bill against the
door of his pickup truck.

Bill's head rose slowly from his chest. He smiled sweetly.
" 'Lo, love," he said.

"What on earth—" I began.

"Think we'd best get him inside," Derek suggested.

Adrian Culver stepped past me. "May I be of assistance?"

Bill favored Adrian with a toothy grin. " 'Lo, love," he
repeated.

I stood aside as Derek and Adrian maneuvered my husband into the hallway, where they propped him against
the wall. He seemed content to lean there, humming quietly to himself.

Adrian's gray eyes had filled with compassion, and I
suddenly remembered that he hadn't been paying attention when I'd told him that the "expat Yank barrister" he'd
met in the pub was my husband.

"I'll be off," Adrian said.

I shook my head. "No, wait, I can explain—"

"No need, Lori." Adrian gave my hand a sympathetic
squeeze and departed.

I closed the door and rounded on Derek. "What have
you done to my husband?"

Bill cleared his throat. "Pegger . . . Peggry . . . Peg-
gle . . ."

"Peggy Kitchen," Derek translated, "brought her petition round to the pub this evening. She spotted Bill and me having supper, came over to ask if Bill'd worked out the legal solution you'd promised her."

I winced. I'd forgotten to warn Bill about the lies I'd spun to keep Peggy away from the schoolhouse.

"Never fear," Derek went on. "Bill's a lawyer. Knows how to improvise. Told Peggy that in order to have enough time to explore the appropriate legal avenues he'd be forced to give up morris dancing."

"No . . . more . . . danshing," Bill stated, fairly firmly.

"Quite right, Bill, no more dancing." Derek patted Bill's shoulder. "That's why Peggy assigned you to the mead-tasting committee for the Harvest Festival. Said it'd take up less of your valuable time."

"Mead." Bill giggled softly.

"Bill doesn't know the first thing about mead," I said, bewildered.

Bill tried again. "I tol', tol', tol' . . ."

"That's what he told Peggy," Derek interjected. "And that's why Peggy took it upon herself to educate your husband's palate. Had him sample all twelve jugs of Dick Peacock's finest mead."

Bill made a complicated attempt to hold up twelve fingers.

I groaned.

"Chris called me away to help her fit the new pub sign with hooks," said Derek. "By the time I got back, Bill was blotto. Took some time to persuade him that his bed would be more comfy than the floor. Took even longer to pry him off of that blasted bicycle. And there's something else. . . ." Derek put an arm out to keep Bill from sliding down the wall. "Peggy pulled me aside and told me some crackbrained story about Francesca and that Culver chap getting up to no good in the churchyard."

I gaped at him, bereft of speech.

"Told her not to be a damned fool," Derek assured me. "Why on earth would Francesca use the churchyard when she has a perfectly comfortable—"

"*Derek!*" I exclaimed indignantly.

"Thought that would bring you round." Derek grinned briefly. "In point of fact, I told Peggy that if she went about talking nonsense about my friends, she'd have to find another handyman. And since I'm the only man in the kingdom who understands her drains, I doubt we'll hear any more out of her." He nodded toward Bill. "Upstairs?"

"Please." As I stood there watching Derek cart my drunken husband off to bed, my indignation gave way to a simmering rage. "That woman," I growled. "That woman must be stopped."

10.

If a hundred Gladwell pamphlets had slithered through my mail slot the following morning, I'd have tossed them on the hearth and set them blazing. I was no longer interested in closing down Adrian's dig. I wanted him to occupy the schoolhouse forever. I was a little out of charity with Peggy Kitchen. And so was Bill.

"May I kill her, Lori? Please? Just this once?"

I wiped his greenish face with a cool washcloth. "Only if you get to her before I do, my darling."

Bill smiled serenely, pushed himself up on his elbows, and was violently sick in the bedside bucket thoughtfully provided by Francesca.

I cleaned him up, got him settled, and went downstairs. As I reached the bottom of the staircase, I noticed Francesca standing in the doorway to the study, a rag in one hand, a jar of furniture polish in the other. She seemed oddly flustered.

"Lori? Would you come in here, please?"

I felt a tiny flutter of alarm as I followed her into the study. The room showed signs of a recent cleaning. The hearth had been swept, the ivy-covered windows were spotless, and the tall leather armchairs gleamed dully in the light from the mantelshelf lamps. Will and Rob observed our entrance solemnly from their bouncy chairs on the far side of the room.

When she reached the wooden desk beneath the windows, Francesca pointed to a bookshelf on her right. "A book fell from that shelf as you were coming down the stairs. It nearly hit me in the head."

"Oh, dear." I didn't have to pretend to be dismayed as I walked over to lay a hand along the blue journal's spine. I did, however, have to keep myself from screeching when the book nudged my palm. "I . . . I should have warned you."

"Warned me about what?" Francesca asked.

I leaned my full weight on the book. "It's an old cottage," I babbled. "The walls are crooked. The floors are uneven. Sometimes . . . when someone comes down the stairs . . . books fall off the shelves."

"But that's dangerous," Francesca scolded. "What if the book had hit one of the boys?"

"She'd never . . ." I cleared my throat. "You're right. I'm sorry. Let's take the boys to the living room, just to be on the safe side."

Francesca complied, but as we were leaving the study, carrying one baby-filled bouncy chair apiece, she gave me a sidelong look. "How did you know it was the blue book that fell?" she asked.

"You . . . um . . . pointed to it," I said, avoiding her eyes. We transferred the boys from their bouncy chairs to the playpen, and I backed toward the hallway. "I've got some phone calls to make," I said. "I'll be in the study, if you need me."

"All right," said Francesca, observing me closely.

I darted up the hallway, praying that she'd blame my jumpiness on hormonal fluctuations. I slipped into the study, paused to take a calming breath, and gently closed the door. Then I grabbed the blue journal from the shelf and banged it open on the desk.

"Dimity, what do you think you're doing?" I demanded. "Do you *want* Francesca to think I'm nuts?"

I wanted to get your attention. If handwriting could appear petulant, Dimity's did.

"You've got it," I said, "but I wish you'd come up with a more discreet way of attracting it."

Your anger was filling the cottage.

"Why shouldn't I be angry?" It wasn't easy, venting my spleen in an undertone, but I managed. "Peggy Kitchen's got the town in an uproar. She's making the vicar's life hell, she tricked Adrian Culver into signing her stupid petition, and she got Bill plastered last night because he tried to quit morris dancing. If that weren't enough, she's spreading filthy rumors about Francesca and Adrian." I thumped my fist on the desk. "You bet I'm angry."

I wanted to remind you of something before you let your anger carry you away.

"What?" I said impatiently. "What did you want to remind me of?"

Your eighth birthday.

"My . . ." I stared at the words on the page, then straightened slowly and touched a hand to my forehead. "My eighth birthday?"

Do you remember what your mother gave you for your eighth birthday?

"Of course I remember." I looked from the journal to the archival boxes that held the letters my mother had written to Dimity over a span of some forty years. I didn't have to refer to them to remember the most glorious birthday gift my mother had ever given me.

"My bicycle." I lowered myself onto the desk chair, rested my elbows on either side of the journal, and stared at the sunlight flickering through the ivy. "My first bicycle. Mom got it secondhand, but I thought it was the most beautiful bike I'd ever seen. It was blue with white hand-grips and a white seat."

It had a silver bell on the left handlebar. You rang it with your thumb.

I glanced down at Dimity's words and smiled. "Mom came out and watched me ride it up and down the block all afternoon. I felt like I was flying. I'll never forget it."

Nor will Peggy Kitchen ever forget her eighth birthday. The sirens sounded as her mother placed her cake on the kitchen table. By the time the raid was over, the cake was gone. As were the table, the kitchen, the house. Peggy spent her eighth birthday huddled in the basement of a church while Birmingham was pulverized by the Luftwaffe.

I turned my face away. I didn't want to know more. I fought to hold on to my anger, but I could feel it slipping from my grasp. She'd been no older than Rainey. . . . I felt my chest tighten and forced myself to look back at the journal, where the loops and curves of Dimity's fine copperplate were scrolling inexorably across the page.

Peggy Kitchen came to Finch to escape the blitz in Birmingham. When she and her mother arrived, they possessed nothing but the clothing they wore and a photograph of Peggy's father in his Tank Corps uniform. They were here when they got word that he'd been killed. He was burnt to death when his tank was shelled during an encounter with Italian troops in North Africa. Three months later, Piero Sciaparelli arrived, a prisoner of war, to work for old Mr. Hodge.

"Francesca's father . . ." I murmured.

The first time Peggy met Piero, she threw stones at him. Some of the villagers, I'm sorry to say, rallied around her. Piero Sciaparelli spent the rest of his life, as many soldiers do, trying to put the horrors of war behind him, but Peggy Kitchen never stopped throwing stones. From what you've told me, she's throwing them still.

"I wish she'd stop," I said softly. "The war's been over for a long, long time."

Perhaps we can help her.

"I think it's a little late for that," I said.

Lori, my dear, haven't you learned by now that it's never

The writing stopped. I heard a scrabble of claws and a strange snuffling noise in the hallway, slid the journal back into place on the bookshelf, and turned to face the hall.

"Emma?" I called.

The door opened and Ham trotted in, nearly tripping Emma in his eagerness to greet me. Ham—short for Hamlet—was Nell Harris's black Labrador retriever. Like Rocinante, he'd been left in Emma's charge while Nell was in Paris.

"We've come to view the corpse," Emma intoned while Ham frisked about my knees.

"I don't recommend it. Bill's not a pretty sight." I bent to fondle Ham's ears. "He should've known better than to spend an evening drinking Dick Peacock's mead."

Emma's eyebrows rose as she sank into one of the tall leather armchairs near the hearth. She was wearing black Wellington boots, baggy cotton trousers, and a gardening smock over a violet tank top. "I can't believe it," she said. "You're blaming Bill's condition on *Bill?*"

I ducked my head. "No, I've just been talking with—" I looked at the open door, then jutted my chin toward the blue journal. "How about a walk in the garden?"

Emma got the message. "Ham needs a run," she said, getting to her feet. "Poor pup's been stuck in the car with me all morning. I've brought first aid for your stricken husband," she added as we left the study. She reached into the pockets of her smock and pulled out a ceramic honey pot and a brown paper packet. "Homemade thyme honey and strawberry leaf tea. Harris's patented cure for hangovers."

"Bless you," I said. "I wouldn't trust anything Peggy Kitchen dug out of Xanadu."

"Peggy did help me find an awfully nice birthday present for Rainey in that back room of hers," Emma countered.

"Was that before or after she forced you to sign the petition?" I asked.

"After," Emma admitted sheepishly. "But she didn't so much force as encourage."

"With a two-by-four," I muttered. "Horrible old cow."

Emma patted my shoulder. "You're beginning to sound more like yourself again, Lori."

Francesca seemed to think that a walk in the garden would do wonders for my unsettled nerves. "Take your time," she urged, shooing us out. "I'll look after the boys—all three of 'em."

Ham bounded ahead of us, through the solarium, across the sunken terrace, over the low retaining wall, and into the wildflower meadow that ran down to the brook. Emma and I took a slightly more conservative route, going through a gap in the stone wall instead of jumping over it, and strolled across the meadow at a leisurely pace.

It was too hot to go any faster. There wasn't a cloud in the sky, the air was perfectly still, and a deafening chorus of insects sang in the rustling grasses. Emma slipped out of her gardening smock, and I wished I'd worn shorts instead of jeans. As the sun baked our foolishly unprotected heads, I made a point of praising each flower we passed. I managed to misidentify every single blossom, but Emma seemed to appreciate the effort.

"I'd like to do the same sort of thing with the meadow behind the vicarage." She raised a hand to shade her eyes as she surveyed her handiwork. "The vicar's field runs down to the river instead of a brook, but I could give it a similar treatment—sprinkle it with drifts of bluebells and daffodils. If this dry spell keeps up, though, I'll have to consider using desert plants."

"How bad is it?" I asked.

"Burt Hodge is beginning to worry about his crops," Emma replied, "and if you didn't have a stream running through your property, you wouldn't have any flowers at all." Emma pointed to her boot-clad feet. "I plan to start on the Buntings' garden as soon as I leave here."

"Thanks," I said. "Any luck on the computer search for the Gladwell pamphlet?"

Emma shook her head. "Nothing so far. I'll keep looking, but most libraries don't list that sort of thing in their on-line catalogs."

"We'll just have to hope that Stan's word-of-mouth search succeeds." I walked on a few steps before I realized that Emma hadn't moved.

"Why are you walking like that?" she asked, staring at me.

"Like what?" I said.

"Like this." She strode past me with her head down and her shoulders hunched.

I contemplated her performance in puzzled silence. Then the penny dropped. "Diaper bag," I said, hunching one shoulder. "Toy bag," I went on, hunching the other.

"Rations and medicine kit." I bowed my arms as though imitating a fat man, held the pose, then flung my arms over my head and spun a circle in the grass. "Look at me! I'm weightless! Race you to the bridge. . . ."

It was only fifty yards, but by the time Emma and I reached the brook, we were sweltering. She kicked off her boots, I kicked off my sneakers, and we leaned on each other for balance as we wrestled with our socks. We rolled up our pant legs and sat side by side on the split-log bridge, trailing our toes in the water and relishing the cool breeze rising from the shallow, rushing stream. Ham plunged right in, then splashed upstream and out of sight, his tail wagging like a banner with damp fringes.

"I'd almost forgotten what it was like to be strap-free," I said when I'd caught my breath.

"You should get out more often," Emma said. She leaned back on her hands. "How did you fare yesterday? Bill told Derek you were trolling the square for suspects."

Emma gave me her full attention while I expounded on Sally Pyne's one-woman uprising, Christine Peacock's cleaning frenzy, Katrina Graham's excessive devotion to her boss, and Adrian's possible involvement in the Culver Institute.

"Wouldn't you agree that Sally, Chris, Katrina, and Adrian qualify as suspects?" I concluded "They've each got a pretty strong motive to steal the Gladwell pamphlet."

"I suppose so." Emma lifted a hand to adjust her wire-rim glasses. "I suppose some of the motives might even intersect. Sally and Christine, for instance, have sound business reasons for wanting Adrian's museum to pull in tourists. They might have stolen the pamphlet in order to keep him here." She flicked up a splash of water with her toes. "I suppose I can understand Katrina Graham's motives, as well. I had a huge crush on my advisor at MIT."

"See?" I spread my hands. "Katrina might have stolen the pamphlet in order to protect her mentor."

"I'd have stolen anything for Professor Layton," Emma said, with a wistful sigh, "but Professor Layton would never suppress evidence in order to keep a project going. Does Adrian Culver strike you as unscrupulous?"

"Hard to say. I keep meeting him under unusual circumstances." I turned to Emma. "Do you believe in love at first sight?"

She looked away, with a ghost of a smile tugging at the corners of her mouth. "Yes," she said, "as a matter of fact, I do." She rubbed a thumb against her wedding band. "Why do you ask?"

"Because Adrian took one look at Francesca," I said, "and turned to mush. She treated him like dirt, but he didn't care. She could've stomped on his toes and he would have apologized for putting his foot in the wrong place."

"Why was she so rude to him?" Emma asked.

"She doesn't want outsiders invading Finch," I said, "and she thinks Adrian's pulling a fast one on the vicar. Plus, she's anti-archaeology—thinks it's rude to dig up dead people's possessions. I think she inherited that point of view from her father." I listened for a moment to the water gurgling over the smooth black stones. "All I can say about Adrian is that he *seems* genuine. He seemed surprised by the amount of equipment his students packed, and flabbergasted when I told him about the Culver Institute."

Emma pursed her lips. "Sally Pyne has been known

to turn a crumb of information into an entire loaf. We don't know for certain what she found in Katrina's room, do we?"

"It should be easy enough to check out," I said. "No one gets financial backing for something as unwieldly as a museum without leaving a trail." I glanced at Emma. "Would you . . . ?"

Her nod lacked enthusiasm. "I'll search the Net for any mention of the Culver Institute, but . . ."

"But?" I prompted.

"But I think you're on the wrong track." She put a hand up to hold her glasses in place, slid off the bridge, and landed with a controlled splash. "Come on in; the water's fine."

The water was, in fact, just this side of arctic, but I jumped in anyway and tottered after Emma, gripping the slippery rocks with my toes as the brook foamed around my calves and ankles.

"The eyewitnesses don't seem to be coming to you," Emma was saying, "so you should be going to them. Nothing goes unnoticed in a village. I'd suggest you try— No! Stop! *Heel!*"

The cry came too late. Ham had exploded from the bank like a furry avenging angel, tickled pink to find a pair of playmates in the water. He barreled into Emma midstream, Emma grabbed at me, and we both sprawled backward, arms windmilling wildly. Our landing made a splash that should have flooded the meadow.

Emma floundered, spluttered, then sat up, laughing. "I'm not hot anymore," she managed, "but I think parts of me are going numb."

I clambered to my feet, pulled Emma to hers, and scrambled up the bank. We grumbled halfheartedly at

Hamlet as we followed him into the meadow, and he responded by giving us a bone-chilling shower as he shook himself dry. When Emma ordered him to sit, he stretched out in the sunlight and closed his eyes.

I pushed my wet curls back from my forehead and followed his example. "Should've dumped Bill in the brook last night," I commented, turning my face to the sun. "It would've sobered him up faster than thyme honey and tea."

Emma wiped droplets from her glasses. "You seem awfully complacent about Bill's delicate condition," she observed. "Derek said you were breathing fire last night. How did Dimity manage to calm you down?"

"She reminded me that people are complicated." I wrinkled my nose. "I hate it when she does that."

Emma stretched out next to me on the grass. "How complicated is Peggy Kitchen?"

I folded my hands behind my head, gazed up at the cloudless blue sky, and told Emma about Peggy Kitchen's eighth birthday. "Hard to imagine, isn't it?" I said. "Spending your childhood scanning the sky for German bombers?"

"It's the part after the bombs drop that I find hard to imagine," said Emma. "How would I react if my world was blown to bits?"

"You'd plant a victory garden in the craters," I said, with great conviction.

"No, I wouldn't," Emma retorted. "I'd run for my life, just like Peggy and her mother." She took off her glasses and rolled onto her stomach, pillowing her cheek on her hands. "I wonder if that's why Peggy came back to Finch. She must have felt grateful to the people here for taking her in."

"I doubt if the people who took her in live here anymore." I brushed at a fly buzzing around Ham's head. "I used to think we were the only outsiders in Finch, but it seems I was wrong. Everyone in the village seems to be from somewhere else."

Emma closed her eyes and lay so still that for a moment I thought she'd drifted off to sleep. I scratched Ham's damp chin, then let my hand fall to the ground. The sun felt deliciously warm after our icy plunge, and the baked earth gave off the heavy, sweet scent of high summer. I'd nearly succumbed to the brook's soothing murmur when Emma spoke.

"I know where I'd go to look for witnesses," she said.

"So do I." I rubbed my eyes. "I should have thought of it yesterday. As soon as Bill's fully recovered, I'm going to visit the Buntings' neighbors."

"Don't bother with the cottages across the lane," said Emma. "They're owned by weekenders. They'd be back in London by Sunday night."

"More émigrés," I muttered. "How about the people who live on either side of the vicarage?"

"They're your best bet, but . . ." Emma put her hand out and waggled it. "I've heard they're very private. You may have trouble getting them to talk."

"What if I tell them . . ." I thought for a moment, then sat up, proud of my ingenuity. "I'll tell them I'm helping Lilian Bunting with her parish history. No one wants to be left out of history. And I'll bake a batch of cookies to bring along as a—"

"Bribe?" Emma put in.

"As a thank-you," I amended, "to anyone willing to answer a few simple questions."

"Brilliant." Emma snuggled deeper into the grass. "And once you're inside . . . ?"

"I grill 'em till they squeal." I screwed my face up horribly, but Ham ruined the moment by licking my nose. I pushed him aside and got to my feet. "Up, woman," I commanded, "and pull on your boots. You have a jungle to conquer, and I have a batch of cookies to bake."

11.

Since I had a bag of lemons on hand, I made lemon bars. When Francesca made a passing reference to the dozen or so blue ribbons Lilian Bunting's lemon bars had won, I laughed lightheartedly and assured her that I was baking for the fun of it—which was the truth, if not precisely the whole truth.

Harris's patented cure for hangovers—and twelve hours of uninterrupted slumber—got Bill back on his feet by the following morning, though he was reluctant to consume anything other than dry toast and Emma's strawberry-leaf tea at breakfast. When I dropped him off at his office, he refused categorically to eat lunch at the pub.

I watched as he unlocked his office door, then craned my neck to survey the square. A large delivery van was parked near the tearoom, and two husky men in back-support belts were unloading a pair of long, heavy cylindrical objects covered with brown paper. Simon was lugging an armful of pointy trowels from the schoolhouse to the paneled van. I called a hello and Simon replied so cheerily that I knew without asking that Adrian had finally

given him a shot at doing some hands-on work in Scrag
End field.

Buoyed by the young man's sunny smile, I drove up
Saint George's Lane and parked in front of the vicarage,
intent on finding out more about Lilian's parish history
before I presented myself to her next-door neighbors as
her representative.

I patted the supply of lemon bars stacked neatly on
the passenger seat, took up the red spiral-bound notebook, and climbed out of the car, then stood for a moment, gazing over the low stone wall, astonished by the
change that had taken place in one short day.

Emma had been hard at work. She'd slashed the shrubs
ruthlessly, torn up the brambles, and freed the walls from
a burdensome tangle of vines. The garden was still dotted
with odd tufts and straggly bits, like a crew cut cropped
with a blunt blade, but Emma had made it much harder
for a sticky-fingered intruder to slip into the vicarage
unobserved.

I heard voices coming from the back of the house and
crept along the side to see who was speaking. I peered
around the corner, then quickly drew back. Emma was
sitting at the bottom of the library stairs, showing Rainey
Dawson how to pull weeds up by the roots. Rainey wore a
child-sized pair of gardening gloves—Nell's castoffs, no
doubt—and her braids were pinned like a flyaway halo
around her head. She'd already acquired smudges of dirt
on her nose, her knees, and her elbows, but they didn't
look out of place in a garden. Perhaps, I thought, Rainey
had found her life's work.

I didn't want to distract the little whirlwind, so I made
my way quietly to the front stairs and rang the bell. The
door was opened by a woman I didn't recognize. She held
a broom in one rubber-gloved hand, however, and wore

a flowing kerchief as well as a loose-fitting duster, so it seemed safe to asume that she was the Buntings' cleaning lady.

"The missus is out," she informed me. "Vicar's on the telephone, but he shouldn't be long."

I nodded toward the garden. "Lilian must be happy about the new landscape."

"Says it's a fine thing not to snag her stockings when she goes down the front walk. Vicar claims he didn't know there *was* a front walk." The woman grinned slyly at the Buntings' strained communion with nature, then introduced herself. "I'm Annie Hodge."

The name rang a bell. "As in Hodge Farm?"

The woman nodded. "Hodge Farm belongs to my husband."

"It's right next to Scrag End field, isn't it?" I said. "Have you gotten a chance to visit Dr. Culver's dig?"

"There's five acres of barley between us and Scrag End," Annie informed me, "and we've too much work at hand to mind what this doctor chap's up to." She glanced over her shoulder. "Here's the vicar."

"Lori, my dear girl," said the vicar, joining us on the doorstep, "I'm so sorry to keep you waiting."

"Pot of tea, Vicar?" Annie offered. "You don't look at all well."

"Tea," said the vicar absently. "Yes, by all means." He heaved a forlorn sigh. "Bring it to us in the library, if you please."

I gave Annie a friendly nod and followed the vicar up the hall. He looked as though he'd aged ten years since I'd last seen him.

"Will Lilian be home soon?" I asked as we entered the library.

"Lilian?" The vicar paused to consider. "I believe she

promised to be back in time for lunch. She's attending a lecture at the village hall in Stow." He sat behind the desk and gestured vaguely at the green velvet couch. "Please, make yourself comfortable."

The room was suffocatingly hot and as dark as a tomb. The windows and the French doors were closed, the drapes closely drawn. The desk lamp was on, but its shade was tilted so that its meager circle of light illuminated only the black telephone and the vicar's folded hands.

"Mr. Bunting," I said, "would you like me to turn on a few lamps?"

"Hmmm?" The vicar looked up from a silent contemplation of his hands. "Lamps, did you say?" He peered across the room. "It is a bit gloomy in here, isn't it. I've kept the drapes closed since I spoke with you about the, er, incident. Lilian thinks I'm overreacting."

"You've had a shock," I said, turning on the pole lamps at either end of the couch. "It would be strange if you didn't have some sort of reaction."

"It's the invasion of privacy, you see." The vicar glanced over his shoulder at the muted sound of Rainey's chatter coming from the library stairs. "It's rattled me. As has a phone call from the bishop. I've just finished speaking with him. He rang to tell me that he'd received Mrs. Kitchen's petition. She presented it to him at seven o'clock this morning."

I winced sympathetically.

"The bishop made it quite clear that he doesn't want Mrs. Kitchen bothering his old chum Dr. Culver. He ordered me to . . . to *keep a lid* on Mrs. Kitchen." The vicar held out his hand imploringly. "Is he mad?"

"I think he underestimates Peggy Kitchen," I soothed. "He's only met her once."

"One would think once would be enough," murmured

the vicar. "But what am I to do? The wretched woman cornered me after morning services and told me that I hadn't heard the last of her." He shuddered gently.

"I called Stan," I said, hoping to distract him from his woes. "Dr. Finderman, that is. He promised to do everything in his power to find another copy of the Gladwell pamphlet."

"How kind of him." The vicar made an effort to sound elated, but the prospect of keeping a lid on Peggy Kitchen was clearly weighing on his mind.

"While Stan's working on that end," I went on, "I thought I'd do some research of my own. Do you think Lilian would mind if I looked through her notes for the parish history?"

"She'd be flattered by your interest," said the vicar. He motioned toward the long table at the end of the room. "Please, feel free to browse."

I seated myself at the long table and rummaged through Lilian's copious notes. Annie delivered the tea tray, but left it to the vicar to pour a cup and bring it over to me. I resisted the urge to sip. Annie's tarry brew was strong enough to turn Will and Rob into lifelong insomniacs.

The vicar settled into his armchair with his cup of tea, and I paused occasionally to scribble a word or two in the red notebook. I soon realized that the vicar had spoken the truth: Finch's history had been as dull as ditchwater. It took less than a half hour to travel from the Iron Age to "The Village Today."

"All done," I said finally, tapping the papers back into a pile. "Thanks much. I'll let you know if, er, *when* I hear from Stan."

A rare smile lit the vicar's face. "Lori, my dear, you are an angel."

"And you," I said, "are bound to be a saint."

His face resumed its mournful contours. "A martyr, more likely."

"Stop fretting, Vicar," I urged. "God's on our side, remember?"

"That's what the French said at Agincourt," the vicar murmured.

He retired, muttering gloomily, and I returned to the Mini to fetch a bag of lemon bars. Notebook, pen, and thank-you bribe in hand, I headed for the schoolmaster's house, a modest, single-story cottage that deserved better care than its present owner was giving it. The limestone facade was filthy, paint flaked from the window frames, and missing slates gave the peaked roof a gap-toothed appearance.

The current owner—a man by the name of George Wetherhead, according to Lilian's notes—had kept his garden under control, however. There were no shrubs, no flowers, scarcely any lawn, nothing to block his view of the lane, the vicarage, and the meadow. If Mr. Wetherhead had been looking out of a window on Sunday night, he might have seen something peculiar going on next door.

The man who answered the door was short and slightly built, with a round face and long wisps of gray hair combed across an otherwise hair-free scalp. His forehead was marked with a horizontal indentation, as though he'd just removed a tight-fitting hat or cap. He wore a white shirt with epaulets and a pair of dark-blue trousers, and leaned heavily on a three-pronged metal cane.

"Mr. Wetherhead?" I asked. "My name's Lori Shepherd. Lilian Bunting's asked me to help her gather information for her parish history. I wonder if you might—"

"I'm busy," he said, reaching for the door.

I slid my foot over the threshold. "You don't want to be left out of the parish history, do you?" I wheedled. "Your house is extremely, um, historic. There are all sorts of . . . of legends associated with it."

"Legends?" Mr. Wetherhead's eyes narrowed. "What sort of legends?"

"All sorts." I took a half step forward and rested my palm on the open door, a marketing technique I'd learned while selling Girl Scout cookies in my youth. "I'd love to tell you about them, if you have the time."

"No. I'm sorry, but—" He turned his head suddenly and stared back into the house.

"Is something wrong?" I asked. I was about to inch another half step forward when the little man seized my arm and hauled me inside. The heavy door had scarcely swung shut behind me when the air was torn by a piercing, high-pitched scream.

12.

"You'd no right to push yourself into my cottage." Mr. Wetherhead stood in the doorway, as though to block my only escape route. "No right to come poking and prying. I insist that you tell no one what you've seen here today. It's no one's business but my own."

The windows in the raftered room were small and heavily curtained. A large trestle table, lit by a shaded ceiling lamp, rested on sheets of plywood laid over the scuffed pine floor. I circled the room slowly, my back to the wall, unable to tear my gaze from the table.

"Your neighbors haven't noticed?" I murmured skeptically.

He tightened his grip on the metal cane. "The houses across the lane are used only on weekends, and the Buntings have never had cause to complain." A note of desperation entered his voice. "If word gets out, I'll be ridiculed, shamed in front of the entire village. Is that what you want?"

A shrill scream rent the air once more as the diminutive locomotive entered a tunnel at the base of the plaster mountain. It emerged a moment later, chugged past the dairy farm and through the Victorian village, crossed the iron bridge above the silvery trout stream, changed tracks, and began the slow ascent that would take it to the ski resort on the mountain's upper reaches. The miniature landscape was a world unto itself and filled the entire trestle table.

"I don't know why you *want* to keep it secret," I said, bending low to get a better view of the tiny chairlift and the geranium-filled window planters in the Swiss-style chalet. "People would pay to see what you have here."

Mr. Wetherhead fingered an engine-driver's cap hanging from a peg just inside the doorway. "You don't find it . . . ridiculous? For a grown man, I mean."

"Ridiculous?" I clapped my hands with delight as a guardrail descended to block the tracks. "It's spectacular . . . brilliant. . . ."

Mr. Wetherhead peered at me anxiously. "Do you really think so?"

I put my hand over my heart and looked him straight in the eye. "I really think so."

The small man hobbled over to fiddle with the control panel. "I suppose I could answer a few of your questions. What does Mrs. Bunting want to know?"

"She's collecting material for her chapter on contemporary Finch." I consulted the red notebook. "She hired me to do some research—find out a little about all of Finch's residents—backgrounds, feelings about the village, funny sights any of you may have seen . . ."

Mr. Wetherhead's hand jerked and the guardrail lifted. The train rounded a curve, chugged smoothly into the village, and came to a halt at the station platform. Mr. Wetherhead flipped a switch on the locomotive, and the chugging stopped. "Cup of tea?" he asked.

"Yes, please." I stood back to give him room to limp ahead of me.

Walking through Mr. Wetherhead's house was like touring a railway museum. Station signs covered the faded wallpaper, signal lanterns hung from the ceiling, and the floor was a maze of boxes containing extra track, bits of scenery, and a seemingly endless variety of model trains.

"It must've taken forever to glue all of those fir trees onto the mountain," I said, pausing to admire a shiny black steam engine.

Mr. Wetherhead shrugged diffidently. "I've had a great deal of time on my hands since I left my job."

"Did you work for the railways?" I asked.

"I was a track inspector on the Southwestern Line. They pensioned me off after my accident." He looked back over his shoulder. "Will you mind taking tea in the kitchen?"

"That'll be fine," I said. There wasn't enough room to lift a teacup anywhere else.

The kitchen wasn't spacious, but it was large enough to accommodate a Formica-topped table and a pair of folding chairs. Mr. Wetherhead filled the teakettle, motioned for me to take a seat, then began to search through his cupboards.

"I know I have biscuits here somewhere," he murmured, a frown puckering his forehead.

"Will these do?" I put the bag of lemon bars on the table. "I brought them as a way of thanking you for your help with the parish history. I hope you'll accept them as an apology, as well, for intruding on your privacy."

"I pulled you into the cottage," Mr. Wetherhead reminded me, coloring slightly at his own audacity. "I had to shut the door before the train whistle sounded. My mother was very strict about disturbing people with my bells and whistles."

I pretended to take notes while Mr. Wetherhead gave me the potted version of his life. We all have them, I mused, gazing at the meagerly stocked cupboards. Our minds are filled with prepackaged anecdotes as handy as instant soup. Just add an audience, and they spill out. Not all of them, however, were as sad as Mr. Wetherhead's.

Mrs. Wetherhead hadn't much cared for anything her son loved. She ridiculed his passion for trains and belittled his decision to work for the railways. When a fall from a moving freight car shattered his pelvis and ended his career, she told him it was high time he grew up and stopped mucking about with choo-choos.

"I'm afraid I disappointed her yet again." Mr. Wetherhead placed the teapot on the table and lowered himself laboriously into the other chair. "An uncle left this house to me when he died. I came here as soon as I was ambulatory and brought with me my collection of *choo-choos.*"

"It's a shame that Finch doesn't have a train station," I observed.

"Is it?" Mr. Wetherhead filled my cup with fragrant chamomile tea. "My mother never learned to drive, you see, so it was difficult for her to visit me here. She was entirely dependent on the railways." He picked up a lemon bar and regarded it thoughtfully. "She died last year, God rest her soul."

Mr. Wetherhead, I thought, might act like a frightened rabbit, but he'd inherited something of his mother's iron will. It had taken no small amount of courage for a man of his mild temperament to escape the clutches of a carping old crone, but he'd done so, in the end. I regarded him with respect and admiration—gratitude, as well, for reminding me of the power a mother exerted, for good and evil, over the lives of her children.

My growing admiration shot sky-high when he praised my lemon bars.

"They're on a par with Mrs. Bunting's," he said. "Have you considered entering them in the Harvest Festival?"

I ducked my head modestly. "The thought never crossed my mind."

"I'd consider it, if I were you," he advised. "You might find yourself with a blue ribbon." He passed the plate of lemon bars to me, apparently unaware of the difficulties surrounding the festival.

"Have you been to Kitchen's Emporium lately?" I asked.

"I never go to the Emporium," he replied. "Mrs. Kitchen reminds me too much of my mother. I use the Naunton post office when I sell my trains."

"Sell your trains?" I said, frowning. "Why would you sell your trains?"

Mr. Wetherhead looked pointedly at the red notebook. "Will my response be off the record?"

I laid my pen on the table.

"The changes in the National Health have made it difficult for me to live on my pension alone," he confessed, "so I occasionally sell one of my trains through the post. There's a good market out there among model railroad hobbyists." He refilled my cup. "But you didn't hear it from me."

I twiddled my thumbs for a moment, dissatisfied with the state of a world in which a man had to sell parts of his dream in order to pay his medical bills. "Have you ever thought of turning your house into a museum?" I asked.

Mr. Wetherhead looked so startled that I could almost

hear his mother's voice, nagging away inside his head. "No one would come," he protested.

"I think they would," I told him. "I wasn't joking when I said that people would pay to see your collection. Why don't you try it out during the Harvest Festival? You could charge a nominal fee and—"

"Mrs. Kitchen is running the festival, isn't she?" Mr. Wetherhead began stirring his tea with nervous, jerky swipes of the spoon. "I couldn't possibly bring myself to work with her. I've a quiet, peaceful life, and I don't want Mrs. Kitchen interfering in it."

I saw his point much too clearly to object, so I let the subject drop and asked instead if I might bring Will and Rob around to see the mountain layout.

"Anytime you please," he said, with a bashful smile. "I've enjoyed talking with you," he added. "Have I given you the kind of information Mrs. Bunting wanted?"

"Mrs. Bunting?" I'd become so caught up in our conversation that I'd lost sight of my cover story. "Er, yes," I said hastily. "She'll be delighted."

"Hardly that." Mr. Wetherhead turned his teacup slowly in his hands. "I'm probably the dullest person you've interviewed. I'll wager my house has a more interesting history than I do." He glanced up from the teacup. "You said something about legends, didn't you?"

"Certainly." I'd entirely forgotten the whopper I'd told as I was worming my way into Mr. Wetherhead's house. It would have made things easier if he'd forgotten it, too. Legends had been conspicuously absent from Lilian Bunting's notes.

"Will you tell me about them?" he prompted.

I flipped open the red notebook and scanned its pages, hunting for information on the schoolmaster's house.

"Your uncle's house was built just over a hundred years ago," I informed him, "to house the master of the village school."

Mr. Wetherhead waited politely, clearly hoping for something a little less prosaic.

Hadn't Lilian told me something about the school-master's house? "The last master to live in here was a . . . a bit of a lad," I said, echoing Lilian's words. "It seems he was a bachelor, but that minor technicality didn't stop him from fathering a classroomful of little scholars. I guess he wanted to keep those seats filled. Fascinating, huh?"

The expression on Mr. Wetherhead's face made it plain that he considered scurrilous gossip a poor substitute for the promised legends. I was ashamed of myself for leading him on. He'd overcome considerable shyness for my sake—surely I could invent a legend or two for his. I put down my pen and closed the notebook, fairly certain that I could rely upon my own firsthand experience to satisfy Mr. Wetherhead's craving for myth and magic.

"And then, of course," I added in a confidential murmur, "there's the ghost."

Mr. Wetherhead's palm smacked the table. "I knew it!" he cried. "But it isn't *my* ghost. Brother Florin belongs to the vicarage!"

13.

"Excuse me?" I said faintly. "Did you say Brother Florin?"

Mr. Wetherhead flushed scarlet. "That's what Mrs. Morrow calls him. Does Mrs. Bunting call him by another name?"

"N-no," I said, my brain in a whirl. "In fact, Lilian doesn't know very much about him at all. She was hoping you might—"

"Yes, of course. I'll tell you everything I know. It isn't much. I've only seen him once." Mr. Wetherhead sat back in his chair and mopped his brow with a bright-red handkerchief. "It's such a relief to know that Mrs. Bunting is aware of Brother Florin. I was afraid to tell anyone I'd seen a ghost, apart from Mrs. Morrow, and I only consulted her because she's an expert on the subject."

"Is she?" I squeaked.

"Mrs. Morrow's a professional," Mr. Wetherhead assured me. "She knew all about Brother Florin. She told me I was lucky to see him so clearly. There was a full moon on Sunday night, you know."

"Sunday night?" I said, blinking. "You saw him on Sunday night?"

Mr. Wetherhead demurred. "Technically speaking, it was Monday morning. I saw him at precisely eight minutes past midnight."

Mr. Wetherhead's eyes were dancing. He was smiling broadly and twisting his handkerchief into knots, hardly able to contain his excitement. Brother Florin was probably the most thrilling thing that had ever happened to him. How could I demote his spine-tingling specter to common criminal? I opened the red notebook and decided, for the time being, to go with the flow.

"Brother Florin *always* appears after midnight," I stated firmly. I picked up my pen. "Where were you when you saw him?"

"In the room next to this one," said Mr. Wetherhead. "It's my bedroom. I was having trouble sleeping because of the heat, so I got up to open the window and I saw him. He rose out of the mist and went round the vicarage twice." Mr. Wetherhead moved his hands through the air to illustrate Brother Florin's queer perambulations. "He glided about, shifting this way and that, with his arms folded across his stomach and his hands tucked into the sleeves of his robe."

"He was wearing a robe?" I said.

"The hooded robe of his order," Mr. Wetherhead explained. "That's why I couldn't see his face. But he was shaped a bit like Paddington Bear."

I scribbled *Paddington Bear in a cowl* in the notebook. "What happened after he circled the vicarage?"

"He vanished." The little man's eyes twinkled. "One moment he was moving about, and the next he was gone. Just like that. That's when I knew he was not of this earth." Mr. Wetherhead smiled sheepishly. "I thought at first that he might be a burglar."

"But you don't think that anymore?" I said.

"No, I don't." Mr. Wetherhead chuckled. "If the vicarage had been burgled on Monday morning, the police would have visited by now, and I would've known about it, living next door as I do."

I began to feel a headache coming on.

"I stayed at my bedroom window for two hours that night," Mr. Wetherhead continued, "and I've watched for him every night since, but he hasn't rematerialized. Is that the usual thing?"

"Absolutely," I replied smoothly. "Sometimes Brother Florin goes for years between appearances. Mrs. Morrow was right when she said you were lucky to see him. She lives on the other side of the vicarage, doesn't she?" I intended to have a word with Finch's so-called ghost expert.

The small man didn't answer directly. He began to turn his teacup in circles again as he informed me, hesitantly, "Mrs. Morrow's business depends on her ability to keep confidences."

"Your secret is safe with me," I assured him.

"You know how people are," he went on. "I wouldn't want my name bandied about at Kitchen's Emporium or the pub."

"I understand," I said, with feeling. "And I give you my solemn oath that I won't breathe a word about Brother Florin at Kitchen's Emporium or the pub."

I kept my promise to Mr. Wetherhead. I didn't breathe a word about Brother Florin at Peacock's pub or Peggy's shop, but while Bill and Francesca put the twins down for their naps after lunch, I exhaled half a dictionary to Dimity.

"Is it true?" I asked, huddled over the blue journal, with the door safely shut. "Is there really a Brother Florin?"

I don't think so. Let me see. . . . There's a Brother Glorin at Pricknash Abbey, near Gloucester, but no one knows about him yet—he's still keeping his vow of silence. And there's Brother Florian at Craswall Priory in the Marches—a lonely outpost for such a gregarious soul. It's a pity the two can't trade places. Perhaps I'll suggest it to—

"Brother Florin, Dimity?" I prodded gently.

No, I can't say that I know of a Brother Florin. I can assure you, however, that the Buntings have the vicarage entirely to themselves.

"So Mrs. Morrow is telling fibs about ghosts," I said thoughtfully.

She wouldn't be the first to do so. The long casualty lists of the 1914–1918 war created a market for mediums. I grew up in a world in which spiritualism was all the rage. It's come back in vogue lately, hasn't it?

I shrugged. "A lot of people are searching for answers in unconventional places these days."

They conducted the same search when I was young. Séances, crystals, planchettes, palmistry . . . As the vicar will gladly tell you, there's nothing new under the sun.

"Does any of it work?" I asked, curious.

I've no idea. I would never respond to anyone who accepted money to contact me, but there are others who feel differently. I wouldn't call myself an expert on the subject.

I laughed. "Well, if you're not, then Mrs. Morrow certainly isn't. Thanks, Dimity. I'll let you know what I find out."

I closed the journal, put it back on the shelf, and trotted up to the nursery. I hadn't yet told my husband about

Brother Florin. We hadn't had the chance to talk in the car because Bill had bicycled home, and Francesca had been with us during lunch. I hoped to catch him before he went back to the office.

"Francesca?" I said as I entered the nursery. "Has Bill left yet?"

"Ten minutes ago." Francesca was sitting in the rocker near Rob's crib, knitting a blue bootie that made the products of my own clicking needles look more than ever like abstract art. "He told me to tell you that he'd catch up with you later."

The nursery was scented with the irresistible perfume of baby shampoo and talcum powder. The boys, freshly bathed, were sleeping on their tummies in their cribs, their heads turned in the same direction, their fists curled in identical positions before their rosy faces. I walked over to stroke Will's back. I wasn't worried about waking him. The twins had inherited their father's gift for sleeping soundly.

"Do you know Mrs. Morrow?" I asked Francesca.

Francesca looked up from the bootie. "Tall woman, lives next to the vicarage?"

"That's the one," I said.

"I don't know much about her," Francesca admitted. "She loves cats, lives in London, hired Briar Cottage six months ago. Word has it that she's writing a book. She's no wedding ring, so there's some who say the *Mrs.* is just for show. Doesn't go to my church or Saint George's— keeps herself to herself, by and large. Some say she's got weird wiring."

I straightened slowly and turned to face the rocker. "Pardon me?"

"She had the wiring in Briar Cottage redone when she moved in," Francesca explained. "Had extra phone lines put in. But as I say, I don't know much about her." Francesca uttered the preposterous disclaimer without a trace of irony. I wondered, somewhat nervously, what she'd say if asked to describe her new employers.

My nanny seemed to know an awful lot about a woman she didn't really know, yet she hadn't said one word about ghosts. Six months seemed like plenty of time for the village telegraph to pick up on Mrs. Morrow's unusual field of expertise. Had Francesca been out of the loop, or was she exercising discretion? I decided not to probe. If Mrs. Morrow had managed to keep one corner of her life hidden from the villagers' prying eyes, more power to her.

Francesca lifted her needles and resumed knitting. "I heard that the bishop sent Mrs. Kitchen away with a flea in her ear." She smiled complacently. "I told you it was a lot of nonsense. The bishop's thick as thieves with Adri— Dr. Culver." Her smile became a scowl as she added, "He came here again today."

"Who?" I asked.

"Dr. Culver. Claimed he was looking for his hat." Francesca snorted. "He wasn't even wearing that old hat of his when he was here the other night. It would've looked out of place with those nice gray slacks he'd changed into."

Adrian Culver's persistence, it seemed, was beginning to pay off.

Smiling inwardly, I told Francesca that I was off to the village again but that I'd be home in plenty of time for dinner. I bent low to kiss Will's temple, planted a tender smooch on Rob's plump cheek, and set out to find out just what Mrs. Morrow was up to.

Briar Cottage was concealed from Saint George's Lane by a thorn hedge so tall that I couldn't see over it, and so dense that a half-starved rabbit would have had trouble squeezing through. The hinges on the tall wooden gate screeched raucously as I pushed it open. Silence followed, broken only by birdsong and the distant sound of Rainey talking Emma's ear off in the vicarage garden. I stood for a moment, just inside the gate, taking a careful look at Mrs. Morrow's house.

Most houses in Finch had exchanged thatch for slate when they were modernized in the 1960s, but the roof of Briar Cottage was as shaggy as the day it had been woven. The overhanging thatch had been trimmed to accommodate a pair of upstairs windows that were, like their ground-floor counterparts, neatly curtained in starched calico.

Briar Cottage was made of the same honey-colored stone as the rest of the buildings in Finch, but it was very small, not quite half the size of the schoolmaster's house. Its walls were crooked and slightly bowed, as though it had begun settling onto its foundations before the Royalists rode through town and hadn't finished settling yet. I found the little house strangely appealing.

As I strode up the front walk, I reminded myself that whether Mrs. Morrow was a crook or a crank, she might still prove to be a valuable witness. It didn't matter if she took pleasure in misleading innocents like Mr. Wetherhead. If she could corroborate his story—or better yet, add to it—I'd be one step closer to catching the Buntings' Paddington-shaped burglar.

I knocked on the front door, waited, then knocked again. I'd raised my hand for a third and final attempt when the door was flung open by a willowy woman with vivid green eyes.

"But darling, I've told you a thousand times," she cried, *"no sex before the full moon!"*

14.

It took no more than a few eye-blinking seconds for me to realize that the woman was neither hallucinating nor addressing her advice to me, but speaking into the thin, curved mouthpiece of a telephone headset.

"No, no, and no!" she continued, motioning for me to come inside. "It doesn't *increase* your power—it drains you dry! Put Keith on, will you?"

I closed the door and waited politely for her to finish her conversation.

"Miranda knows best, Keith darling. Try again next month and let me know how it turns out. Good-bye, duck. Give my best love to Wormwood. Keith's cat," she explained, removing the headset. "Hideous name for a poor old mog, don't you think? I can just imagine what *she* calls *him*." She held out her hand. "Miranda Morrow, at your service. Are you collecting for the church roof fund or have you come for a consultation? Or"—she waggled her eyebrows—"are you one of us?"

"I, uh . . ." I was so busy gawking at my surroundings that Miranda's questions scarcely registered.

She followed my astonished gaze around the cramped, low-ceilinged room. "Not exactly *Country Life*, eh?"

"N-no . . ." I agreed. It was more like *Country Coven*.

A three-legged cauldron stood upon the hearth, beneath a chunky wood-beam mantelpiece littered with tarot cards, dousing twigs, faceted crystals, and small piles of polished stones. Astral charts were pinned to the walls, cabalistic symbols chalked on the faded redbrick floor, and bunches of dried herbs, hanging upside down from the rafters, filled the room with a pungent fragrance.

Between the curtained windows a black velvet–covered table held a crystal ball as big as my head. A blackened twiggy broomstick had been mounted in a rack over the front door. I wasn't remotely surprised when a black cat with luminous yellow eyes came over to rub his head against my ankles. As I bent to scratch his chin, however, I caught sight of a table tucked into a nook beneath the staircase.

"Wow," I said, recalling Francesca's comment on weird wiring. "That's a pretty fancy setup you've got there."

Miranda smiled benignly on an array of compact electronic equipment that made Houston Mission Control look like a sideshow. "Couldn't do my job without it," she said simply. "I'm taking calls this afternoon, but I spent all morning answering my E-mail."

"What, exactly, is your job?" I said. "If you don't mind my asking."

Miranda seemed amused by my diplomacy. "I'll give you three guesses," she said. "Nuclear physicist, milkmaid, or . . . witch."

I ducked my head, embarrassed. "I wasn't sure you'd want to be called by that name."

"Some women are sensitive about it," she said, nodding her approval. "I'm not. Witch, sorceress, psychic, healer, crone—I don't care what people call me, so long as they call."

"So you're a . . . a telephone witch?" I asked, wondering how the vicar would react to his neighbor's extremely nonconformist beliefs.

"I'm writing a book at the moment," she replied, "but it wouldn't do to abandon the faithful while I enjoy the quiet pleasures of my rural hideaway. They're helpless without me." She placed the headset on the table beneath the stairs. "Now, are you going to introduce yourself, or are you hoping that I'll read your mind?" She raised a hand to forestall my answer. "Wait. . . . Wait. . . . I'm getting an impression. . . . It's stronger now. . . . Yes. . . . I can see it clearly. Your name is . . . *Lori Shepherd!*"

I folded my arms and gave her a sidelong look. "I take it you've spoken with Mr. Wetherhead?"

"He came knocking at my door the minute you'd driven off," she said, laughing. "Care to sit down?"

I gestured to the headset on the table. "Your phone calls?"

"They can leave messages," she said. "Come. . . ."

Tucked in among the arcane paraphernalia, and placed at an angle to the fireplace, was a fat little sofa draped with a dozen paisley shawls. I sank onto—and into—the sofa while Miranda stooped to light a row of candles in the fireplace.

She looked more like a farmer's daughter than a witch. Compared to the other villagers I'd met so far, she was a stripling youth—in her mid-thirties, I guessed, not much older than me. Her face had a fresh, natural bloom and a sprinkling of faded freckles. She was barefoot and wore a loose-fitting blue chambray dress that swirled about her ankles. Her reddish-blond hair hung in long sun-streaked tresses to her waist.

"A summer fire," she explained when the candles were lit. "Lovely flames without inordinate heat." She closed her eyes and stretched her hands toward the candles, palms upward, as though in silent prayer. "Don't worry," she murmured from the corner of her mouth, "I'm not casting a spell. I'm simply giving thanks for the gift of light. I try not to take things for granted."

She lowered her hands, dropped into a well-worn armchair, and stretched her long legs across a burgundy-fringed ottoman. "I'm sure you're wondering why in the world I chose to live so near a vicarage."

"It does seem a tiny bit . . . aggressive," I acknowledged.

"It wasn't meant to be," said Miranda. "I hired Briar Cottage sight unseen, and never thought to ask who my neighbors were. That's why I don't give tea parties. I don't want the vicar to think I'm poaching on his patch." She leaned her chin on her hand. "Besides, not everyone is as tolerant of my religion as dear old Mr. Wetherhead—though it appears to be gaining in popularity. I may hang out my pentangle yet."

"Speaking of Mr. Wetherhead," I said, trying not to let myself be sidetracked, "I was hoping you'd tell me a little more about Brother Florin."

"Good gods," she said, sitting up. "Have you seen him, too?"

"How could I?" I said nonchalantly. "You invented him." I expected a staunch denial or a careful equivocation. Instead, I got a cheerfully guilty chuckle.

Miranda leaned back in her chair, nodding happily. "It was naughty of me," she confessed, "but Mr. Wetherhead wanted a ghost so *badly* that I couldn't resist the temptation to give him one. Apart from that, I didn't want him blabbing about what he'd seen. I don't think Finch is quite ready to deal with a coven in its midsts, do you?"

I was so far at sea that I could hear whales singing. "Coven?" I repeated, bewildered. "What coven?"

The merriment faded from Miranda's green eyes. She stared at me for several long seconds, then lowered her lashes as the black cat leapt onto the arm of her chair and insinuated himself into her lap. His purr filled the room as she tickled the top of his head with her fingertips.

"I'm sorry," she said. "I think I may have taken something for granted after all. I assumed that you went along with the Brother Florin story in order to conceal your activities on Sunday night."

"The only activities I was engaged in on Sunday night involved lullabies and dirty diapers." I informed her. "Are you telling me you're not the only witch in Finch?"

Miranda got to her feet, with the purring cat draped limply over her shoulder. She paced to the crystal ball and back, taking care to move between the hanging herbs, then stared down at the candles, deep in thought. Finally, she lowered the black cat onto the tapestry chair and beckoned me to follow her upstairs.

Miranda Morrow's bedroom filled the space beneath the rafters. It was as spartan as the parlor was gothic. A bed without a headboard, a deal table with an oil lantern, an old oak wardrobe, and a plain wooden bench were the only furnishings. The calico curtains provided a spot of color, but the windows were set so low in the walls that the sills were nearly level with the floor.

Miranda ducked below an exposed tie-beam and sat cross-legged before a window in the back wall. "I'll tell you what I saw on Sunday night," she said, motioning for me to sit beside her, "and let you be the judge."

I lowered myself to the floor as she pulled the curtain aside. The window overlooked the back end of the vicarage garden and the rolling meadow beyond, though the river was hidden from view.

"I can't be absolutely certain," Miranda began. "It's a long way off and the mist was very dense." Miranda rested her hands on the windowsill. "I always come up here when there's a full moon, to say my prayers and meditate." She pointed to the line of trees that marked the river's course on the far side of the meadow. "She rose just there on Sunday night. She was exquisite, once she got above the mist, perfectly pure and silvery white, so bright that she cast shadows. I closed my eyes, to commune with her, and when I opened them again, there was a flash of light, as though someone had turned a torch toward my cottage. That's when I saw the two women." Miranda tapped a finger on the sill. "At least, I *assume* they were women."

"Why?" I asked.

"Because they were worshiping the moon," Miranda replied, as though it were self-evident. "Men don't go in for moon worship, as a rule. They can't seem to get the hang of cycles."

"What . . . form did the worship take?" I inquired awkwardly. My experience with witches had, until now, been limited to items printed in the gutter press, and I was anxious not to give offense.

Miranda sniffed. "The usual amateur nonsense. Not my style at all. They jumped up and down, bowed to each other, raised their arms in supplication—they were probably chanting, as well, but I couldn't hear them from here."

I tried to picture Sally Pyne and Christine Peacock hopping up and down in the vicarage meadow at midnight. Had they been jumping for joy because they'd gotten hold of the Gladwell pamphlet?

I turned to Miranda. "Did either of them approach the vicarage before the, um, ceremony?"

Miranda sighed. "One did, the one Mr. Wetherhead mistook for Brother Florin. It was the ringleader showing off, I expect—thumbing her nose at Christianity. Childish, of course, but try convincing a woman in a hood that she should seek harmony, not conflict. At any rate, she circled the vicarage twice, then . . ." Miranda paused.

"Then what?" I coaxed.

"I'm not quite sure what happened next," she replied. "As I said, there was an awful lot of mist about. The ringleader probably heard a noise and scarpered off to join her chum in the meadow." A tolerant smile took the sting out of her words. "I didn't want to give them away. That's why I invented Brother Florin."

The black cat bumped my elbow with his head, and I let him curl up in my lap. I stroked his gleaming fur and gazed out at the meadow, wondering if the hooded witches had, like the hooded Brother Florin, sprung from Miranda Morrow's fertile imagination.

"If you're so concerned about protecting those two women," I said slowly, "why are you telling me about them?"

A strange light seemed to flicker in the depths of Miranda's vivid green eyes. "I read auras," she said simply. "Yours tells me that you didn't come here to uncover a coven." Her green eyes narrowed. "You've got quite a different agenda altogether."

"Witches in Finch?" Bill exclaimed.

"Keep your voice down," I urged. "Francesca might hear."

I leaned back against the pile of pillows at the foot of the bed in the master bedroom, facing Bill, who reclined against his own pillows piled against the headboard. Will was curled up on Bill's chest, and Rob was snoozing soundly next to me. I'd spent so much of the day away from my boys that I couldn't bear to part with them at bedtime.

"Witches in Finch," Bill repeated.

"And a ghost who looks like Paddington Bear," I reminded him. "Let's not forget about Brother Florin."

Bill nodded absently.

"That was supposed to be a joke," I pointed out. "We know that Miranda Morrow invented Brother Florin. I'm willing to bet a bucket of lemon bars that our local coven doesn't exist, either. Although *someone* was in that meadow. . . ."

"Hmmm?" said Bill.

"The meadow takes a sudden dip as it rolls down to the river," I explained, using a pillow to illustrate my words. "When you're standing at the bottom of it, you can barely see the vicarage. The dry grass was crushed and snapped in a circle at the bottom of the dip. I checked on it after I'd finished speaking with Miranda. Someone was there, all right, and I think I know who."

"Hmmm . . ." Bill stared into the middle distance and gave a vague nod.

"Look . . ." I finger-walked both hands along the bottom of the ridge I'd made in the pillow. "Sally Pyne and Christine Peacock walk along the river until they come to the dip in the meadow. Then one of them tiptoes over to the vicarage to reconnoiter." My right hand fingertip-toed to the top of the dip. "She circled the vicarage twice, to check for signs of life; then she snuck in through the French doors, snatched the pamphlet, and scooted back to the dip." My finger-figures hopped about in triumph. "Chris and Sally stole the Gladwell pamphlet to make sure that the pub and the tearoom would profit from Adrian's museum. I'm sure of it."

"Hmmm," Bill said.

I folded my hands, having become aware of a curious one-sidedness to our conversation. "Hard day at the office?" I inquired politely.

"No . . ." Bill frowned in concentration. "I'm trying to remember something Chris Peacock told me, the night I was poisoning myself with Dick's mead. It had something to do with the meadow. I wouldn't have thought of it if you hadn't put the two together just now."

My heart leapt. "What did she say? Did she tell you she was there on Sunday night?"

Bill stroked the mustache space above his upper lip, a habit he'd established in his hirsute youth. "Chris didn't want Peggy Kitchen to hear," he said slowly, "so she took me aside and . . ." He shook his head, discouraged. "I'm sorry. It's gone. All I can remember is that she was agitated about something that happened in the meadow. The mead seems to have erased her actual words."

"Did she mention Sally Pyne?" I suggested.

"I don't know." Bill gently rubbed Will's back. "Miranda Morrow may be right about the coven, though. Christine Peacock's a bit of a nutcase when it comes to the supernatural. It's not hard to imagine her taking up the broomstick. Why don't you stop by the pub tomorrow and talk to her?"

"I intend to. I still have half a batch of lemon bars left and"—I smiled slyly—"Dick Peacock just happens to be judging the pastry competition at the Harvest Festival."

15.

"Shepherd! Rise and shine! Got news for you!"

I squinted at the bedside clock. It was midnight back in Boston—two hours past Stan's usual bedtime and a half hour before the twins' first feeding. "Stan? Wh-what are you doing up so late?"

"Provost's dinner. Gave me gas. The provost, I mean. The food was pretty tasty. You want my news or don't you?"

Bill moaned and buried his head in the pillows, so I carried the phone into the walk-in closet, flicked on the light, and shut the door.

"Yes, Stan, I want your news," I said, too groggy to be properly enthusiastic.

"I can get you Gladwell pamphlets on transubstantiation, the virgin birth, and the efficacy of faith without good works," Stan boomed. "Zilch on archaeology."

I should have shouted "Way to go!" because no one but my old boss could have dug up *any* Gladwell pamphlet on such short notice. Instead, I slumped onto the hamper and mumbled dejectedly, "Nothing at all about the hoax?"

"Nada," Stan replied, overlooking my ingratitude. "I found a guy in Labrador who's nuts for Gladwell pamphlets, but he's never heard of *Disappointments in Delving*. Offered me a bundle if I found a copy. Might take him up on it. I've always wanted to drive a Lamborghini."

"Is the guy in Labrador your only lead?" I asked.

"Yeah, but he's solid," Stan answered, with astonishing forbearance. "He's overnighting a pamphlet from his collection. I'll overnight it to you as soon as it gets here."

"Why?" I asked.

"So you'll know what you're looking for!" he bellowed. "What's the matter with you, Shepherd? The twins suck your brains dry?"

"But if the pamphlets aren't the same—" I began.

Stan cut me off. "Some Victorian pamphleteers stuck to patterns," he lectured. "If they didn't own two dozen fonts or a paper mill, they couldn't change their style at the drop of a hat. They used and reused the same fonts, the same type of paper, and usually the same page layout."

"Oh," I said, feeling almost as thickheaded as Stan wanted me to feel. "So *Disappointments in Delving* may look like the pamphlet we'll be getting from our man in Labrador."

"The kraken wakes," Stan quipped. He paused for a prolonged belch. "Gotta go. I need another bicarbonate."

"Thanks, Stan," I said, suppressing a yawn. "I mean it. You've done a great job."

"I'm not done yet," he said. "And, Shepherd, you should get more shut-eye. You're gonna set a bad example for the nippers."

I glared blearily at the telephone as Stan rang off, then roused myself to get ready for my visit to the pub. If I was quick about it, I could bake a fresh batch of lemon bars before Bill came down for breakfast.

* * *

Grog, the Peacocks' basset hound, gazed dolefully at the ladder upon which Dick Peacock stood, as though anticipating its imminent collapse. Our local publican was not a small-boned man. He weighed three hundred pounds if he weighed an ounce, and the sight of him preparing to hang a brand-new sign from the wrought-iron gibbet over the pub's entryway was enough to draw a crowd of nervous onlookers.

The sign itself excited speculation. Demurely veiled in burlap, it leaned beneath the pub's sparkling windows, still smelling of fresh paint. I stood among a knot of murmurers that included Mr. Barlow, Buster, Mr. Farnham, and Mr. Taxman.

At the outer edge, forming a subknot of their own, stood Miranda Morrow and George Wetherhead. The dark circles under Mr. Wetherhead's eyes suggested that he was keeping up his fruitless midnight vigils, but he seemed otherwise cheerful, leaning on his cane and acknowledging my nod with a shy smile. I nodded to Miranda, then looked back at Dick, hoping that his ladder had been designed for heavy-duty use.

Despite his excess poundage, Dick Peacock cut a dashing figure in Finch. He had a neatly trimmed goatee and mustache, wore a Greek fisherman's cap tilted at a jaunty angle, and favored richly colored shirts. Today's was a deep shade of raspberry.

A poorly suppressed gasp went through the assembled throng as Dick began his descent, followed by an even less tactful whoosh of relief when he made it safely back to earth. He bent to pat Grog's head, then turned to address his audience.

"Not yet," he announced. "I need another S hook for the chains."

"Oh, come on, Dick," prodded Mr. Barlow. "Let's have a peep."

"It's as much as my life's worth," Dick confided, "to let my own mother have a peep before Chris gives me the go-ahead." He picked up the sign. "You'll just have to come back later."

"Don't know why he needs a sign anyway," grumbled Mr. Farnham, taking hold of Mr. Taxman's proferred arm. "Never needed a sign before. It's always been Peacock's pub and it'll always be Peacock's pub. Don't know what's got into Dick. It's that wife of his, I reckon. She's soft in the head, they say. . . ."

I watched as Mr. Taxman guided the fragile greengrocer over the uneven cobbles. Peggy Kitchen's suitor might be a bit tight-lipped, but I couldn't help liking him. I recalled the gentle way he'd spoken of Rainey after she'd tumbled from the counter at Kitchen's Emporium, and noted a similar kindliness in his handling of Mr. Farnham.

Rainey Dawson hailed me from the tearoom's front doorstep, then pelted across the square and flung her arms around me, as though we'd been separated for two years instead of two days.

I returned her hug one-handed, so as not to drop my pretty tin of lemon bars. "That's a great hat you've got on. Where'd you get it?"

Rainey pranced back a few steps and spun in a circle to display her new attire. I recognized one of Nell Harris's old gardening smocks—now daubed indelibly with yellowish mud—and the pair of work gloves I'd seen the day before, but the straw sun hat was new.

"Mrs. Kitchen found it in her back room," Rainey told me. "Emma said I needed a hat to keep the sun from broiling my brains. Emma's teaching me how to pull weeds, and plant seeds, and water *everything* because it's been a *dreadfully* dry summer and if we don't get rain soon Emma's cabbages will curl up and die and *so will she!*"

"I don't think she'll die, Rainey," I said, laughing. "Emma's made of pretty tough stuff." I glanced at the sheet-shrouded tearoom and wondered how much longer it would be before the renovations were complete. Sally Pyne would owe Emma a month of free meals for keeping Rainey occupied while the all-new Empire tearoom took shape. "How's your grandmother doing?"

"Gran's back hurts," Rainey reported, "and her knees hurt and her shoulders hurt and her neck hurts because—" Rainey froze self-consciously and clapped a gloved hand over her mouth. "I promised Gran I wouldn't tell."

The words were muffled but intelligible, and they made sparks fly in my suspicious mind. Damp meadows, I mused, were known to be hard on aging joints. Perhaps our little pitcher had overheard her grandmother and Christine Peacock discussing a certain event that had taken place outdoors, in secret, on Sunday night?

I bit my tongue to keep myself from asking the obvious questions. I was willing to do many things for the Buntings, but the list did not include tricking a little girl into ratting on her grandmother.

"If you promised your gran that you wouldn't tell," I said, "then you'd better keep your lips locked tight."

"I've got to go help Emma," Rainey said, bouncing back to life. "We're putting pots of 'santhemums by the vicar's back steps. See you later!"

Leave it to Emma to combine security with botany, I thought, as Rainey dashed toward Saint George's Lane. A maze of flowerpots would add a touch of charm to the library steps—and make it trickier than ever to negotiate them in the dark.

Dick Peacock had gone into the pub, taking Grog and

the burlap-swaddled sign with him. Opening time was eleven A.M., so I would have the publican and his wife all to myself for a couple of hours. I gave the tin a last-minute polish with the hem of my cotton blouse, then walked over and knocked on the door.

Christine Peacock answered my summons. She was a tall woman, in her mid-fifties, with a fair complexion, bright blue eyes, and shoulder-length silvery white hair. Chris was nearly as big around as her husband, but she carried her weight easily and wore what she pleased. Today she'd donned a pair of plaid shorts and an eye-popping cherry-red T-shirt.

"Good morning," I said.

"We aren't open till eleven," said Dick, joining his wife in the doorway.

"I know," I said. "I just stopped by to say hello. I haven't been into the pub for a while, so I thought I'd just . . . stop by . . . to say . . ." I cleared my throat, disconcerted by the Peacocks' blank stares. "I was in . . . last year sometime," I offered weakly. It wasn't the sort of place a pregnant woman frequented. "I'm Lori Shepherd, Bill Willis's wife."

Christine's cheeks flamed. She gave Dick a look that should have taken the back of his head off, and snapped, "Dick's sorry. Aren't you, dear?"

"I am," said Dick.

"And if he ever serves that pig's swill to your husband in my pub again—"

"*Your* pub," Dick said, affronted. "*Pig's* swill?"

"Flavored meads, I ask you . . ." Christine tossed her head. "It's as bad as the banana wine you made last summer."

I swallowed hard. "Banana wine?"

"An unsuccessful experiment," Dick admitted, with great aplomb.

Christine turned to me. "We've apologized to Bill. I'm glad you stopped by so we could apologize to you, as well."

"Thanks, but there's no need," I assured her. "I know how hard it is to resist Peggy Kitchen's suggestions."

Dick nodded sagely. "Like trying to resist a tidal wave."

"In fact," I said, thinking on my feet, "I've come here to apologize to you. Derek Harris told me what a nuisance my husband was the other night, so I baked a little something." I held up the tin of lemon bars. "Peace offering?"

"Accepted." Dick practically snatched the tin from my hands, then held the door wide. "I was just sitting down to a fresh pot of tea. Care to join me?"

My life had changed considerably since I'd last stepped foot inside the pub, but the pub hadn't changed one bit. The gleaming mahogany bar had polished brass beer pulls, an overhanging framework filled with spotless glasses, and a set of rear-wall shelves resplendent with bright bottles—but there the splendor ended. The rest of the pub still looked as shabby, dim, and dusty as it had when Bill and I had last stopped in for a drink.

The Peacocks had furnished the place with rickety chairs and a dozen or so scarred wooden tables lined up before a hideous banquette covered in protective plastic and upholstered in lime green–and–orange brocade. The back wall featured a beautiful walk-in hearth, but a patron would have to be very drunk indeed to draw a chair up to it, because the space in front of the fireplace formed the flyway for the dartboard.

In the middle of the wall above the banquette—at a safe distance from the dartboard—hung a framed photograph of Martin, the Peacocks' only child, standing straight and tall in his army uniform. I'd never met Martin, but rumor had it that his bedroom had been turned into a shrine, that not so much as a particle of dust had been disturbed since he'd packed his bags and reported for duty twenty years ago.

Dick ushered me to the table directly beneath Martin's portrait, where a teapot, cup, and saucer had already been arranged, then bustled off to fetch an extra cup and saucer. Grog snuffled amiably around my sneakers as I sat on the banquette, but Christine went behind the bar, where she appeared to be conducting an experiment.

Before her sat a row of ten pint-sized beer glasses. Seven were filled to the brim with what appeared to be pale ale, but the first three held a frothy red liquid. As I watched, Christine lifted a small plastic bottle and squeezed a drop of food coloring into the fourth glass. She stirred it with a swizzle stick, contemplated the result, then added another three drops.

"Here we are," said Dick, returning to the table. "I hope you don't mind gentian tea. I've been taking it for my gout."

"Do you make it yourself?" I asked, eyeing the teapot suspiciously.

"Good heavens, no," said Dick. "I got it from that Morrow woman, the one who hired old Miss Minty's cottage. She says there's nothing in it but nature's goodness."

"Miss Minty's cottage?" I said as Dick filled my cup. "I thought Mrs. Morrow's place was called Briar Cottage."

"That's true enough," Dick conceded, "but it was old Miss Minty's cottage when I was a little lad. I suppose I'll call it that until my dying day, whatever the deed books may say."

As Dick spoke, Mr. Farnham's words came back to me: *It's always been Peacock's pub and it'll always be Peacock's pub.* Was I in the presence of that rarest of rare breeds, a native villager? I looked at Dick with fresh interest.

"Mr. Peacock . . ." I began.

"We're Dick and Chris to you," called Christine from the bar.

"And I'm Lori," I replied. I watched while Dick loaded his gout-relieving tea with six teaspoonfuls of sugar, then began again. "How long have you lived in Finch, Dick?"

"Fifty-nine years," he answered. "My whole life, that is. Only time I left was when I joined the army. That's when I met Chris."

"Our Martin's in the army," Christine informed me, pointing to the photograph that hung directly above my head. "He's followed in his dad's footsteps."

"Our Martin's done better than his dad ever did," said Dick proudly. "I hoped he'd come home one day to help me and his mother run the pub, but the army's done so well by him that I've stopped expecting it." Grog rested his jowly muzzle on Dick's shoe, and Dick reached down to pat him on the back. "Couldn't ask a rising star like Martin to settle in a quiet place like Finch, now, could we?"

"Maybe we could," Christine said, bending over her array of glasses.

A flicker of pity lit Dick's eyes as he looked over at his wife. "I suppose we can try," he said quietly. "Chris has some new ideas."

"Is that why you're fixing up the pub?" I asked. "I thought it was a general cleanup campaign, what with Sally Pyne renovating the—"

Christine snorted. "Sally Pyne wouldn't know a good

idea if it bit her on her big fat bum. She thinks more about her waistline—what there is of it—than about what's good for the village."

"Now, Chris," Dick remonstrated, "if Sally wants to dress her place up Roman, it's her business and none of ours."

"It's her business going down the drain," Christine snapped. "She's a fool if she thinks Dr. Culver's going to bring tourists to Finch." She sniffed disparagingly. "Him with his old hole in the ground."

"He might discover something important," Dick pointed out.

"Roman ruins?" Christine mocked. "What's Finch need with Roman ruins? There's Cirencester and Chedworth and Crickly Hill not forty miles from here," she went on, listing three of the Cotswolds' better-known archaeological sites. "You think Dr. Culver's grubby hole can compete with them?"

"You've got to start somewhere," Dick reasoned.

"That's what I'm doing," said Christine. "But I'm not looking backward, like Fat Sally. I'm looking ahead." She lifted one of the glasses of ale and examined it closely before adding another drop of food coloring. "What color would you say Mars is, Lori?"

I blinked, jarred by the abrupt change of subject. "The planet Mars?" I asked.

"That's right." Christine leaned her chin on her hand and stared at me fixedly. "What color would you say Mars is? Looking at it from the ground, I mean, with your own two eyes."

"Well . . ." I scratched my head. "I supposed I'd describe it as a . . . a glittery garnet-red. On a clear night," I added hastily.

"Oh, that's lovely, that is," said Christine. "We can put

that in the brochure, Dick. *Red Planet Special—a glittery garnet-red ale with a taste that's out of this world.* It's got a ring to it."

"It does," Dick agreed, his gaze fixed on the bottom button of his black brocade waistcoat.

I looked from his face to the row of red, frothing glasses. "Are you developing a new beer?"

Christine stood tall and squared her shoulders. "We're developing more than that, aren't we, Dick? Show Lori the new sign I've painted."

Dick hefted his large frame from the chair and trudged dutifully to the sign, which he'd left just inside the doorway. He took a penknife from the pocket of his waistcoat and cut the brown string that held the burlap covering in place. He gave me a brief, embarrassed glance as the burlap fell away, and I was assailed by an awful premonition.

"What do you think?" Christine asked. "That'll do the trick, eh? That'll bring the crowds in, and then our Martin'll have a *reason* to come home."

The Peacocks' new pub sign depicted two faces on a dark ground. One face was slightly larger than the other, but apart from that, they were identical: hairless, triangular, and delicate, with enormous eyes, plug holes for nostrils, and thin slits for mouths. They wore dark-brown hoods, and their skin was painted a pale shade of greenish-gray.

"The Green Men . . ." I murmured, reading the pub's new name aloud.

"That's right," said Christine triumphantly. "That'll fetch more tourists than Roman ruins *or* the Harvest Festival. We'll have 'em hanging from the rafters once word gets out that aliens have landed in Finch!"

16.

"I tried to tell your husband about it when he was here the other night," Christine said as Dick returned to the table. "To see if I'd need to swear before a judge that I'd seen the little buggers. But he was too far gone by then to listen."

"Christine," I said gently, "are you absolutely sure about what you saw?"

"Positive." Christine came out from behind the bar and pulled another chair up to our table. "I'd taken Grog out to do his business late Sunday night," she began. "The old boy's been having plumbing troubles, so he has to go out more often than usual." She leaned forward, with her elbows on the table. "Grog and me were walking along the river, down by the vicarage meadow. There was a full moon rising, but it was still behind the trees and the ground mist was as thick as slurry. Grog had just finished lifting his leg when it happened." She paused dramatically and leaned in even closer. "Never seen anything like it before in my life. The mist over the vicarage meadow lit up all swirly and bright, like headlamps in the fog, but these lights"—she pointed upward—"were coming from the sky."

"From the sky," I echoed solemnly.

"That's when I saw 'em," Christine continued, "just for a minute, mind. They were lit up from behind, then they were gone—poof—lights and all. I think they found out I was watching and hoped to lure me closer, so they could suck me up into their ship and perform experiments on me."

I decided that a knowing nod would be my best response. Dick stared at his hands and said nothing. As his wife had become more animated, he'd become more subdued. He hadn't once looked over at the new sign.

"Did you hear anything?" I asked.

Christine frowned. "I thought I heard a sort of chuffing noise just before the sky lit up, but it was hard to tell, with the river so near and all."

"You must have gotten close enough to see their faces," I said.

"I did not," Christine declared. "I got out of there as fast as Grog could trot. Came straight back to the pub and locked the door behind me. Aliens can be dangerous, you know. I've read all about 'em."

"But if you didn't see their faces," I said, looking past her at the sign, "how do you know what they looked like?"

"Everyone knows what aliens look like," she replied. "The papers are full of 'em."

The papers were full of something, I thought, and it wasn't aliens.

"It all happened just before midnight," Christine continued.

"*Before* midnight?" I repeated.

"About fifteen minutes before," Christine said. "I know,

'cause I looked at the clock when I came in. I tried to rouse Dick, but he was dead to the world."

"Chris told me about it next morning," Dick said quietly, "and took me over to have a look at the vicarage meadow."

"And there it was," Christine crowed. "A circle of bent grass, where the alien ship had landed."

"It must've been an awfully *small* alien ship," Dick put in, "because the circle wasn't more than ten feet across."

"Size doesn't matter," Christine insisted. "They've got *powers.*" She folded her arms obstinately. "I know what I saw, Richard Peacock. What's more, I know that we're going to make a packet out of the little green buggers when word gets out that they've been to Finch. Our Martin'll have a good job waiting for him here. He'll *want* to come home."

Grog whimpered urgently and Christine got to her feet. "Time for walkies," she said. "You won't tell anyone but Bill about this, will you, Lori? I want it to come as a surprise. I can't wait to see Sally Pyne's face when she sees she's missed the boat."

Pity flooded through me as I watched Christine fetch Grog's leash from under the bar and lead him out into the square, whistling a jaunty tune. I gazed sadly at the dreadful sign and waited for Dick to break the silence his wife had left behind.

Wordlessly, he opened the tin of lemon bars and offered me first choice. He took one for himself but left it lying untasted on the table while he stared down, nudging crumbs this way and that with a fingertip.

He spoke almost apologetically. "She wants him to come home so *badly,* you see."

"I can understand that," I said.

"Can you?" Dick folded his hands across his waistcoat

and pursed his lips. "I wonder. You and Bill are just start-
ing out. You've got your boys at home and you can't imagine it ever being any different. But the day'll come when
they'll be off, when they'll be too busy to call or write
or visit." He nodded patiently. "It's the way of things.
Children're supposed to grow up and have their own lives.
They're supposed to stop needing you." He lifted his gaze
to the framed photograph. "But you never stop needing
them. And that's a fact."

I looked away, unable to bear the hunger in Dick's eyes.
It doesn't have to be that way, I told myself. No one is
too busy to pick up a telephone, not even a big-shot army
officer.

"Doesn't Martin ever come to see you?" I asked.

"He's been home ten times in twenty years," Dick
answered. "It's not his fault," he added quickly. "The
army's sent him all over the world—Singapore, India,
South America. He's in England, now, though. We'd
hoped to lure him home with the Harvest Festival, until
Dr. Culver showed up. From what we've heard, the festival don't stand a chance against the likes of him. That's
why Chris . . ." He glanced at the sign and fell silent.

I gazed at him steadily. "Do you believe that Christine
saw aliens in the vicarage meadow on Sunday night?"

"Chris saw what she wanted to see." Dick lifted the
lemon bar to his lips and took a surprisingly dainty nibble.
"She's right about one thing, though," he added, brushing
crumbs from his goatee. "Once word gets out that the little buggers've visited Finch, the crowds'll come all right.
Nutters 'n' fruitbats, every one. Our Martin won't come
within fifty miles of 'em. Or a pub named after 'em. He's
got his rank and reputation to consider." Dick's second
bite was larger than his first. Three-quarters of the lemon
bar disappeared in one chomp.

"What if the Harvest Festival were to go on as planned?" I asked. "Would Martin visit you then?"

"He promised his mother he would," said Dick. "But there's not much chance of that, is there? Not with Dr. Culver parked in the schoolhouse." He polished off what remained of his lemon bar and reached into the tin for another. "It's a pity," he added, "because you know a thing or two about baking. I'm not saying you'd win a blue ribbon, Lori, but you'd give Lilian Bunting a run for her money. And that's a fact."

The sound of hammering smote my ears as I emerged from Peacock's pub. Mr. Taxman was nailing a scalloped swath of red-white-and-blue bunting to the edge of a wooden platform that had risen from the cobbles in front of Kitchen's Emporium. A handful of spectators, full of bantering advice, were silenced by the discordant jangle of sleigh bells as the Emporium's front door swung open and Peggy Kitchen strode forth.

Peggy's encounter with the bishop had done nothing to quench the fire in her eyes. She paused to survey Mr. Taxman's handiwork, tweaked the bunting to straighten a few wrinkles, then began distributing sheets of familiar harvest-gold paper from a stack cradled in one arm, exhorting each recipient to "Stand and be counted!" The flock bleated submissively, then scattered. Within minutes the square was deserted, save for Peggy, Mr. Taxman, and me.

Peggy waved me over, but I was already on my way. I hadn't forgotten her attempt to blacken Francesca's reputation.

"Grand, isn't it?" Peggy boomed, thrusting a flyer in front of my face. "Jasper's done a fine job. Knows how to put words to paper, that man does. Listen:

HEAR YE! HEAR YE!
CITIZENS OF FINCH!
Ye are herebye called to attend
A RALLY!
Defend your village from the Onslaughts of Outsiders!
Show your support for Time-Honored Traditions!
DON'T LET THE BISHOP DICTATE VILLAGE POLICY!
Raise your voices in a righteous cause!
Sunday Noon on the Square
For God hath not given us the spirit of fear,
but of power.
—*II Timothy 1:7*

"Rousing, that's what I call it," said Peggy, her mad eyes glinting behind her pointy glasses. "Just the ticket to grab folks by the guts, don't you think?"

The new flyer closely resembled the one announcing Peggy's petition, but it evoked in me a quite different set of emotions. Four days ago, I'd been afraid of Peggy Kitchen. Now I found myself, perversely, cheering her on. Peggy was a brawler and a bully, and her manners made me want to kick her shins, but I couldn't fault her tenacity, or her willingness to work for what she wanted. It would take a bigger man than the bishop to knock Peggy Kitchen down for the count.

"It's very nice," I acknowledged stiffly. "However—"

"I know Bill's working hard on the legal end of things," she said, "and I know you've ordered that nanny of yours to whittle away at Dr. Culver's willpower, but we need to get the villagers worked up, as well."

"Peggy," I said sternly, "you have no right to talk about Fran—"

"I'll admit," she conceded, "that I misunderstood your plan, at first, but Derek Harris set me straight. It's dead clever, Lori, throwing that woman at Dr. Culver's head to distract him while we cut the ground out from under him."

I shook my head in vigorous denial. "That's not—"

"Credit where credit is due." Peggy swept an arm through the air to encompass the entire square. "We'll march down here directly after church on Sunday. Jasper'll do the introductions, I'll say a word to get the troops wound up, then you'll speak your piece and touch their hearts."

"Me?" I wheezed.

"Picture it," said Peggy, framing the platform with an outstretched hand. "The little mother, clutching her babes to her meager breast, pleading for a chance to show her young ones the ways of her ancestors."

"But I'm not even English!" I exclaimed. "And my breasts aren't—"

"Your husband's got English relations," Peggy countered, "and that's close enough. You'll see. It'll go down a treat on Sunday. If we can't force the bishop to change his mind, we'll *shame* him into it. Must run." She patted the stack of flyers, pivoted in place, and strode purposefully toward Saint George's Lane.

For a moment the square was as still as a battlefield in the wake of an artillery barrage. I sensed a dozen fearful eyes peering from shop windows while a dozen lungs began to breathe again. Gradually, the tide of life resurged. Birds recommenced their interrupted chirping, Mr. Taxman resumed his hammering, Mr. Barlow tossed another rubber ball, and Buster gladly chased it. On the whole, I thought, as Christine and Grog crept furtively from behind the war memorial, the citizens of Finch would probably *prefer* an alien invasion to a run-in with Peggy Kitchen on the square.

"What's going on, Jasper?"

I snapped to attention and nearly licked my chops because the question had been uttered by none other than my prime suspect. Sally Pyne was walking gingerly toward Kitchen's Emporium, as though to minimize each necessary knee bend.

Despite constant dieting, Sally Pyne remained steadfastly grandmother-shaped. Her body was close to the ground and amply cushioned, custom designed to scoop grandkids off their feet and envelop them in suffocating hugs. She had a round, determined chin and wore her silver hair in a short but stylish chop. She'd dressed for the day in a queen-sized royal-blue tracksuit and thick-soled purple running shoes, an ensemble selected, I suspected, to coddle joints stiffened by a damp and damning night's work, burgling the vicarage.

"Sally," I said, with a show of heartiness. "Where have you been hiding yourself?"

"In a minute, Lori." Sally hobbled past me to address a second question to Mr. Taxman. "Now, Jasper, what's all this about a rally on Sunday?"

"See for yourself." Mr. Taxman picked up a flyer from a small stack Peggy had left on the platform and handed it to the frowning Mrs. Pyne.

Sally mumbled her way through the text, growing paler with each exclamation point. Then she crumpled the flyer into a ball and tossed it expertly into the center of the platform. "It's off," she snapped.

"Pardon?" said Mr. Taxman.

Sally Pyne gave a good impression of an armored tank as she squared off in front of Peggy Kitchen's suitor.

"You tell Mrs. Kitchen that if she *dares* create a disturbance on the square this coming Sunday, I will personally see to it that she's covered, head to toe, with rotten eggs."

Mr. Taxman smoothed his brown tie. "But why?" he inquired.

Sally glared at him ferociously. "Because, you nitwit, Sunday's my granddaughter's birthday! *And* the grand opening of the Empire tearoom!"

17.

Bill and I sought sanctuary in the study. I sat huddled on the ottoman, with Bill behind me in the tall leather armchair nearest the door. Francesca, Will, and Rob were taking a turn in the back garden, working up an appetite for lunch.

"If I had to guess," Bill murmured, kneading my shoulders, "I'd say that you didn't speak with Sally about her whereabouts on Sunday night."

"I panicked and ran," I confessed miserably. "All I could think about was standing next to Peggy on that platform, covered in rotten eggs. What am I going to do, Bill? If I don't go to the rally, Peggy'll kill me, and if I do go, Sally'll turn me into an extremely runny omelette."

"Deep breaths," said Bill. "Deep breaths. Your morning wasn't wasted, you know. You've eliminated Christine Peacock from our list of suspects, for a start. She may have seen the burglars, but she wasn't one of them."

My spirits lifted half an inch. "True."

"You learned something else, as well," Bill went on, in his most soothing voice. "Brother Florin, Miranda's witches, and Christine's aliens all wore hoods. It shouldn't be too difficult to find out if Sally owns a hooded raincoat or jacket."

"Everyone in Finch owns a hooded jacket," I grumbled. "This is England, the land of the green and the home of the rain."

"You've narrowed down the time frame, too," Bill pointed out, undeterred. "Christine saw her aliens about a half hour before Mr. Wetherhead saw his ghost. Maybe someone saw a pair of hooded figures sneaking in or out of the tearoom between, say, eleven-thirty and half past twelve."

I rubbed my tired eyes and tried to focus on something other than raw eggs. "I doubt if anyone stays up that late in Finch."

Bill's magic fingers went to work on a knot in my right shoulder. "And let's not forget about Rainey's secret," he continued. "Did Rainey overhear her grandmother moaning indiscreetly about what brought on her aches and pains?"

"Rainey's out of bounds," I said bluntly.

Bill switched to my left shoulder. "Then what about Simon or Katrina? They're staying with Sal—"

"Katrina!" I exclaimed, sitting bolt upright. "Of course. How could I forget about our little hero-worshiper?"

"Because she's scarcely showed her face in the village since Tuesday," said Bill. "She seems to spend every waking hour at Scrag End." He chuckled suddenly. "Derek calls her the little blond weight lifter."

"She's in great shape," I agreed. "You should've seen her unloading boxes from the van. She made Simon look like a wimp. She could hop the vicarage wall without working up a sweat. I'll bet Sally told her about the pamphlet, just to get up Peggy's nose. . . ." I leaned back against Bill, revitalized, and pieced together what must have happened.

"Adrian Culver arrives in Finch on Sunday morning, right? And Sally Pyne sees a golden opportunity to infuriate Peggy Kitchen. So while Peggy rants at the vicar, Sally visits the schoolhouse and offers to house Simon and Katrina.

"She shows Simon and Katrina to their rooms. She discovers Katrina's cache of fund-raising letters and begins to dream her own imperial dreams: The Empire tearoom is born. Are you with me?"

"Lead on," said Bill.

"Later that same day, the village grapevine begins to crackle." If I closed my eyes I could almost hear the distant thrum of wagging tongues as the gossip drifted through the leafy lanes:

They say that specky chap's not goin' to stay. . . .

Word is, Vicar's got somethin' up his sleeve. . . .

I heard it were on his desk. . . .

Bill seemed to hear the same voices, because he followed through on my speculations without missing a beat. "Sally, unlike Peggy Kitchen, knows how to keep her mouth shut and listen. She listens hard all afternoon, and by dinnertime she's winnowed out the truth: The Gladwell pamphlet, a document guaranteed to send Adrian Culver packing, is lying on the vicar's desk, not five feet from a pair of well-concealed and unsecured French doors."

"Exactly." I nodded eagerly. "She knows she has to act quickly. She's not built to clamber over walls, so she enlists the help of a younger, fitter, but equally enthusiastic accomplice. She and Katrina wait until Simon's asleep, then don hooded jackets and slip out of the tearoom, carrying flashlights." I shivered as Bill's lips brushed my ear.

"They creep along the riverbank," he whispered, "and climb to the top of the dip in the vicarage meadow. Someone slips on the slick grass and drops a flashlight—the sudden glare catches Christine's attention. The thieves regroup, switch off the flashlights, and hug the ground, hoping the mist will swallow their fumble."

"Stop whispering," I said. "You're giving me the creeps."

Bill laughed, then spoke in his normal voice. "While Christine and Grog skedaddle for the pub, Katrina moves toward the vicarage. Sally waits in the dip while Katrina—Brother Florin—circles the vicarage, checking for lights."

"And when she's sure the Buntings are safely tucked in bed," I continued, "she darts into the library, snatches the Gladwell pamphlet from the vicar's desk, and returns, trophy in hand, to the dip. She and Sally do a victory dance—Miranda's moon-worship ritual—and crush the grass beneath their feet. Voilà—the landing site of the alien invaders."

I rested for a moment, stunned by the elegance of our recital, then turned to Bill. "Well?"

"One thing," he said. "Wouldn't Katrina object to continuing a dig that might land her boss in hot water? It won't help Adrian's reputation to be accused of perpetrating a fraud."

I thought for a moment. "Katrina might not know about the fraud," I said. "Sally could have told her that the *pamphlet* was a hoax, something cooked up by Peggy and Mr. Taxman—like those flyers—to fool the Buntings, Adrian, everyone."

"It's plausible," Bill allowed. "Katrina had already had one run-in with Peggy by the time she met Sally. She must have thought Peggy capable of anything."

"Katrina thought Peggy was crazy," I stated firmly. "She told me so, the first time I met her." I got to my feet. "I'm positive that Katrina Graham and Sally Pyne stole the Gladwell pamphlet. All we have to do is prove it."

"It'd be helpful to prove it before Sunday comes around," Bill reminded me. "Sally'll be less likely to throw eggs if she's already got 'em all over her face."

Emma added a new and unwelcome wrinkle to my theory when she showed up on my doorstep an hour later, bearing a briefcase full of computer printouts.

"Sally took my undergardener off to find a party dress," she announced, "and since I promised Rainey I wouldn't plant a seed without her, I've given myself a half holiday."

"Come on in," I said.

Emma was the only person I knew who didn't demand to see the boys the minute she stepped into the cottage. I found it quite refreshing.

"Rainey's been a Trojan," she told me, as we settled on the couch in the living room. "I wish I had her energy."

"Don't we all," I said.

"She's a trouper," said Emma. "She carted flowerpots up and down the library steps all morning, without a single squawk—and she seems to thrive on dirt. She's so different from Nell that it makes me wonder if they're from the same planet."

I recalled Nell Harris's sense of style, her air of sophistication, and nodded my agreement. "Night and day," I said.

"I've brought a present for Reginald," Emma said. "Nell sent it from Paris, on Bertie's behalf."

Bertie was a chocolate-brown teddy bear. Nell carried him with her everywhere, without apology or explanation. Bertie and Reginald were cousins, of a sort, both having sprung from Dimity's sewing needle, and Bertie never failed to remember Reg during his travels abroad.

Emma opened her briefcase and removed a box wrapped in gold foil. "Marrons glacés," she said. "Straight from the Champs-Elysées."

I looked toward the playpen, where Rob and Will were chewing contentedly on their toes. "I don't think Reg'll mind if we open his present for him. I'm sure he'd *want* us to enjoy . . ." My words trailed off as I strolled over to scrounge through the stuffed menagerie that kept the boys company. "That's odd," I said, straightening. "I could've sworn I put Reg in the playpen before I went into the village this morning. Francesca?" I called, heading for the kitchen. "Have you seen Reginald?"

Francesca looked up from the bread dough she was kneading. "He's in the playpen, isn't he?"

"Not anymore," I said. "I thought you might have moved him."

She gazed at me, perplexed. Then her dark eyes sparked with sudden illumination. "The sneak," she whispered. Flour flew as she gave the dough an angry punch. "The underhanded, conniving—" She caught my eye and clamped her mouth shut, then turned to the sink to rinse her hands. "Will it be all right if I slip out for a bit?"

"Sure," I said. "I'll be home for the rest of the day." I had a vague suspicion who the sneak might be, but I wasn't going to be the first to mention his name.

"May I use the Mini?" she asked, stripping off her apron.

"Take the Mercedes," I said, following her to the front door. "You know where the keys are."

"Grazie. I won't be long." Francesca took the keys from the hall drawer. She paused before the mirror to brush a smudge of flour from her chin, then marched outside. The Mercedes's engine roared and its tires spat gravel as Francesca spun out of the drive.

"Brrr . . ." I said, shivering theatrically. "I wouldn't want to be in Adrian's shoes when Francesca catches up with him."

"What's going on?" asked Emma.

"I'm not sure," I admitted, returning to the couch, "but I suspect that Dr. Culver came a'courtin' this morning, and left with Reginald in his rucksack."

"Don't be silly," said Emma. "Why would he take Reginald?"

"I didn't say he *took* Reginald. Not on purpose, anyway. Not consciously." I looked over at the playpen. "My guess is that Reg just sort of accidentally *fell* into Adrian's rucksack."

Emma looked as though she thought I'd lost my mind.

"Oh, come on, Emma," I said. "You know what a sucker Dimity is when it comes to true love. I'll bet she's using Reg for a spot of matchmaking. She's done it before."

Emma bit her lip and stared down at her briefcase. "I hate to say it, but I think Dimity may be backing the wrong horse this time."

My smile faded. "What do you mean?"

"You remember the on-line search you asked me to do, regarding the Culver Institute?" Emma reached into her briefcase and produced a sheaf of computer printouts. "This is what I found."

"You're kidding," I said.

"I'm serious." She shuffled through the printouts. "I was able to retrieve a set of E-mail follow-ups to surface-mail solicitations asking people to support the Culver Institute." She looked up uncertainly. "You don't seem very pleased."

"I'm not," I said as a wave of disappointment washed through me. "Adrian seems like such a nice guy. You should have seen him the other night, when he showed up here with Reg. He was so cute, like a little kid spiffed up for a school dance. He behaved impeccably when Bill came home, drunk as a skunk, and he didn't lose his temper when he found out that Peggy had tricked him into signing her petition." I sighed. "He just laughed and said she'd make a great prime minister. And he's such a *goop* when he's around Francesca. I can't help liking him, Emma."

"No one ever said nice guys can't be ambitious," Emma pointed out.

"But nice guys don't lie," I said, shaking my head sadly. "And Adrian's lied to everyone—to me, to the Buntings, to his staff, maybe even to the bishop. He's got everyone believing that he has no long-range plans for Finch. But these"—I tapped the printouts—"prove otherwise. They confirm what Francesca told me about the cache of letters Sally found in Katrina's room."

"In that case," said Emma, "I guess we have to face facts. Adrian's got more at stake in Finch than we realized."

"Which puts him at the top of my list of suspects," I said, "because he's got more to lose than anyone else. His museum will go down in flames if his backers find out about the Gladwell pamphlet." I buried my face in my hands and groaned. "The arrogance! To foist a fake on his unsuspecting backers and think he can get away with it!"

Emma listened sympathetically while I recounted my thrill-filled morning. If she smiled over Christine's aliens or my role as Peggy's poster child in the upcoming rally, she had the decency to do so when I wasn't looking. She also pointed out, quite sensibly, that Adrian's inclusion on the suspect list didn't necessarily exclude Sally Pyne or Katrina Graham.

"Adrian could have told Katrina and Sally about the pamphlet after he'd learned about it from the vicar," Emma reasoned. "They may have planned the burglary together, or he may have talked them into it, then sat back and watched while they did the dirty work. He should have known that others would be watching, too."

"Nothing goes unnoticed in a village," I murmured, sick at heart.

"I know what I'd like to do next," Emma said. "I'd like to break into the schoolhouse to see if I can find a hooded raincoat, or copies of the solicitation letters, or, best of all, the missing pamphlet."

"*You?*" I said, thunderstruck. "When did the keyboard bandit turn into an action heroine? Rainey's energy *has* rubbed off on you, my friend."

"Hey," Emma protested, "Finch is my village, too. I don't want to see this civil war get any bigger."

"Okay," I said doubtfully, "but you'll have to come up with another plan. Crime—even a piddling little crime like the burglary—has too many unintended consequences." I thought of the vicar, sitting in his darkened library, and of George Wetherhead's futile enthusiasm. Most of all I thought of Christine Peacock, yearning for her son, hoping to coax him home with a scheme that wouldn't have entered her mind but for a chance encounter with the burglars. I wondered if Adrian had ever stopped to consider the hidden costs of building a monument to his ego.

"Then how about this?" Emma proposed. "I'll talk Simon into giving Derek and me a tour of the schoolhouse tomorrow. A really *thorough* tour."

"What'll I be doing while you're ransacking the cupboards?" I asked dryly.

Emma thought a moment. "You'll be taking Dr. Culver up on his invitation to visit Scrag End field. And you'll keep him and Katrina there until my tour is finished."

I looked over at the playpen and nodded. "Rob, Will, and I should be able to keep Katrina out of your hair for quite a while." I turned my gaze to Emma's briefcase and smiled grimly. "I'll leave Adrian to Francesca."

18.

Will and Rob watched from their bouncy chairs as I shut the study door and reached for the blue journal. Emma had departed and Francesca had not yet returned, so the boys and I had the cottage to ourselves. It seemed a good time to give Dimity some pointers on the delicate art of matchmaking. If I had to lose my nanny, I didn't want to lose her to a two-faced, puffed-up popinjay like Adrian Culver.

I gave the boys' chairs a jiggle before I settled into an armchair, and they gurgled with unabashed delight. An hour with my bambinos did me more good than a whole week of Bill's backrubs. I jiggled their chairs again, to show my gratitude, then sat back and opened the blue journal. Before I could say a word, Aunt Dimity's looping scrawl began to fill the page.

What an exciting time you're having, Lori! Witches and ghosts and Martians, oh, my. I hardly know where to begin. And now there's the rally, the birthday party, and the reopening of the tearoom, all on the same day. You've so much to look forward to!

"That's one way of looking at it," I said, leaning my chin on my fist.

I've got to hand it to you, my dear. Your timing is extraordinary. I've seen many confrontations between Peggy Kitchen and Sally Pyne, but you'll witness what promises to be the climax of their feud. How I wish I could be there to see it.

"If you can figure out a way to trade places with me, Dimity, I'll be only too glad to . . ." I fell silent as the implications of Dimity's comments filtered through. "Wait a minute," I said. "Peggy and Sally didn't move to Finch until after you . . . departed." I winced at the euphemism but continued doggedly. "How did you manage to witness *any* of their confrontations?"

Peggy and Sally came to Finch long before they settled here for good. I remember when they first arrived. Peggy and her mother were taken in by Mr. Harmer, the shopkeeper on the square. Sally lived with Miss Shuttleworth, who ran the tearoom. Little Billy Barlow followed a few weeks later—he stayed with Mr. Diston, the blacksmith—and the Farnhams took in Jasper Taxman. It wasn't easy, what with ration books, food queues, and the blackout, but it was necessary. Birmingham, Bristol, and Plymouth were under the gun in those days.

"In those days . . ." I repeated slowly. "Dimity, are you saying that Mrs. Pyne, Mr. Barlow, and Mr. Taxman were brought to Finch as children, because of the blitz? Were they evacuees, like Peggy Kitchen?"

They were evacuees, but they weren't a bit like Peggy. They hadn't lost a father, so perhaps it was easier for them to be kind.

"Kind to whom?" I asked.

To Piero Sciaparelli, of course. Not everyone threw stones, you know. Sally Pyne loved Piero, and Peggy never forgave her for it.

I closed my eyes, bruised by the sudden revelation.

Peggy and Sally weren't simply two strong-willed women angling for dominance in a small community. They were lifelong enemies. They'd hated each other for more than forty years, and now, the day after tomorrow, on the square in Finch, their long-running feud would come to a head. Would the rotten eggs turn into stones? I wondered. Would sly theft give way to open warfare?

I looked down at the journal. "Did Jasper Taxman and Billy Barlow get involved?"

Billy was too busy being a little boy to pay attention to a pair of bickering girls, but Jasper . . . Ah, poor Jasper. He allowed Peggy to lead him around by the nose, I'm afraid. A potent case of puppy love.

"It didn't get him anywhere," I pointed out. "In the end, Peggy became Mrs. Kitchen, not Mrs. Taxman."

Widows have been known to remarry.

My eyes widened. "Jasper moved back to Finch in hopes of marrying his childhood sweetheart? Golly. That's potent puppy love, all right. I wonder why the others came back."

Who can tell? Perhaps they had fond memories of Finch. Perhaps they felt they owed something to the village that had given them shelter from the storm so many years ago. I expect they came back for many different reasons.

"Peggy didn't come back until after Piero Sciaparelli's death," I said. "I'll bet she was majorly annoyed to find Sally here—and vice versa. From what Mr. Barlow told me, it sounds as though they picked up where they left off during the war—Finch's longest long-running feud."

It's such a pity. Piero sought nothing but peace in his adopted country, yet he found himself, time and again, at the center of conflict. He'd lost far more than Peggy Kitchen, yet he was as kind as summer. I wish you could have known him.

"So do I," I murmured.

I'm sorry, Lori. I've let my recollections run away with me. I had another reason entirely for wishing to speak with you today.

"What's that?" I asked, pushing aside memories of a man I'd never known.

I wanted to remind you that Rainey's birthday is less than three days away. Have you gotten her a gift?

I gave a weak laugh. At the moment, finding a birthday present for Rainey was the least of my worries. "Not yet. Emma found something for her in the back room at Kitchen's Emporium, but I'd rather not go that route."

You needn't rely on Peggy. All you have to do is look in the attic.

"Which attic?" I said.

The one above your head, my dear. Look for a trunk, a green trunk with brass hinges. I think you'll find exactly what you need. There was a pause. *I'm sorry, Lori, but I must fly. Thank you for letting me prattle on about Piero. And do let me know how Emma's search of the schoolhouse turns out!*

"Dimity! Wait! I wanted to . . ." I watched as Dimity's fine copperplate slowly faded from the page. ". . . ask you about Adrian," I muttered, knowing that no one could hear me but Will and Rob. I closed the journal, returned it to the shelf, and faced the boys. "Well, troops, let's see what's waiting for us in the attic, shall we?"

The attic wasn't much more than a crawl space, a dim and dusty hollow beneath the eaves, where Dimity had stored old picture frames, worn quilts, ancient cameras— odds and ends she couldn't use but couldn't throw away.

I peered down from the trapdoor to make sure the boys were okay. Francesca was, presumably, still tracking Adrian down in her pursuit of Reginald, and Bill was still at work. It was patently unsafe to cart the boys up the narrow pull-down ladder that gave access to the attic, so I'd left them down below, nestled in their bouncy chairs, where I could see them.

I thought I knew the trunk Dimity had spoken of. I'd gone through it when I'd moved into the cottage, then returned it to its place under the eaves. It had been filled with elegant old clothes more suited to the Pym sisters than to a mud-pie princess like Rainey.

I crawled over to sit cross-legged before the trunk. It was covered with forest-green leather and trimmed with brass metalwork; the latch plate bore Dimity's initials. I raised the lid and removed a fitted tray filled with kid gloves, silk scarves, and linen handkerchiefs. Dust wafted gently into the musty air as I carefully placed the tray on the rough wooden floor, and a spider crept out on an overhead beam to see what was disturbing her cobweb. I mumbled an apology for the intrusion, peered into the trunk's main compartment, and gasped.

"Oh, my," I whispered, lifting the stuffed tiger from his bed of beaded dresses. "Oh, Dimity . . ."

I gazed into the tiger's black button eyes and felt a flood of love flow through me. He was perfect. His brown stripes would conceal grubby handprints, and he was sturdy enough to withstand being dropped, trodden on, and tripped over by a little girl better known for vigor than for grace. He was happy-go-lucky, fearless, nigh on indestructible—and he'd need to be.

I touched a finger to the tiger's hand-stitched whiskers and wondered, for a moment, what his name was. Then I hugged him to me and murmured to the spider, "Rainey will know."

Bill found me grating carrots for our salad when he came home that evening. The rich aroma of rosemary chicken drew him to the kitchen doorway, where he stood, eyeing me speculatively.

"You're in a good mood," he observed, with the air of a man who'd worked out a knotty problem. "Has the rally been canceled?"

"Nope." I laid the grater aside, gave the carrot stump to Rob, and tossed the salad.

Bill snapped his fingers. "I know! You've booked a flight back to Boston."

"Don't be ridiculous," I said. "I've got a speech to make on Sunday."

Bill came over to feel my forehead. "No sign of fever, but I suggest you lie down anyway and let Francesca finish preparing dinner. Where is she?"

"I sent her to her room." I shrugged at Bill's sharp intake of breath. "It was either that or let her burn the cottage down. She's been in an absolute daze since she got back from seeing Adrian."

Bill stumbled back against the sink in mock amazement. "Francesca went to see Adrian? Voluntarily? Has the world gone mad since lunchtime or have the two of you been at the cooking sherry?"

"Go wash your hands," I ordered. "I'll tell you all about it over dinner."

Francesca had returned from Scrag End field so preoccupied that she'd put Rob's T-shirt on him backward and dropped Will's socks in the toilet bowl.

"As I fished them out," I said, passing Bill the new potatoes, "I heard her say to her reflection in the mirror, 'Adrian *means* well.' At which point I steered her to her room and closed the door."

"Did she find Reginald?" Bill asked, spooning potatoes onto his plate.

"Oh, yes," I said. "But not before she'd accused Adrian of theft, dishonesty, and a wanton disregard for the feelings of a pair of helpless infants. Imagine her chagrin when Simon spotted Reginald in the backseat of the Mercedes."

"Ow," said Bill, grimacing.

"Adrian was very good about it," I said. "He stopped by with a bouquet of wildflowers, to make sure Francesca knew there were no hard feelings." I put my fork down, assailed by a sudden loss of appetite. "I can't take Francesca with me to Scrag End field tomorrow. Adrian's already charmed her into thinking he means well. God knows how much further he'll get, now that her guard is down."

Bill reached over to squeeze my hand. "I'm sorry, love. I know how it pains you to see handsome princes tumble off their chargers. You're an incurable romantic, and I wouldn't have you any other way."

A few moments and several mouthfuls later, he said thoughtfully, "I suppose Reginald got into the Merc the same way he got into Father's briefcase last summer. Dimity seems to be going out of her way to throw our two ill-matched lovebirds together."

"She can't be right all of the time," I said, "but when she is, she's spot on. Wait until you see Rainey's birthday present."

"Extraspecial?" said Bill.

"Way beyond extra," I replied. "Reginald has a new cousin. A tiger. He'll be the hit of the party."

"Ah, yes," said Bill, "the party. The birthday party that's scheduled to coincide with Peggy's rally." He paused to savor another bite of juicy, aromatic chicken before asking, "Did I hear you correctly? Are you really going to get up on that platform and make a speech?"

"I am." Something of the tiger's spirit had entered into

me in the attic. I was no longer afraid of what would happen on Sunday. In truth, I was rather looking forward to placing myself between Sally Pyne and Peggy Kitchen. It would be a dangerous job, but someone had to do it.

"Do I get a sneak preview?" Bill coaxed.

"Of my speech?" I shook my head. "Sorry, but you'll have to wait till Sunday, just like everybody else."

"I'll alert the media." Bill let the subject drop and concentrated fully on his food. When he'd finished, he pushed himself back from the table and groaned contentedly. "I am replete," he announced, patting his stomach. "You know, Lori, Francesca's a good cook, but she's no match for you."

I had a sudden vision of the glop Bill had been eating for the past ten months or more, of the meals put through strainers, sieves, and food mills. With a guilty twinge I realized exactly how much he'd missed my cooking, and I blessed him for not mentioning it sooner. I watched him take his plate into the kitchen and felt my heart swell even as my throat constricted. Some handsome princes, I thought, knew how to stay in the saddle.

19.

My conscience was no match for Francesca's. Once she'd laid eyes on the wildflower bouquet, there was no stopping her from accompanying me to Scrag End field.

"I let my temper run away with me yesterday," she said stolidly, as we loaded the boys' strollers into the trunk of the Mercedes. "I said some things I shouldn't've. I should be apologizing to Dr. Culver, not the other way round."

I studied her covertly as we went back into the cottage. The disease had progressed more rapidly than I'd realized. Four days ago she'd have bitten her tongue in two rather than say a kind word to Adrian.

"Have you changed your mind about the Culver Institute?" I inquired, curious to see just how far gone she was.

She gazed down at the diaper bag for a moment, then gave a minute head-shake. "No. It'd be wrong to build a museum in Finch. It'd change the village too much, and the village doesn't need changing."

I put a few squeaky toys, a patchwork platypus, and a plush brontosaurus into the toy bag but left Reginald in the playpen—he'd caused enough trouble already.

We finished loading the trunk, then went back to fetch Rob and Will. As she passed the hall mirror, Francesca paused to smooth her hair and straighten the collar on her shirtdress. She needn't have bothered. Adrian would find her enchanting if she showed up in a bandana and bib overalls. She was an ideal diversion.

Derek and Emma were supposed to meet Simon at the schoolhouse at one o'clock for their tour. As Francesca steered the Mercedes over the humpbacked bridge and into the square I spotted Derek greeting Simon, who'd just emerged from the paneled van. Emma stood near Kitchen's Emporium, discreetly flagging us down, while Rainey hopped up and down on Jasper Taxman's platform, waving wildly and calling out, "Over here, Lori!"

Francesca parked in front of Bill's office, and I hastened over to confer with Emma. We met in the middle of the square.

"I've got another passenger for you," she said, looking slightly frazzled. Emma lowered her voice as Rainey ran circles around us. "I don't want her to break anything in the schoolhouse."

"She does better in outdoor settings," I agreed.

"May I go to Scrag End with you, Lori?" Rainey pleaded. She'd divested herself of the gardening smock and work gloves but retained the sun hat. Its broad brim was, like Emma, beginning to fray around the edges. "I'll be good, I promise, and I've always wanted to see Scrag End and Emma says you've brought WillanRob and—"

"Yes," I interrupted. "You may come along." I jutted my chin toward the Mercedes. "Ask Francesca to buckle you into the front seat."

Rainey dashed off, jubilant.

Emma let loose a sigh of relief. "That child may be a joy in the garden, but she's a handful everywhere else."

"I don't know why I'm bothering to go to Scrag End," I said, with a wry smile. "Francesca and Rainey make a perfect SWAT team. They'll keep Adrian and Katrina pinned at the dig for hours. All set for your tour?"

Emma nodded. "Derek has his instructions. He'll look high, I'll look low." Since Emma was a foot shorter than her husband, it seemed an eminently sensible division of labor.

Francesca drove up Saint George's Lane, past the vicarage, the church, and the belt of trees that lay beyond the churchyard. At the far edge of the forested land, she turned right, onto a narrow, unpaved track.

The rough track followed the course of the river and appeared to mark the boundary between forest and farmland. To our left, across the river, a vast field of ripening grain rose gradually to a hilltop where a cluster of farm buildings huddled among a handful of sheltering trees. Hodge Farm, I thought, remembering the vicar's words.

To our right lay airy woodland fringed with a tangle of wildflowers, some of which had no doubt found their way into Adrian's bouquet. About fifty yards in from the main road, the forest opened up into a clearing.

"Is this it?" I asked.

Francesca nodded.

"The vicar told me it was useless for cultivation," I said. "I think I see what he means."

"It's useless for much of anything," said Francesca, parking the Mercedes. "The lower part floods and the upper part's nothing but rocks."

I could well believe it. Scrag End field was a singularly

charmless piece of real estate—a sloping, lumpy meadow tufted with spiky grass and pathetic, tumbleweed-like bushes. I'd expected more from a place that had my village up in arms—an air of mystery, a brooding atmosphere, an intangible *something* to suggest that this was a field worth fighting over. But even Miranda Morrow would be hard-pressed to detect mystery in Scrag End's aura. It exuded about as much drama as a municipal parking lot.

There were, however, signs of habitation. At the field's eastern edge, near the lane and partially sheltered by the trees, a blue tarpaulin on poles shaded a motley collection of folding tables and canvas chairs. The upper half of the field had been marked out with a gridwork of staked ropes and pennants on thin rods. Between the tarpaulin and the grid lay a trail of buckets, brushes, sieves, and trowels— the tools of the archaeologist's trade.

Katrina Graham, dressed in a blazing orange tank top, a red sweatband, and a pair of baggy shorts, was emptying a bucket of dirt into a wheelbarrow at the center of the grid. She paused to look up as our car rumbled into view. Adrian, clad in his dusty work clothes and disreputable hat, sat in a folding chair beneath the blue tarpaulin, with a large sketch pad propped on the table before him. The moment he spied the Mercedes, he jumped to his feet and hurried toward the lane.

Rainey was as good as gold. She didn't budge until Francesca had removed the key from the ignition, released her seat belt, and unlocked the doors. Then she exploded from the car and tore across the field like an escaping convict.

"Whoa," said Adrian, scooping her up as she came within reach. He set her on her feet and placed his hands on her shoulders. "You'll have to be more careful, Rainey.

We don't want you tripping over those ropes." He lifted his head and shouted, "Miss Graham!"

Katrina dropped the bucket into the wheelbarrow and trotted down the sloping field to Adrian's side. Her skin glistened with sweat and her headband was soaked through, but she didn't seem in the least fatigued. "Yes, Dr. Culver?"

Adrian bent to retrieve the hat that had tumbled from Rainey's head. "We have a new recruit," he said, placing the hat back where it belonged. "Please see to it that Miss Dawson is issued with sunscreen, then show her how to utilize the waste dump."

Katrina gave a husky laugh. "Yes, sir," she replied. "Come along, Miss Dawson." She took Rainey's hand and led her to the work area beneath the tarpaulin.

Adrian strode over to the Mercedes. "Welcome to Scrag End, Lori. I'm so glad you've come."

I eyed him doubtfully as I extricated Will from his car seat. "The waste dump?"

"It's where we put the soil we've removed from the trial trench," Adrian explained. "It seems the best way to deploy Rainey's talents."

"Oh," I said. "I'm new at archaeology."

"You'll be an old hand by the time you leave here today. Please, Miss Sciaparelli, allow me." Adrian hurried over to help Francesca lift the strollers from the trunk.

"Thank you for the flowers," Francesca murmured, concentrating on unfolding Rob's stroller. "It was kind of you to bring them."

Adrian wobbled slightly, as though staggered by Francesca's passionate words. "I'm . . . you're . . . it's . . ." He might have gone on all day if I hadn't intervened.

"Adrian," I said, "would you please hold Will while I get Rob?"

Adrian stopped stuttering. "Me?" he said, retreating a step or two.

"Just for a second," I coaxed. "My son won't bite. He can't. His teeth haven't come in yet."

Adrian took a deep breath and wiped his palms on his shirt. He stood stiffly at attention as I placed Will in his arms, but my son was adept at dealing with inexperienced adults. Will wriggled and squirmed until Adrian loosened up, then snuggled his head into the crook of Adrian's neck.

The look of abject terror faded from Adrian's eyes. "Such soft skin," he murmured. "The sun won't do it any good at all, old chap. We must get you into the shade."

I turned to inform him that Will's stroller had a perfectly adequate awning, but he was already striding toward the tarpaulin, with my son cuddled close to his chest.

Francesca seemed taken aback by his desertion. As she clicked the sturdy awning into place, she muttered, "You'd think the man had never held a babe before."

"Maybe he hasn't," I said.

"A man his age?" Francesca protested.

"Bill never held a baby until he had his own. Does Adrian have any children?" I asked, putting Rob in the stroller.

"No," said Francesca, "nor a wife, neither." She flushed suddenly and bent low over Rob's straps. "Or so I've heard."

Katrina was still annointing Rainey with sunscreen when Francesca, Rob, and I arrived at the tarpaulin. Adrian had returned to the folding chair near the propped sketch pad and appeared to be entirely absorbed in watching Will grasp his index finger. While I piled an empty table with the miscellaneous baby-bags, he peered curiously from one twin to the other.

"How do you tell them apart?" he asked.

Rainey piped up unexpectedly: "You look in their eyes."

All heads turned in her direction, but Francesca was the first to speak.

"What d'you mean, Rainey?" she asked.

"I . . . I don't know," said Rainey, unnerved by the attention her remark had drawn. "It's just that . . . when I look at Will, Will looks back at me. And when I look at Rob, Rob looks back at me."

Francesca's full lips curved into a slow, sweet smile as she bent down to lift Rainey's chin. "It's their souls you're seeing," she told the little girl. "You can't mistake one soul for another, any more than you can mistake a cat for a cabbage. D'you see?"

Rainey nodded eagerly. "Rob's is silvery blue and Will's is sort of golden. Is that what you mean?"

Francesca gave an astonished laugh. "I believe you see 'em more clearly than I do," she said. "Those are the lights of their souls, sure enough."

I looked from Rainey to my boys. I'd always been able to tell Will and Rob apart, but I'd never known how to explain it to the nurses or Dr. Hawking or anyone else who asked—leave it to an eight-year-old to do it for me.

"Your soul is a soft, dark brown," Rainey added, gazing into Francesca's eyes, "like Mummy's brown velvet hat. Isn't that right, Dr. Culver?"

Adrian fielded the question gamely. "I've, er, never seen your mummy's hat," he replied.

"I'll ask her to wear it to my party," Rainey assured him. "Mummy can stand next to Francesca and you can stare into Francesca's eyes, the way you always do, and—"

"Dr. Culver," Katrina interrupted. "Do you think we'll be much longer? We have to get those soil samples back to the lab for analysis."

Adrian had all but buried his face in Will's T-shirt. Now he got up, with my son cradled in his arm, and bustled over to one corner of the work area to retrieve a dirt-filled bucket.

"The soil samples can wait until our guests have departed," he said, carefully avoiding Francesca's eyes. "I believe you were about to show Rainey the waste dump. While you're there"—he handed the bucket to Katrina— "don't forget to discard this detritus, as well."

It was a gentle reproof, but a reproof all the same, and Katrina didn't take it well. She shot a hostile glance at Francesca before trudging across the field to the wheelbarrow, with Rainey trotting happily in her wake.

"Miss Graham is apt to take her science a bit too seriously," Adrian observed when Katrina was out of earshot.

"She's sweet on you," Francesca commented, eyeing the muscular little blonde dispassionately.

Adrian looked alarmed. "Surely not," he protested.

"Plain as the nose on your face," Francesca told him, taking Will from his arms. "And why shouldn't she be? You're the famous professor, the man with all the answers."

"I can assure you that I have far more questions than answers," Adrian said, with a self-deprecating wave of his hand. "But I am being remiss in my duties. Won't you have a seat? May I offer you a glass of cold water?" Adrian tossed his hat aside, opened an ice chest, and took from it a bottle of the springwater Katrina had ordered from Mr. Taxman at Kitchen's Emporium. He filled a pair of plastic cups.

"Scrag End has me baffled," he said, handing us our

drinks. "Miss Graham has advanced several theories to explain what's going on here, but I find them less than convincing."

Francesca and I exchanged puzzled glances. It was a queer remark, coming from a man who planned to finance a museum on the strength of his finds at Scrag End field.

"Is there something wrong with Scrag End?" I asked.

"Everything's wrong," Adrian replied. "We're finding the wrong artifacts from the wrong periods in the wrong places." He reached for the sketch pad, flipped to a blank page, and pulled a chair over, so he could sit between Francesca and me.

"Archaeological sites have their own logic," he began, resting the oversized pad on his lap. "To put it simply, if you find a lot of broken pottery, it's reasonable to assume that you've happened upon a potter's shop. And if you find nothing but fifth-century pottery, it's reasonable to assume that the potter lived in the fifth century. Furthermore . . ." He pulled a pencil from his shirt pocket and drew five horizontal lines on the sketch pad. "Layers of soil are like layers of time. As a general rule, the deeper you dig, the older the artifacts."

As he bent once more over his sketch pad, my heart began to race. I'd read enough picture captions in *National Geographic* to follow Adrian's argument. Archaeologists expected to find artifacts from different periods clustered in different layers of soil. A fifth-century spearhead lying beside a first-century statue of Minerva would set off all sorts of alarms. If Cornelius Gladwell had been stupid enough to dig a hole and simply dump his Roman gewgaws into it, then his hoax was doomed to failure. Not even an Oxford-trained archaeologist like Adrian could fake enough documentation to cover such a colossal blunder.

Adrian finished adding a series of dots to the horizontal lines. He pointed to the dots nearest the top of the page. "These represent my initial discoveries. They range in date from the second to the fifth century. Do you see my problem?"

I tried to sound nonchalant. "Too many artifacts from too many centuries in the same place."

"Exactly." Adrian tossed the sketch pad onto the table. "And the trial trench isn't clarifying the situation."

I looked at him in confusion. He seemed to be admitting that his site was highly suspect, but he showed not the slightest sign of dismay or disappointment.

"Would you care to see the trial trench?" he offered.

"You go ahead, Lori," said Francesca. "I'd sooner stay in the shade with the boys."

The heat hit like a wet velvet curtain the moment Adrian and I left the shade of the tarpaulin. I glanced across the field at Rainey, hidden under her hat and helping Katrina shovel dirt from the wheelbarrow into what appeared to be a large wood-framed sieve. I was grateful to Adrian for providing her with sunscreen.

Adrian gazed skyward. "It's beginning to cloud up. I believe we may be in for a good soaking before the weekend's through."

I looked up and saw a flock of fleecy clouds streaming across the sky, harbingers of heavier rain clouds to come. "The gardeners will rejoice."

"The farmers, as well," said Adrian, with a glance at the stunted crops across the river, "but I'm afraid it won't make my work any easier. Please, watch your step." He took me by the elbow and guided me carefully through the maze of staked ropes to the edge of a yawning hole the size and shape of a grown man's grave.

"Not a textbook trench," Adrian observed, with a wry

smile, "but nice work, nevertheless. Miss Graham is willing to work long hours, and her fitness fanaticism has paid off—she's very strong—invaluable traits in a budding archaeologist."

"Do you consider honesty an equally invaluable trait?" I asked.

"Naturally," said Adrian.

"Then why did you lie to the vicar?" I demanded.

"I beg your pardon?" said Adrian.

I turned to face him squarely. "You told Mr. Bunting that you'd never heard of the Gladwell pamphlet, yet you've all but admitted that Scrag End is a hoax."

"I never called Scrag End a hoax," Adrian protested. "I merely pointed out a few anomalies, and Miss Graham has come up with some interesting explanations to account for—"

"Dr. Culver!" Rainey's shout smote my eardrums like a clap of thunder. "Look what I found!"

20.

Rainey raced across the field and hurdled the staked ropes with the agility of a track star, then spoiled the effect by crashing into Adrian and nearly knocking him into his trial trench. As he caught his balance—and hers—Katrina dashed up, apologizing for the disruption. Adrian waved her to silence as Rainey held out a grubby fist.

"Look, Dr. Culver! Isn't it grand?" Rainey gazed up at Adrian, transported.

Adrian bent low to examine the silver coin in Rainey's filthy palm. "What luck!" he exclaimed. "It's not many archaeologists who find a silver denarius on their first trip out."

Rainey's gaze dropped to the coin. "I thought it was money."

"It *is* money," Adrian assured her. "It's a kind of money people used long ago." He squatted beside her and pointed at the coin with his little finger. "See here? This is a picture of Constantine, a Roman emperor. After you've brought the denarius to the schoolhouse, Miss Graham will tell you all about the emperor Constantine."

Rainey's face fell. "I can't keep it?"

"You don't want to keep it for yourself," Adrian told her.

"I don't?" Rainey closed her fist over the coin.

Adrian shook his head. "When we find things here, they don't belong to us. They belong to everyone. That's why we put them in museums, where everyone can see them."

Rainey gave the proposition some serious thought. "May I bring Mummy and Daddy and Jack and Gran to your museum to see my denarius?"

Adrian let *your museum* pass without comment. "Of course you may. Let's go back to the work station. We'll put Constantine's denarius in a box, so you won't mislay it. It's a splendid discovery, Rainey. I'm very proud of you."

I almost sympathized with the resentful look that flashed across Katrina's sweaty face. She'd put a lot of hard work into the dig. It had to be galling for her to be upstaged by a scrawny eight-year-old.

"Katrina," I said, "why don't you take a break? You look as though you could use one."

"I don't need a break," she said shortly, looking down at the trench.

"That's too bad," I said. "I was hoping you'd explain your theories to me."

She glanced up. "Did Dr. Culver mention my theories?"

"Yes," I said, "and he gave you full credit for them."

"He's too generous," she said, thawing slightly. "All I've done is recapitulate his lectures."

"I'd love to hear your interpretation of his lectures," I coaxed.

Katrina cast a sour glance toward the tarpaulin. "Are you sure I won't interrupt—"

"Don't be silly," I said firmly, taking her by the arm.

"Our visit wouldn't be complete without a lecture from an expert."

Katrina's resistance crumbled. "I'm not an expert," she said, allowing herself to be tugged along, "but I'll be happy to explain my theories, if you're really interested. . . ."

By the time we reached the tarpaulin, Adrian had deposited Rainey's silver coin in a small cardboard box labeled RAINEY DAWSON'S DENARIUS. It seemed to me to be an oddly imprecise annotation—no date, no provenance— and when Katrina saw it, she looked sharply at Adrian. He responded with a sly wink, and Katrina relaxed, grinning sheepishly.

Adrian, it seemed, had taken a page from Cornelius Gladwell's pamphlet. He'd planted the coin in the bucket of dirt he'd given Katrina, in hopes that Rainey would find it. I gazed at him with grudging admiration. He couldn't have thought of a better way to introduce Rainey to the joys of his profession. Archaeology, I suspected, would give gardening a run for its money when it came time for the little blunderbuss to choose her life's work.

While I pulled Rob's socks up and Will's T-shirt down, Katrina opened a second bottle of springwater. She filled glasses for herself and Rainey, refilled the rest of the glasses, and perched on the edge of a table. I gulped my water greedily, then returned to my chair.

"Lori's asked me to explain my theories," said Katrina.

"Excellent." Adrian sat down, stretched his long legs out before him, and folded his hands over his flat stomach. "Proceed, Miss Graham."

Katrina pulled off her headband and swiped a hand across her spiky blond crop. She looked very young but curiously invulnerable—a confident doctoral candidate, ready to ace her orals.

"I'd like to start by saying that my theories are based almost wholly on Dr. Culver's lectures," she began. "He spoke once of the effects of erosion on soil, of the way artifacts can be washed from one place to another by rain, melting snow, or floods. That might explain why we're finding things in odd places."

I shifted uncomfortably in my chair. Katrina's first theory wasn't without merit. Francesca had said that Scrag End field was prone to flood.

"Or," Katrina continued, "we might have stumbled on a tip."

"A what?" I asked.

Katrina cocked her head to one side. "A garbage dump," she said. "I believe that's what it's called in the States. If Scrag End had been used as a tip, we'd expect to find artifacts from different periods all jumbled up together."

"You're diggin' up rubbish?" Francesca asked incredulously.

"What's wrong with that?" Katrina demanded. "You've no idea how much information can be gleaned from a civilization's rubbish. Some of our most valuable—"

"Miss Graham," Adrian broke in gently, "you've made your point and you'd do well to moderate your tone. You're speaking to guests, not colleagues."

"I'm sorry, Dr. Culver." Katrina's biceps bulged as she twisted her hands together in her lap. She took a sip of water, then resumed more calmly. "A third possibility is that the site's been disrupted by cultivation. Farmers may have plowed through the soil, dislodging and rearranging—"

"No," Francesca said abruptly. "Scratch that one. No one's ever farmed Scrag End field."

Katrina's blue eyes flashed angrily. "How can you possibly know what was going on here five hundred years ago?"

"Because I've lived here all my life and know Finch's history." Francesca pointed to a tree standing a few yards away from the tarpaulin. "That's the only thing the Romans planted this side of the river."

"A tree?" Katrina scoffed.

"It's a sweet chestnut," Francesca informed her. "The Romans planted them so they could make flour out of the chestnuts. A tasty thing, chestnut flour."

Katrina looked for help from Adrian, but he was staring at Francesca. I, too, had turned toward my nanny. I was on the verge of asking how she'd come by her in-depth knowledge of ancient arboriculture when Dimity's words came floating back to me: *Piero worked as a farm laborer for old Mr. Hodge until VE Day. . . .*

Francesca's father had worked at Hodge Farm. If old Mr. Hodge had befriended Piero Sciaparelli, he would have given Piero's children the run of his land. Mr. Hodge might have taken Francesca to see the floods in Scrag End field, and filled her head with stories about the sweet-chestnut trees. It seemed strange that Francesca hadn't mentioned the connection when Hodge Farm had first come into view.

Rainey's voice interrupted my musings. "It must be a very *old* tree," she observed gravely. "Katrina told me that the Romans lived here years and years ago."

Francesca's face softened. "It's not the same sweet chestnut as the Romans used," she explained patiently. "It's the many-times-great-grandchild of the ones they planted."

"A fascinating sidelight, Miss Sciaparelli," said Adrian.

I thought Katrina would twist her fingers right off. She wasn't having the best of days. Our arrival had delayed the testing of her precious soil samples, Rainey had upstaged her by "discovering" the denarius, and Francesca had interrupted her lecture.

"Yes, Miss Sciaparelli," she said, with as much grace as she could be expected to muster. "Fascinating."

"As are your contributions, Miss Graham," said Adrian, bowing to Katrina. "They reveal a creative imagination—an essential tool in any scientist's kit, but particularly useful when one is attempting to reconstruct the past. My compliments."

Katrina smiled radiantly.

"Unfortunately," Adrian continued, "your theories don't overturn my main objection to Scrag End field." He rose from his chair and paced deliberately as he spoke. "If Scrag End was used as a tip, where did the rubbish come from? Similarly, where did the artifacts reside before floods or rain or melting snow carried them to Scrag End field? For either of these theories to work, we must posit the existence of a villa close at hand." He held his hands wide. "I find it difficult to conceive of any self-respecting Romano-British citizen building a home in such an unpropitious location."

Katrina held her head high, undaunted by the assault. "I believe I can account for that anomaly, as well," she said.

Katrina pushed herself off the table and strode across the lane to stand at the river's edge. Adrian went with her, with Rainey trotting at his side and Francesca walking a step or two behind him, pushing Rob's stroller. Will and I took up the rear.

Katrina waited until we'd gathered around, then raised a hand to shade her eyes as she peered out over the sea of grain. "If I were a Romano-British citizen," she said, pointing, "I'd build my villa on the top of that hill."

"Very good," murmured Adrian, looking up at the farm buildings. "Please continue."

"If a Roman villa occupied that location," Katrina went on, "the artifacts could have been washed down the hill to Scrag End field, or placed there by the villa's inhabitants. Furthermore—" She broke off suddenly, then turned to Adrian, muttering, "He's back again."

"Who?" I asked.

"Our watcher," Adrian replied.

I followed his gaze and saw a motionless figure standing among the stone buildings at the top of the hill.

"He's been observing us all week with a pair of binoculars," Katrina murmured. "I caught the light glinting off the lens just now."

"I expect it's Burt Hodge," said Adrian, "or his wife, Annie. The vicar tells me they own the farm. They're probably wondering what we're doing down here. I must remember to stop by and invite them to tour the site."

"Annie Hodge," I said, searching my memory. "She's the vicar's housekeeper, isn't she?"

Adrian nodded. "I believe so."

"In that case, there's no use inviting her for a tour," I told him. "I spoke with her the other day. She said that she and her husband were too busy to waste—" I felt Katrina's gaze on me and quickly revised my statement. "To *spend* time in Scrag End field."

"I should let them know they're welcome nonetheless." Adrian grabbed Rainey, who was testing the stability of an alarmingly wobbly rock that jutted into the flowing stream. "Perhaps, Miss Graham, you'd like to show Miss Dawson some of the artifacts you've discovered. While you're doing so, you can describe your latest theory more fully to the rest of us."

Adrian, Katrina, Francesca, Rob, and Rainey returned to the tarpaulin's shade, but Will and I stayed at the water's edge, watching the watcher, until the distant figure had retreated to the shelter of a stone barn.

"I don't like it," I said to Francesca after we'd dropped Rainey off at the tearoom. "Feelings are running high in the village. I don't like the thought of someone spying on Adrian with binoculars."

"Burt Hodge means no harm," Francesca declared, keeping her eyes on the road.

"Why do you think he's watching Adrian?" I asked.

"If I know Burt," said Francesca, sounding as though she did, "it's because he thinks it a waste of petrol to drive over and find out what's going on in Scrag End."

"You sound pretty sure of yourself," I commented.

"Burt and I grew up together," Francesca told me. "My father worked for his father when he first came to this country."

"Did he?" I was growing adept at negotiating Francesca's oblique conversations. "I wondered how you knew so much about Scrag End field."

"Old Mr. Hodge was a good man," said Francesca. "He let me and my brothers and sisters roam all over his land. Some folk didn't like him for it, but he never paid them any mind."

"Why would anyone object to an old man being kind to a bunch of children?" I knew I was treading on thin ice, but I wanted to hear Piero's story from Francesca's point of view.

"We weren't just any children." Francesca's knuckles whitened on the steering wheel, but her foot remained steady on the gas pedal. "Hasn't Mrs. Kitchen told you about my father?"

"No," I answered honestly. "Mrs. Kitchen hasn't told me a thing about your father. What about him?"

Francesca touched the medallion at her throat. "My father didn't come to England voluntarily," she said. "He was shipped here, as a prisoner of war. He was held in a detention camp in Yorkshire for six months before they sent him off to work for Mr. Hodge. So many farmers had joined up that they had to use what labor came to hand." She paused. "Was your father a soldier?"

"Yes," I said. "He landed at Normandy on D Day and fought his way to the Rhine, but he wasn't even wounded. He was lucky. Like your father."

"You think my father was lucky?" Francesca asked, as though the idea was new to her.

"He survived the war," I pointed out. "He lived long enough to raise a family. I'd call that lucky, wouldn't you?"

Francesca didn't reply directly. "It wasn't easy for him," she said. "Nor for his family. Most folks were decent enough, but some were . . ." Her lips tightened. "They needed someone to blame, and Papa was right in front of them, with his accent and his funny-sounding name."

I marveled, not for the first time, at how the cruelty of a few could diminish the kindness of many. "Seems like Mr. Hodge was one of the decent ones," I commented.

"He was a good man," Francesca repeated. She slowed as we approached the Pym sisters' curve. "Which is more than can be said for his son." She sped up again as we came out of the curve. "What did you think of Dr. Culver making out that Scrag End was no good? You think he's given up on the museum?"

The abrupt change of subject signaled an end to Francesca's brief spate of self-revelation. I let it go but made a mental note to ask Dimity about old Mr. Hodge's son once I'd figured out what was going on in Scrag End field—which might not be any time soon.

"Francesca," I confessed, "I don't know what to think about the museum. At the moment, Adrian Culver has me flummoxed."

21.

The cottage was blissfully silent. The boys were asleep in the nursery, Francesca had retired to her room, and Bill's regular breathing indicated that he'd joined his sons in dreamland. As I lay awake, staring at the ceiling, it occurred to me that I hadn't had a single sleepless night since Francesca had arrived. A week ago, I'd risen once an hour to make sure the boys were still breathing. Tonight I tossed and turned because of Adrian Culver.

I didn't know what to make of the man. Emma's printouts of his E-mail proved that he was raising money to build the Culver Institute right here in Finch. Why, then, was he going out of his way to prove that Scrag End field was a bust? If it hadn't been for Katrina's brainstorm about a Roman villa standing where Hodge Farm now stood, he might have called it quits that afternoon.

I sat up and ran a hand through my disheveled curls. If Adrian was willing to judge Scrag End on its lack of merits, why would he bother to steal the Gladwell pamphlet? Had he changed his mind about the museum? Had Peggy Kitchen's determined resistance frightened him off? Or had he decided that Scrag End was simply too anomalous to serve his purpose?

The only thing I could be sure of was his devotion to Francesca. He'd stopped by after dinner, ostensibly to bring the boys a colorful picture book about Pompeii. I'd tried to take him aside, to ask him again about the museum, but by then the phone had started ringing.

Emma had called to report that her schoolhouse tour had been a waste of time. She'd found nothing that pointed to the museum or the burglary. When she proposed breaking into Katrina's lodgings, I suggested that she consult a therapist before her obsession with break-ins got her into trouble.

A call from Stan had completed my day. The pamphlet from our man in Labrador would arrive on Monday morning. I should have been excited, but I wasn't. I didn't see how the pamphlet Stan had obtained would help me find *the* pamphlet. I wasn't even sure if *the* pamphlet mattered anymore. Adrian seemed perfectly willing to let the hoax reveal itself, with or without the vicar's printed proof.

I looked at the clock on the dresser as it chimed the hour. Eleven o'clock, and all was extremely perturbed. If I didn't settle down soon, I'd be fidgeting until dawn. I listened to Bill's steady breathing, then slipped out of bed and tiptoed downstairs to put the kettle on. A pot of tea and a chat with Dimity might still my spinning head.

Are the boys still breathing?
I smiled ruefully as Dimity's handwriting appeared on the blank page. "Yes, Dimity. The boys are fine. As if you didn't know." I curled my legs under me in the tall leather armchair, my teacup within reach on the table at my elbow. "I've been meaning to thank you for the tiger in the

trunk. Rainey'll love him. I just hope she doesn't love him to pieces."

If Reginald could survive your childhood, my dear, the tiger can survive Rainey's. You were never the daintiest of creatures, you know. I seem to recall repeated attempts to send Reginald to the moon. . . .

"Did Mom write to you about that?" I said, amused by the memory. "Poor Reg. The liftoffs weren't so bad, but the splashdowns nearly did him in." I poured a cup of tea from the pot on the tray. "Reginald's been a busy bunny lately, hopping from the playpen to the Mercedes with no visible means of transport."

He's done well, hasn't he? Francesca was being terribly stiff-necked about Adrian. It's nearly impossible, I've found, to be stiff-necked when one is eating crow.

"He embarrassed Francesca," I said sternly.

Dimity was unrepentant. *Francesca needed a push in the right direction, and Reginald provided her with one. A moment's embarrassment is a small price to pay for a lifetime of happiness.*

"A lifetime of happiness?" I exclaimed. "How can you be so sure about Adrian? Didn't you hear what Emma said about those computer printouts?"

Computer printouts are open to interpretation. Adrian's feelings for Francesca—and hers for him—are not.

"But Dimity . . ."

You don't understand, my dear. It's vitally important that Francesca learn to trust her heart again. She fancied it broken, once, and she's never allowed anyone near it since.

I leaned my chin on my hand. "I had no idea."

How could you? Francesca's engagement to Burt Hodge was broken off long before you came to Finch.

I nearly dropped the journal. "Burt Hodge? Francesca was engaged to old Mr. Hodge's son?"

She was, until Burt jilted her and married Annie.

Annie Hodge's image floated through my mind, complete with rubber gloves, broom, and cleaning-woman's kerchief. Perhaps Burt Hodge preferred a sturdy workhorse to an exotic, sometimes temperamental beauty.

I sipped my tea and looked down at the journal. "Would it surprise you to learn that Burt Hodge has been spying on Scrag End field for the past week?"

Burt was always very protective of Francesca.

"So Burt's checking out the new guy in town?" I clucked my tongue. "Sounds to me as though Burt's being pretty presumptuous. It's none of his business if—" I jumped as the telephone rang, and made it to the desk before it rang a second time.

"Hello?" I said, half expecting to hear Stan's usual robust greeting.

"Miranda Morrow, here," said the voice on the other end. "If you want to see our local coven in action, come to Briar Cottage right away."

I cupped my hand over the receiver. "You're sure?"

"Positive, darling," she replied. "Hurry."

"Dimity," I said, hanging up the phone, "I've got to go. I've got a pair of burglars to catch."

Be sure to bundle up, my dear, or you'll catch a cold, as well. . . .

As I scrambled into a dark-blue sweatshirt and black sweatpants, I whispered Bill's name softly, several times. I jostled the bed slightly as I poked my feet into black socks and dark-blue sneakers. I scratched pen on paper as loudly as I dared while scribbling the brief note telling him my plans. And I sang a silent hymn of thanks when nothing woke him. Bill needed his rest—and I wanted to catch our burglars single-handed.

I watched for lights to come on in the cottage as I eased the Mercedes out of the drive, but the engine's purr roused no one. When I reached the humpbacked bridge, I cut the motor and coasted to a stop. I would go to Briar Cottage, but not right now.

I knew exactly where I'd find the burglars: in the dip below the ridge, where the vicarage meadow swept down to the river. That's where Christine had spotted her alien invaders, where Dick had seen the circle of broken grass, and where I would shine the bright beam of my emergency lantern, when the time was ripe. Until then, I'd use my penlight, to avoid alerting my prey.

Lantern in hand, I closed the car door gently and flicked the switch on the penlight. I glanced briefly at the darkened windows in the village, then climbed down from the bridge to the narrow tree-lined path along the riverbank.

The path was wreathed in bands of dank gray mist. Wisps flimsy as spiderwebs gave way to cloying curtains that parted at my passage, then swirled silently together in my wake. Droplets blurred my vision, soaked my sneakers, and chilled each indrawn breath, but I kept the penlight focused on the ground, kept the river's susurration to my right, and trotted confidently along the beaten path. I felt like a commando embarking on a raid, moving swiftly as a panther, slyly as a serpent, boldly as a lioness, until a slight flaw in my plan began to dawn.

I had no idea where I was. I didn't know how far I'd come or how much farther I had to go to reach the vicarage meadow. I could still hear the river rushing between its reedy banks, but I couldn't see a thing. I'd trotted blithely into a cloud of fog so dense that I had to raise my foot to see my shoelaces.

"Brilliant," I muttered, peering futilely into the murk. "If I shout for help, maybe the burglars'll rescue me." I was on the verge of pounding my stupid head against the nearest tree trunk when I heard a noise.

I stood stock-still, straining to separate the fleeting sound from the insistent murmur of the river. I closed my eyes to concentrate and heard it again—a faint, rhythmic thumping that seemed to be coming from the left.

I slipped the useless penlight into my pocket and let my ears guide me toward the thumping sound. I'd gone no more than five yards when the pocket of fog thinned and I found myself standing at the edge of the vicarage meadow. I shivered suddenly and dropped to my knees, thankful that I'd doused the penlight before emerging from the gloom.

Silken shreds of mist swirled and curled across the meadow like an undulating shroud. Clammy fingers brushed my face, twined sinuously around my neck, and drifted sluggishly down the ridge to fill the hollow where Dick had seen the broken grass.

The thumping noise was coming from the hollow. As I crept closer, the noise grew more complex. Grunts and groans accompanied the thumping. It didn't sound to me like the engines of an alien spaceship. It sounded like a person being beaten to a pulp.

I swallowed hard and wished fervently that Bill were by my side. I no longer felt like a commando, but I couldn't back off now. Someone had to put a stop to those dreadful muted moans, and it looked as though that someone would be me. I gripped the lantern tightly, prepared to use it as a club, and crawled closer to the bottom of the hollow. As I moved forward, the pooled mist thinned, parted, and revealed two shadowy figures, not ten yards from me. I gasped, and fumbled with the lantern, but before I found the switch, a blinding beam of light came from above.

"I say," called a mild, curious voice from the top of the ridge. "Is that you down there, Mrs. Pyne? And . . . Miss Graham, isn't it?"

"Vicar?" chorused Sally and Katrina.

"Freeze!" I shouted, jumping to my feet. "We've got you covered!"

"Lori?" Bill's voice sounded from on high.

"*Bill?*" I exclaimed.

"Lori?" said Sally Pyne, turning her hooded head from side to side. "Bill?"

The vicar cleared his throat. "Now that we've introduced ourselves, I'd like you all to join me in the library. Lilian's making cocoa. Come along."

"I can explain, Vicar," said Sally Pyne, scrambling out of the hollow.

"So can I!" I cried. "You're looking at your burglars, Vicar! These two stole your pamphlet!"

"Burglars!" Sally paused in her uphill climb to glare at me. "How dare you!"

"I'll tell you how I dare." I marched toward her. "I have three independent witnesses who'll swear they saw you and your accomplice come here on Sunday night."

"I freely admit to being here on Sunday night," Sally declared stoutly. "But I object most strenuously to the use of the word accomplice. Katrina is—"

"Thank you, Mrs. Pyne," interrupted the vicar. "As you can imagine, I'm eager to hear everyone's story, but I'd prefer to do so over a nice cup of hot cocoa."

"Vicar, wait," I began, but Bill loomed out of the mist, and the words stuck in my throat. I glanced up at him, then quickly lowered my eyes. "Guess you found my note, huh?"

"Freeze?" he said, folding his arms. "We've got you covered? Were you using the editorial 'we' or the royal 'we'?"

I hung my head, knowing full well that it should have been the marital "we."

"I won't bother to point out what might have happened if you'd stumbled into the river," Bill said, "or if Sally and Katrina had turned out to be a pair of hardened criminals. I certainly won't describe what it felt like to wake up in the middle of the night and find you gone."

"Bill—" I quavered, but he waved me to silence.

"I'll simply say that if you ever do something like this again . . ." He bent forward, until I was forced to look into his reproachful eyes. "It won't surprise me in the least. Your mother said you were bullheaded, and she was right."

I leaned into his arms. "I'm sorry, Bill."

"Not as sorry as you're going to be," said Bill, "when I describe your daring exploits to Derek and Emma." He turned toward the vicarage. "What was that again? 'Freeze? We've got you covered?' "

22.

The library was gloriously warm and bright. A fire crackled merrily in the fireplace, all of the lamps were lit, and extra seating had been provided to accommodate the damp and chilly congregation. The vicar sat in his shabby armchair, facing the culprits on the green velvet couch, while Bill and I surveyed the guilty duo from a pair of petit-point chairs we'd brought in from the dining room.

Sally and Katrina stared back at us defiantly. Sally had folded her hood into the collar of her royal-blue track-suit and wiped the condensation from her silver-rimmed glasses before planting her running shoes firmly on the carpet. Now she sat glowering, red-faced and round-bodied, like a furious fireplug. Katrina, clad in silky black jogging shorts and a hooded gray sweatshirt, had disdain-fully refused the cocoa Lilian had offered, requesting a glass of water in its stead.

The vicar had forbidden conversation until he'd fin-ished his first cup of cocoa, so I had time to contemplate a second pair of petit-point chairs, as yet unoccupied. One was obviously for Lilian, who'd returned to the kitchen to warm another saucepan of milk, but the presence of an extra chair, carefully arranged yet conspicuously empty, puzzled me.

The puzzle was solved a short time later, when Lilian flew down the hall to answer the doorbell and returned to the library, escorting a grim-faced, disheveled Adrian Culver. When Katrina caught sight of him, her belligerence faded.

"D-Dr. Culver," she faltered. "What are you doing here?"

"I was about to ask you the same question," said Adrian. He smoothed his uncombed hair back from his forehead and turned to Lilian. "Thank you for ringing me, Mrs. Bunting. If my assistant has inconvenienced you—"

Lilian nodded toward the empty chair. "Please, Dr. Culver, have a seat near the fire. Would you like a cup of cocoa?"

Adrian hesitated, as though he hadn't expected such a civil reception. "Yes, please."

"I'll be right back," said Lilian. She looked at her husband. "Don't start without me, Teddy."

"Wouldn't dream of it, my dear." The vicar slouched comfortably in his armchair and said nothing more until Lilian had finished serving the fresh batch of cocoa and seated herself between her husband and Adrian Culver.

"Now," she said brightly, "who would like to go first?" She pointed to Katrina. "Miss Graham, I think. Please, dear, tell us what you've been doing in that nasty damp meadow so late at night."

"I don't know what all the fuss is about," said Katrina miserably. "We were exercising, that's all."

"Exercising!" exclaimed Adrian.

"It was my idea," Sally put in hastily. "Simon refused to

work out with Katrina, so I offered to join her. I thought a spot of PT might help me lose a few pounds."

"Commendable of you." The vicar set aside his cocoa and tented his long fingers. "But surely you could have found a more hospitable place than the bottom of my meadow. And why work out, as you say, in the dark? I'd have loaned you a torch if you'd asked."

Katrina looked at Sally Pyne. "People have been terribly unkind about Mrs. Pyne's efforts to lose weight."

Sally flushed scarlet. "They've been beastly," she declared. "I didn't want Mr. Barlow joking about Fat Sally's chances at the Olympics, or Mr. Farnham going on about the battle of the bulge, so we slipped out after dark to the meadow, where no one would see us."

Sally's words had a pathetic ring of truth to them. No middle-aged woman in her right mind would want her neighbors looking on while she did jumping jacks. The potential for ridicule would be enough to discourage all but the hardiest of fitness addicts, and Sally Pyne was a rank beginner. Her moans, groans, and aching joints were proof of that.

"We did carry torches, the first night," Katrina was saying, "while we mapped out our route. But then—"

"Then Christine Peacock came along," Sally interrupted, indignantly, "walking that leaky hound of hers. Gave me the fright of my life. After that, we left the torches at home."

I glanced at the bemused smile hovering on Bill's lips and saw a lifetime of false-arrest jokes stretching out before me. It was mortifying to think that I'd nabbed a pair of innocent joggers, but Sally and Katrina had provided explanations for almost everything my eyewitnesses had seen.

Miranda Morrow had observed a ritual taking place, but the worshipers' arms had been raised to the gods of fitness, not to the moon. Christine Peacock's alien engines had been nothing more than Sally's wheezing, Katrina's huffing, and the glare of hastily extinguished flashlights. The circle of broken glass had been produced by two pairs of industriously pounding track shoes.

All I had going for me was Brother Florin. Two separate witnesses—Mr. Wetherhead and Miranda Morrow—had seen a hooded figure circumambulate the vicarage on Sunday night. Sally and Katrina had, by their own admission, been in the vicinity, and both wore hooded sweatshirts. I wondered if a direct attack would catch them off guard.

I leaned forward. "Which one of you approached the vicarage?"

"We didn't go anywhere near the vicarage," Sally protested.

"Why would we?" Katrina chimed in. "We were trying to keep a low profile."

Bill tried another tack. "Did you see anyone else while you were out?"

"Only Christine Peacock," Sally replied. "No one else is daft enough to go walking by the river after dark. That's why *we* were there." She focused in on the vicar. "Now, what's all this about burglars and accomplices? Did someone steal something from the vic—"

Adrian stood abruptly, as though he could no longer contain himself. He clasped his hands behind his back and gazed down sternly at Katrina. "Miss Graham," he said, "it is highly unprofessional to skulk about a host community without advising your supervisor of your intentions." He motioned toward Sally Pyne. "Do you see what kinds of rumors arise from such behavior? Mrs. Kitchen has been difficult enough. She'll leap at the chance to accuse you of being a burglar."

"I'm sorry, Dr. Culver," said Katrina, hanging her head.

Adrian wasn't finished. "Apart from that," he went on, relentlessly, "you need your rest. You've been putting in long hours of hard physical labor at Scrag End. I can assure you that your health will suffer no serious deterioration if you suspend your fitness program for three short weeks."

"Three weeks?" said the vicar, sitting erect. "Did I hear you correctly, Adrian? Do you intend to vacate the schoolhouse in three weeks?"

Adrian turned to him. "I've used up one week," he said, "so I'll be gone in two more. That was our original agreement, wasn't it, Theodore? Three weeks and out?"

"Yes, but I'd heard that you applied for funds to extend your . . ." The vicar's words trailed off. He stared at Adrian for a moment, then bowed his head and gave a mournful sigh. "Gossip. That's what I heard. Groundless rumors from a colleague in Oxford. May God forgive me for believing them." He extended his hand to Adrian. "My dear chap, I do beg your pardon most sincerely."

Adrian stared down as the vicar's outstretched hand, looking thoroughly confused. "I'm sorry, Theodore, but I don't quite follow."

"I do." Sally Pyne got up from the couch. "And you can stop acting innocent, Dr. Culver, because I know all about your plans to build a museum here in Finch."

Adrian closed his eyes and took a deep breath. "Mrs. Pyne," he said, in the rigidly controlled voice of a man rapidly running out of patience, "I can assure you that I have no plans whatsoever to build a museum in Finch or anywhere else. I'm sorry if my idle chatter led you to believe—"

"What kind of a fool do you take me for?" Sally snapped. "Do you think I'd refit my entire business because of idle chatter?" Frowning ferociously, she began to back the dumbfounded archaeologist toward the fireplace. "I've seen the letters, Dr. Culver. I've read all about your fund-raising efforts. I know for a fact that the Culver Institute is a good deal more than idle—"

"Katrina?" Lilian's soft voice interrupted Sally's diatribe. "Are you ill, child?"

I swung around to see Katrina crumple forward and bury her face in her hands. Lilian crossed to the couch and put an arm around the girl's shoulders, but Katrina's only response was a heartfelt moan. Adrian stopped just short of singeing the seat of his pants and dodged past Sally to attend to his assistant.

"What is it, Miss Graham?" he said, bending over her.

"Oh, Dr. Culver," Katrina groaned, still doubled over. "I'm so sorry. I had no idea she'd seen the letters."

Adrian straightened. He looked uneasily at Sally Pyne's triumphant face, then returned to his chair. He sat in thoughtful silence for a moment, then said, very gently, "Perhaps, Miss Graham, you'd care to explain yourself?"

Katrina pushed herself slowly into an upright position. She wiped the back of her hand across her mouth, then sat very still, as though gathering her thoughts. A log fell on the fire, and the hall clock chimed the half hour, but no one looked away from the mute and motionless figure on the couch.

"First of all," she began, looking from Lilian to the vicar, "I don't know anything about a burglary. This is the first time I've set foot in the vicarage, so if something went missing on Sunday night, it's nothing to do with me. Or with Mrs. Pyne," she added, "because we were together the whole time."

"Thank you, Miss Graham," the vicar said gravely. "Your testimony is of the utmost value. Please continue."

Katrina glanced at Adrian, then looked down at her hands. "As for the letters . . . Honestly, Dr. Culver, we were only trying to be helpful."

"*Who* was trying to be helpful?" Adrian asked.

"The twelve of us, the students you chose to work with you at Scrag End field." Katrina slid her tongue across her lips, as though her mouth had suddenly gone dry. "You've always said that fund-raising is the most difficult part of archaeology, so we decided to prepare a grant proposal ahead of time. That way, if Scrag End turned out to be a valuable site, a site worthy of a museum, we'd be able to hit the ground running. We'd have all of the necessary forms and letters ready for your signature. We thought you'd be proud of us for getting a head start on the paperwork."

"But what about that pile of letters next to your computer?" Sally demanded.

"I'm getting to that." Katrina continued speaking earnestly to Adrian. "We've been E-mailing drafts of dummy proposals back and forth to one another for the past few months, critiquing and rewriting them, just the way you said to do in your lectures. Ask Simon. He'll back me up. And we named the museum after you as a . . . a tribute to you, Dr. Culver." Katrina shot a reproachful look in Sally's direction. "It was supposed to be a surprise."

Sally gasped. "Do you mean to tell me that you never intended to build a museum in Finch?"

Katrina gazed hopefully up at Adrian, but he shook his head decisively.

"I'm impressed by your efforts, Miss Graham," he said, "and I look forward to reading your grant proposal, but we won't be using it for this particular site. There's not the remotest possibility of filling a museum with the items we've discovered at Scrag End field."

"But what about my *tearoom?*" Sally squawked. She stared blindly at Katrina, then turned to gaze into the fire, looking bereft. "I'll be a laughingstock. Peggy will never stop crowing. All of the trouble and expense . . . my poor tearoom . . ."

No one had the heart to point out that she'd brought the catastrophe on herself by snooping through Katrina's papers on the sly. The mere idea of being the target of Peggy Kitchen's ridicule made my toes curl and brought out Adrian's most chivalrous impulses. He assured Sally that he would do everything in his power to make sure her tearoom prospered.

"I'll recommend it to all of my friends and colleagues in Oxford," he promised. "I'll mention it whenever I lecture on Scrag End." He looked pointedly at Katrina. "My students won't let you down."

The barrage of goodwill revived Sally's spirits a bit and lit an entrepreneurial gleam in her eyes. "Students always have good appetites," she murmured. "And archaeology students'll like my new decor. . . ."

Lilian glanced at her wristwatch and stood. "Well," she said briskly, "I believe that concludes our business for the evening. You've got a busy day ahead of you, Mrs. Pyne, so we won't keep you any longer."

Adrian sent Katrina off with Sally Pyne, advising them to follow Saint George's Lane rather than the riverbank, but he asked the rest of us to remain in the library. Bill and I exchanged interrogative glances with the Buntings, but it was clear that no one knew what Adrian might add to the night's revelations.

When Adrian returned to his chair, he spoke first to the vicar. "I'm afraid Miss Graham isn't the only one who hasn't been telling the whole truth, Theodore. I'd planned to clear the air when the Scrag End experiment was complete, but it seems better to do so now."

"The, er, Scrag End experiment?" the vicar inquired politely.

"I'm using Scrag End as an outdoor laboratory," Adrian informed him. "It's vitally important for young archaeologists to learn how to spot the difference between an authentic find and an inexpertly contrived hoax."

"A hoax!" exclaimed the vicar. "Are you saying that you knew about Cornelius Gladwell's prank from the start?"

Adrian shook his head. "I'd never heard of Cornelius Gladwell until you mentioned him to me, but I knew that Scrag End was a hoax the moment I laid eyes on it. I've run into this sort of thing before—in Yorkshire, Cumberland, Sussex . . . caches of Roman artifacts buried in all sorts of places for all sorts of harebrained reasons. Scrag End fit the profile perfectly. It was a perfect teaching tool."

I closed my eyes and saw him in the shade of the blue tarpaulin, poking holes in Katrina's arguments, challenging her on every point, forcing her to defend her theories or come up with new ways to explain Scrag End's anomalies.

"You brought your students to Scrag End," I said slowly, "hoping they'd discover the hoax for themselves?"

"That's right," said Adrian.

"Why didn't you tell us what you were doing?" the vicar asked.

Adrian cocked his head to one side. "Would you have been able to hold your tongue when Mrs. Kitchen came to complain about me?"

"I suppose not." The vicar smiled ruefully. "I'd have been sorely tempted to tell Mrs. Kitchen not to take your project seriously."

"And she would have told Dr. Culver's students the same thing." Lilian sighed. "You couldn't allow that to happen, could you, Dr. Culver? If your students don't take their work seriously, they won't learn the valuable lessons you're trying to teach them. Yes, I quite understand."

I, too, understood, much as I hated to admit it. I leaned my head on my hand and sighed—I'd lost three prime suspects in one night.

Bill rubbed his chin thoughtfully. "Why are you willing to trust us now, Adrian?" he asked. "I'm sure we'll all try to keep our mouths shut, but you know how it is in a small village. News spreads by osmosis."

"I don't mind stirring up discussion in a host community," Adrian said. "Discussion can be instructive, even when it's conducted at the top of one's lungs." He paused. "When one of my students stands accused of committing a crime, however, it's time to bring everything out into the open. I do hope you'll keep my secret until my experiment is complete."

"Of course we will." The vicar got to his feet and placed his hand firmly on Adrian's shoulder. "And I, for one, am convinced that Miss Graham had nothing whatsoever to do with the theft."

Adrian let out a rushing sigh. "I'm sorry I misled you, Theodore."

"Not at all," said the vicar. "Come, I'll walk you out."

Adrian bid us good night and left the library with the

vicar. Bill carried the petit-point chairs back into the dining room, and I poked up the fire while Lilian collected
the used cups and brought them to the kitchen. I felt like
a fool and a failure. I'd made a fool of myself in the
meadow and failed to catch the burglar. To make mat-
ters worse, I'd spilled the beans about the theft in front of
Sally Pyne.

It was quite clear to me that Sally hadn't known about
the burglary until I'd opened my big mouth. Her red nose
had practically twitched with curiosity when she'd asked
Now what's all this about burglars and accomplices? The tearoom crisis had provided a temporary diversion, but questions about the theft would reoccur to her come morning,
which meant that by afternoon all of Finch would know
that someone had stolen something from the vicarage on
Sunday night.

I felt Bill's hand on my shoulder and returned the poker
to its brass stand as our little group reassembled. The
vicar stared absently past me at the flickering flames, and
Lilian stood at his side, gazing up at him worriedly.

I stepped toward them. "I'm sorry, Vicar. I shouldn't
have said anything about the burglary. I know how badly
you wanted to keep it secret and—" I broke off abruptly,
startled by a sound I'd never heard before.

Theodore Bunting was laughing. He was leaning on the
back of his worn armchair, whooping and gasping, with
one hand pressed to his chest, and tears trickling from the
corners of his eyes.

"Teddy?" Lilian asked. "Are you quite well?"

The vicar wiped his eyes. "I'm marvelous, Lilian, simply marvelous. My friends," he went on, looking from me
to Bill, "you evidently haven't realized what a good night's
work you've done." The vicar took my hand between both
of his. "Adrian is leaving in two weeks," he said slowly. "I

shall announce in church tomorrow that, in two short weeks, regardless of rumors to the contrary, the school-house will be *empty.*"

I finally caught his drift. "Peggy will call off her rally," I said, dazed with relief. "I won't have to dodge Sally's rotten eggs. The festival will proceed as planned—"

"Mrs. Kitchen will be in her heaven," the vicar crowed, "and all will be right with the world. Lori, my dear girl, I can't thank you enough."

"But what about the Gladwell pamphlet?" I said.

"Hang the Gladwell pamphlet," said the vicar. "Whoever stole the pesky thing is welcome to it. Lilian, I think we might risk a glass of sherry to celebrate this very special occasion."

Lilian fetched the bottle and I raised my glass with the others. But even as I toasted our collective deliverance, I couldn't shake the notion that Brother Florin was still out there somewhere, with the Gladwell pamphlet securely in his possession, laughing at me.

23.

"For God hath not given us the spirit of fear, but of power." The vicar looked down from his pulpit at the record-breaking crowd that filled Saint George's pews and spilled through the open doors into the churchyard. "Those words may sound familiar to some of you. They were printed on a flyer advertising a rally scheduled to take place in our village today. They can also be found in the second epistle of Paul the Apostle to Timothy— chapter one, verse seven, to be precise." He lifted a harvest-gold sheet of paper from the lectern and gazed at it sadly. "I regret to say that whoever used Saint Paul's words on the flyer was far from precise." He held the sheet of paper at arm's length, then slowly and deliberately tore it in half.

A shocked murmur rumbled through the congregation, followed by a handful of isolated snickers as all heads turned toward the front row, where Peggy Kitchen sat, dwarfing Jasper Taxman, who huddled beside her. Peggy's nostrils flared at the sound of tearing paper, and her posture became noticeably more erect, but her pointy glasses never swerved from the pulpit.

"To understand Saint Paul's words, we must read them as they are written." The vicar placed the torn sheet on the lectern, raised a heavy Bible in one hand, and declaimed, with dramatic emphasis, "For God hath not given us the spirit of fear, but of power, and of *love,* and of a *sound mind.*" He returned the heavy Bible to the lectern. "The author of the flyer had distorted Saint Paul's meaning by emphasizing power at the expense of love and wisdom. Yet we all know that power alone is an abomination. Power must be tempered by love, and by intelligent thought, if it is to be used in the service of God and of mankind."

Peggy Kitchen didn't flinch as an approving growl surged through the church, but Jasper Taxman's shoulders drooped an inch or two. I glanced over to see Bill's reaction, but he was gazing at the vicar speculatively, as though wondering where the sermon would go next.

"Precision is vital," the vicar continued, "whether one is quoting sacred texts or speaking to one's neighbor. A lack of precision can lead to grave misunderstandings, which can lead in turn to dissension and discord."

"Ah," Bill said under his breath. "Here it comes."

"I stand before you today," the vicar intoned, "hoping to clear up one such misunderstanding. . . ."

Not one sneeze, cough, or hesitantly cleared throat interrupted the vicar's progress as he guided his flock through the confusion caused by Sally's misreading of Katrina's dummy grant proposal. He mentioned no names. He made no direct accusations. But he made it radiantly clear that, contrary to popular belief, Adrian Culver would be out of the schoolhouse in two weeks' time.

"There is not, nor has there ever been, a single valid reason to believe that our beloved festival might be canceled," he concluded. "The Harvest Festival, during which we will celebrate the glorious bounty our Lord had be-

stowed upon us, will proceed *on schedule, as planned, without fail.* I urge all of you to participate *wisely* and in the
spirit of *love.* In the name of the Father . . ." Through-
out the blessing, the vicar kept his gaze fixed on the wall
painting of Saint George, as though communing with a
fellow dragon-slayer.

Bill bent his head close to mine. "Let's stick around to
offer our support after the service."

I nodded but suspected that the vicar would do just fine
without us. I'd never seen him look so carefree, or so sure
of himself. He conducted the rest of the service with an
unaccustomed bounce in his step and beamed on his
parishioners as they streamed out of the church in a chattering, boisterous swarm.

Peggy Kitchen and Jasper Taxman were the last to leave.
A handful of villagers lingered in the churchyard, but the
prudent majority had hastened down the lane. Bill and I
pushed the strollers within earshot of the west porch and
awaited the empress's reaction to the vicar's reprimand.

"God bless you, Mrs. Kitchen," said the vicar before
she had a chance to speak. "Thank you so much for coming to this morning's service."

Peggy clasped her hands across her stomach and threw
her shoulders back. "I suppose you know what you're
talking about."

"Yes, yes, I assure you, Mrs. Kitchen," said the vicar,
with a merry laugh, "it's quite irrefutable. I'm sure you're
as pleased as I am to learn the truth behind the scurrilous
gossip that's been plaguing our community."

"Yes." Peggy nodded. "Very pleased indeed." Her eyes
narrowed knowingly behind her pointy glasses as she
leaned toward the vicar. "But what's all this about a burglary at the vicarage? More scurrilous gossip?"

"Ah." The vicar's smile wavered as he strained to formulate an honest, noninflammatory answer.

Lilian came swiftly to his rescue. "Something is missing from the vicarage," she stated firmly, "but we can't say positively that it was stolen. It's entirely within the realm of possibility that the item was misplaced. Teddy's so dreadfully absentminded."

The vicar winced at his wife's unorthodox interpretation of the truth and quickly changed the subject. "Will we see you at Rainey's birthday party?"

Peggy drew herself up. "You will," she said. "And it had better be something special, or Sally Pyne'll have her work cut out explaining why she missed church on a Sunday. You leave it to me, Vicar. I'll straighten her out. Come along, Jasper."

As Peggy sailed toward the lane, with Jasper trailing meekly in her wake, Bill and I pushed the strollers to the church's doorstep. Lilian bent to greet the twins, but the vicar gazed mournfully skyward.

"Dear Lord," he murmured, "I beseech Thee to keep Mrs. Kitchen's temper in check until little Rainey's birthday party is over and the grand reopening of Mrs. Pyne's tea shop is complete."

A handful of villagers, peeping out from behind tombs, chorused, "Amen."

Before heading to the cottage, Bill and I paused at Briar Cottage, to have a word with Miranda Morrow, and at the pub, to speak with the Peacocks. Miranda roared with laughter when she heard what Sally and Katrina had been up to in the meadow, but she could add nothing more to her description of the mysterious hooded figure she'd dubbed Brother Florin.

"I can only tell you that he hasn't been back," she said. "Mr. Wetherhead would have been over here like a shot if he'd spotted the ghost a second time." Her eyes twinkled mischievously as she added, "Am I to assume that Brother Florin moonlights as a burglar?"

"You've heard about the burglary?" I said, surprised.

"I'll wager the entire county's heard by now," she said. "The woman who runs the tearoom was delivering the news door-to-door this morning—as a public service, to alert us to the danger in our midst." She touched my arm. "Don't worry, darling, I didn't breathe a word about our ghost, but I'll ring you if he shows up again."

The Peacocks, too, had heard about the burglary but not about Sally's antics in the meadow. Though I broke it to them gently, it still came as a blow.

"Torches and track shoes?" Christine repeated dully. "No aliens at all?"

"I'm sorry," I said. "Anyone could have made the same mistake, with the fog and the noise of the river confusing things."

"In many ways," Bill said consolingly, "I find it easier to believe your story than to imagine Sally Pyne running in place."

Dick put a beefy hand on Christine's shoulder. "It's better to find out now, Chris. What a pair of chumps we'd've looked if we'd found out *after* we'd put up the new sign."

"I suppose you're right." Christine gazed wistfully from Rob's face to Will's, then turned and went back into the pub.

"Never mind," said Dick, stepping away from the door. "Once Chris remembers Martin's promise to come home for the Harvest Festival, she'll perk right up." He glanced cautiously over his shoulder before adding, "I don't mind telling you that I'll be glad to chop that new sign into kindling. Never did like the dratted thing."

A banging noise coming from the tearoom reminded me of Jasper Taxman's platform and my near escape from dodging rotten eggs. The platform was still standing, though denuded of its bunting and its purpose. The tearoom, by contrast, was a beehive of activity. Its windows remained shrouded in obscurity, but shouts issuing from the open doorway indicated that preparations for the day's festivities were under way.

"Two hours to go," said Bill. "Home?"

"Home," I replied.

We headed back to the cottage to have a light lunch, wrap the tiger in striped paper, and change from our Sunday best into lighter clothing. The weather was muggier than ever. Rain, as Adrian had predicted, was in the offing. I hoped it would stay dry until after the party.

While we dressed the boys in their birthday finery, I told Francesca about the mythical Culver Institute. She received the news with outward calm but betrayed her inner turmoil by putting Will's socks on inside out.

"So there's to be no museum in Finch," she murmured.

"There never was," I said. "Adrian was telling the truth all along."

"And he'll be gone in two weeks?" she said, fumbling with the snaps on Rob's romper suit.

"Lock, stock, and barrel," I confirmed. "Just as he promised from the beginning."

When we were ready to go, I took charge of loading the boys into their car seats and left the less breakable baggage to Francesca. She sat in the back, between the twins, staring abstractedly out of the window, but when we pulled into the square she snapped to attention.

"Holy mother of God," she murmured faintly.

"Good grief," muttered Bill, killing the engine.

I, for once, was speechless. In the past two hours the square had been transformed into a cross between a circus and the Colosseum. Sally's familiar collection of wobbly tables and mismatched chairs had been marbelized, gilded, and placed among a half-dozen balloon-covered pillars intended, I surmised, to represent the Forum. Katrina, Simon, and assorted other guests crowned with papier-mâché Roman helmets brandished cardboard-and-foil swords beneath a fluttering flock of pennants strung from the balloon pillars to the war memorial.

A pair of cylindrical concrete pillars, painted blue and garlanded with plastic-looking greenery, flanked the tearoom's doorstep and supported a freshly painted sign.

"The Empire Tearoom SPQF," I read aloud. "SPQ . . . F?" I looked at Bill. "For the Senate and People of . . . Finch?"

Francesca began to quake with suppressed laughter. "Mama bloody mia," she managed, gasping, "if only Papa had lived long enough to see this . . ."

She'd scarcely finished speaking when Rainey passed us, bouncing precariously across the cobbles in a gilded, goat-drawn chariot. The birthday girl was dressed in a snow-white toga, with a wreath of laurel leaves upon her head, a pair of gold-colored armlets clasped about her upper arms, and, incongruously, her usual grubby sneakers on her feet.

Sally had started her fitness program too late to alter the way she filled her toga, but she didn't seem a bit self-conscious as she carried a tray of pastries from guest to guest. Like Rainey, she was adorned with laurel wreath and armlets, but instead of sneakers she wore a pair of thin-soled gold sandals with crisscrossed straps that climbed almost to her knees.

Bill rubbed his chin. "It's the right costume for this weather," he allowed.

I reached for the door handle. "Come on. Let's wish Rainey a happy birthday. If we can catch her."

No one had a better time at Rainey's birthday party than Rainey. When she was finally persuaded to give the goat a rest, she flew from table to table, introducing all and sundry to her tired-looking parents and her placid, brand-new baby brother, Jack. She urged the Pym sisters to tuck into her gran's Hadrian cakes and recommended the Pompeii puffs to the Peacocks, but she slyly snatched all of the Constantine creams for herself. Sticky-fingered and chattering gleefully, she "accidentally" tore the paper from her tiger before the candles on her stunning, two-tiered birthday cake had been lit.

If I had any lingering doubts about the possibility of love at first sight, they were laid to rest by the look on Rainey's face when the tiger emerged from his wrappings. Her chattering stopped midstream, and she sank slowly to the ground, as though her knees had gone too weak to support her. A hush fell over the square as people gathered to see what had tamed the tornado.

Rainey stared down at the tiger for what seemed the longest time. Then she looked up, smiling brilliantly, and gazed directly at me.

"Edmund Terrance," she said, as though answering a question. "His name is Edmund Terrance."

After that, the afternoon became a blur of birthday games, which Rainey won; birthday cake, which Rainey gorged on; and birthday presents, none of which, I noted complacently, held a candle to Edmund Terrance. The party was beginning to wind down when Peggy Kitchen brought it back to life by mounting Jasper Taxman's platform and calling for everyone to gather round. I left Bill with the boys, at Rainey's table, and sidled over to Lilian Bunting, who surveyed Peggy's performance anxiously.

"My friends," Peggy boomed, when the crowd had quieted, "it has come to my attention that a valuable historic brochure sort of thing, belonging to the vicar, was stolen from the vicarage last Sunday night."

Lilian closed her eyes. "Drat Sally Pyne," she muttered.

"I'd like to point out," Peggy thundered, "that it was the theft, and not my flyer, that caused the trouble that's been plaguing our village all week."

Lilian's mouth fell open. "What *can* she mean?"

"She doesn't want to take the blame for stirring everyone up," I murmured, "so she's found a conveniently anonymous scapegoat."

"I'll do whatever it takes to bring the miscreant to justice," Peggy proclaimed. "If anyone has useful information, you can leave it with me or Mr. Taxman at the Emporium. Thank you."

There was a moment of silence, broken by the sound of a scuffle in the vicinity of Rainey's table. I turned just in time to see the birthday girl pin young Paolo Sciaparelli, one of Francesca's numerous nephews, to the ground.

"You give it back," she cried. "It's meant for Dr. Culver."

"You're a liar!" Paolo roared. "You stole it from my aunt!"

Rainey shook the boy until his teeth rattled, then pounced on a small object that dropped from his splayed fist. She sprang to her feet and ran over to stand, panting, before Adrian and Francesca.

"I didn't steal it," the little girl insisted. "I found it when I was helping Emma, and I was going to give it to you, Dr. Culver, to put in your museum, only I wanted to keep it for luck in the chariot races."

"Show me what you've found, Rainey," said Adrian.

Rainey held her hand out flat and I saw that she was holding a bronze medallion identical to the one hanging from the thong around Francesca's neck.

Francesca snatched the *phalera* from Rainey's hand. "Where did you find this?"

Rainey backed away, cowed by Francesca's grim expression. "On the vicar's back steps," she said, "when I was helping Emma carry flowerpots."

Francesca stared down at the *phalera,* then whispered, loudly enough for me to overhear, *"Annunzia."* She looked up at Adrian. "I must go to Hodge Farm."

I leaned toward Lilian. "Who's Annunzia?"

"Annie Hodge, our daily," Lilian replied. "Her maiden name was Annunziazione Sciaparelli. She's Francesca's youngest sister. Annunzia is short for—"

I gripped her arm. "Your cleaning lady is Francesca's *sister?"*

Lilian nodded. "They've been at daggers drawn ever since Burt married Annie."

I felt the world tilt slightly on its axis. "Francesca's *sister* married Burt Hodge?"

"I thought you knew," said Lilian.

"How could I know? No one ever tells me anything." I scrambled after Francesca, who was already climbing into the Mercedes. "Wait! You're not going to Hodge Farm without me! Bill," I called, as I dashed past Rainey's table, "look after the boys!"

24.

Hodge Farm sprawled across its hilltop as though washed ashore by the sea of waving grain. Slate-roofed stone barns and graineries mingled with fiberglass machine sheds and rusting outbuildings fabricated from corrugated iron. Hodge Farm, like Finch, was not an artist's dream of rural beauty. It was a working farm, concerned with substance rather than appearance.

The long drive to the main house was wide and straight, to accommodate the spreading wings of combine harvesters, and broad wagons piled high with baled hay. It ascended the hill, hemmed in by rustling walls of sun-parched barley and ended at a dusty yard littered with farm implements. The farmhouse might have been another barn—no effort had been made to prettify it.

"Why have we come here, Francesca?" Adrian asked, as we pulled into the farmyard. He'd clambered into the Mercedes after me and wedged himself between the boys' car seats in the back. Francesca hadn't challenged his right to come along, and I'd been glad of his company. I found her fierce silence unnerving.

Francesca glanced at the *phalera* in her hand. "My sister

may know something about the theft at the vicarage." She shut off the ignition and turned to me. "Now tell me all about this stolen pamphlet. Be quick about it."

I had to raise my voice to be heard above the savage barking of a gigantic crossbred dog whose job, apparently, was to hunt down and kill uninvited guests. His huge paws thumped against my window and his howls rang in my ear as I rattled off all I knew about the Gladwell pamphlet. When I'd finished, Francesca nodded grimly, then got out of the car to confront the hound from hell.

"Hush, Caesar," she muttered.

Caesar hushed.

"Lie down," she said.

Caesar dropped to the ground.

"Good boy," she added, striding toward the farmhouse.

Caesar wagged his stubby tail as Adrian and I edged gingerly past him to join our fearless leader on the doorstep.

A man stood in the doorway. He was short and stocky, with curly brown hair, leathery skin, and mild, blue-gray eyes. He wore a short-sleeved cotton shirt and, despite the close weather, a pair of heavy corduroy trousers and work boots. He greeted Francesca warily.

"Afternoon, Francesca." His blue-gray eyes scanned my face. "Who're your friends?"

"I've not come to see you, Burt," Francesca said. "My business is with Annunzia."

"Annie's resting," said Burt. "Can't you come back another time?"

"My business won't wait." Francesca brushed the sturdy farmer aside and crossed the threshold. "You tell her to show herself in five minutes, or I'm going after her."

Burt rubbed the back of his head, then motioned for

Adrian and me to follow him into a simply furnished front room. A framed print of the Sacred Heart was the only decoration, and the mantelpiece held nothing but a carriage clock. A pair of Windsor chairs sat on either side of the sagging horsehair sofa that faced the hearth, and a time-darkened table of English oak rested beneath the deep-set window. Francesca looked as out of place in the stark setting as a bird of paradise in a monastic cell.

She stood at the oak table, facing the window, as though rejecting the opportunity to survey her sister's home. I closed the front door quietly and stayed beside it, pretending to be invisible, but Adrian went to Francesca's side and gestured toward the horsehair sofa.

"I'll stand," she said.

I got the distinct impression that she'd have stood barefoot on broken glass before she'd sit in her sister's house.

A moment later, Burt returned with his wife. My vision blurred as Annie Hodge merged with Annunzia Sciaparelli. The woman I'd met at the vicarage had been a cleaning lady—an anonymous archetype clad in head scarf, rubber gloves, and loose-fitting duster. The woman who followed Burt into the sparely furnished front room was unmistakably Francesca's sister.

She had the same auburn hair, full lips, and olive skin, but she was built along more delicate, less voluptuous lines. She was also pregnant. She stood with both hands braced against the small of her back and gazed at Francesca tiredly.

"What do you want?" she asked.

Francesca spoke without turning to look at her sister. "You were at the vicarage last Sunday."

"What of it?" said Annie. "I always go there on Sunday, to pick up my pay packet."

"You overheard the vicar and his wife talking about the Gladwell pamphlet," Francesca continued.

"I might have heard something," Annie allowed. "What business is it of yours?"

Francesca turned slowly and fixed her sister with a piercing stare. "You know the Buntings' habits. You know what time they go to bed and what doors they're likely to leave unlocked."

"What if I do?" Annie demanded.

"Look here—" Burt began, but he fell silent when Francesca turned toward him.

"Farm in trouble, Burt?" she asked. "Drought drying up your crops? Must be worrying, with a new baby on the way."

"We'll manage," Annie said.

"You always manage, don't you, Annunzia?" Francesca's lip curled. "You managed to marry my fiancé. You managed to change your name so no one would remember who's daughter you are. I know how you'll manage to pay the bills if there's a bad harvest." Francesca stepped forward. "You stole the vicar's pamphlet. You wanted Dr. Culver to stay. You thought you could make money off him. You were planning to sell Papa's soul for forty pieces of silver."

Annie shook her head in denial. "I never—"

"You're lying. I know you were there, on the library steps. You left something behind." Francesca thrust her fist toward her sister and slowly uncurled her fingers. The *phalera* glinted dully in the palm of her hand.

Annie opened her mouth to speak, but stopped short as the sound of car tires skidding on gravel mingled with Caesar's sudden, raucous barking.

I yelped and skittered sideways as a weighty fist

pounded on the door. Burt reached for the latch, but before he touched it, Peggy Kitchen burst into the room, followed by a remonstrating Jasper Taxman.

"You mustn't," he said, tugging ineffectually at Peggy's arm while keeping a fearful eye on Caesar's slavering jaws.

Peggy tossed Mr. Taxman aside with a flick of her elbow, slammed the door in Caesar's face, and gazed triumphantly from Annie to Francesca.

"You!" she thundered. "You're the ones who robbed the vicarage. I should've seen it coming. Everyone knows you're no better than your father."

Annie looked quickly at Francesca. "Get out of my house," she said to Peggy, the words more a warning than a command. "Leave here—now."

"I will not," Peggy roared. "I'll say my piece and then I'll have the law on you. They never should've let your father stay here, not after all the suffering he caused. They should've locked him up or sent him back or—"

"*Let* him stay?" Francesca's voice was low and as cold as steel. "*Let him?*"

"No, Francesca," pleaded Annie. "Don't—" Annie stiffened as Francesca turned her head, and Peggy fell back a step.

"I know what Papa taught us, Annunzia." Francesca's voice trembled with suppressed rage. "Forget the past, live now and for the future. But the past isn't easy to forget when it's held to your throat like a knife."

"It was your father held the knife," Peggy retorted. "He was a bloody murderer."

"He was a soldier," Francesca snapped. "He was a foolish boy."

"A *boy?*" Peggy repeated, outraged. "Piero Sciaparelli was—"

"—older than the oldest man in Finch long before you

got round to tormenting him." Francesca tossed her head
contemptuously. "That's what war does to boys, Mrs.
Kitchen. It turns them into old men before their time. If
you'd ever bothered to ask I'd've told you that my father
was fifteen when he ran off to join the army. He was eighteen when he came to work for Mr. Hodge. When Italy
surrendered, he was twenty. I can prove it to you now, if
you like. Do you want to see his papers, Mrs. Kitchen?"

"Eighteen?" said Peggy faintly. "Your father was
eighteen?"

"Annunzia," Francesca ordered, "fetch Papa's papers!"

Peggy waved her hand. "No, please, I . . . I believe you."

"You?" Francesca said. "You believe what everyone
knows. But everyone knows *nothing.*" Her expression remained calm, but her dark eyes burned like smoldering
coals. "No one *let* my father stay here, Mrs. Kitchen. He
stayed because he had nowhere else to go." She turned
to face the window. "Papa did go home, once. When
the war was over, he went back. But there was nothing
to go back to. His village had been bombed to rubble by
the Allies." Francesca paused and I saw tears reflected
in the windowpane. "No one had the courage to rebuild.
They said the place was haunted, that at night you could
hear the screaming of the little ones who'd died. But
it wasn't just the children Papa heard. He heard his family, his friends—everyone he'd ever known. He heard all
the voices of home, screaming in the rubble with the
children."

Francesca glanced over her shoulder. "I'm sorry as can
be that you lost your father, Mrs. Kitchen, but people die
in war. That's just the way it is, the way it's always been.
Those who survive can go on being bitter, or they can
choose to forget the past, to live now and for the . . ." Her
voice quavered, then broke. She stumbled blindly past

Peggy Kitchen, threw open the door, and fled the house. Adrian went after her.

Peggy Kitchen touched a finger to her pointy glasses and looked self-consciously around the room. "I don't know what you're all staring at."

"We're staring at a bloody foreigner." Burt Hodge stepped forward and put an arm around his wife.

Peggy recoiled. "A—A foreigner!"

"You're a bad-tempered old cow from Birmingham," said Burt, "which makes you more foreign here than Piero ever was. Why don't you go back where you belong?"

Annie lifted her chin. "I was born and raised here, Mrs. Kitchen. I know what the villagers think of you. You're not wanted in Finch. Go back to Birmingham."

The words buffeted Peggy like an icy wind. Her eyes widened with shock; then, astonishingly, her chin trembled. She quickly mastered her emotions but for a brief moment she'd seemed as vulnerable as a bullied child.

"I . . . I won't stay here and be insulted," she mumbled, backing toward the door. "Come, Jasper."

"One more thing." Burt clomped forward in his heavy boots. "I don't want to hear any talk about Annie or Francesca breaking the law. If I do, I'll sue you for slander before you can say spit. Understand?"

Peggy opened her mouth but couldn't seem to find the right reply. When Jasper Taxman took her arm, she allowed herself to be led from the farmhouse. A car engine roared briefly, then faded into the distance.

Burt and Annie moved together to the window, as if to make sure that their unwelcome guest had departed, then stood in silence, with their backs toward me. I wanted nothing more than to leave them in peace, but there were too many questions still to be answered.

I cleared my throat. "Annie," I said, "I don't know what's going on between you and your sister, but I promised the vicar that I'd try to find out who stole the pamphlet from his library."

"I didn't take it," Annie said.

"But your bronze medallion was found on the library steps," I pointed out.

"The thong broke a couple of weeks ago. I showed it to Mrs. Bunting at the time. I expect the *phalera* fell off when I was sweeping out the library." Annie turned to face me. "I never wanted Dr. Culver to stay. Francesca's wrong about that."

"Why have you been watching Scrag End field?" I asked. "Dr. Culver saw you—one of you—up here with binoculars."

"I asked Burt to keep an eye on Francesca," Annie told me. "My sister's spending too much time at Scrag End. I'd never betray Papa, but Francesca might, if she fell in love with Dr. Culver."

Francesca, too, had spoken of betrayal. She'd accused Annie of planning to *sell Papa's soul for forty pieces of silver.* "I don't understand," I said. "How would Francesca betray your father by falling in love with Adrian?"

"You'll have to ask Francesca." Annie faced the window and peered up at the sky. "Wind's rising," she observed. "I'd say there'll be rain before morning."

"Please God." Burt's arm slipped around Annie's waist. "One good soak'll save the barley."

It was as if a door had closed between us. They would answer no more questions. They wanted me to go. I left the farmhouse quietly, though my thoughts spun as restlessly as the wisps of hay twirled by the freshening breeze. Why were the two sisters so worried about Adrian Culver?

Adrian was sitting on the hood of the Mercedes, his feet braced on the bumper, his elbows on his knees. Francesca was nowhere to be seen.

"She's back there, somewhere," he said, motioning toward the farm buildings behind the house. "She told me not to follow her. She said she needed to be alone." He rubbed his forehead worriedly. "Did you know about her father?"

"Some of it," I said. "Not all."

Adrian slid off of the hood. He took a few hesitant steps toward the outbuildings, then turned back to me. "Go to her, will you? Someone should be with her, and she won't talk to me."

I entered the complex of stone sheds, pens, and byres, softly calling Francesca's name. A few windows were lit in the farmhouse, but the outbuildings were thronged in shadow. Dusk was moving in and the steady breeze brought a few spatterings of rain. I shuddered as cool droplets splashed my arms, and wondered what the farm would be like when winter winds came chasing up the hill to hurl themselves against the stone walls.

I somehow managed to wend my way outside the maze of buildings, to a spot overlooking the wide fields. I picked out the vague shape of Saint George's tower, an oblong smudge against the darkening sky, and the blurry curve of trees where Scrag End lay. When the rain began in earnest, I darted back to shelter in the doorway of a dark and disused stable.

Since my search had proven fruitless, I put my head down and prepared to make a dash back to the car. Then I heard a soft growl. I froze midbreath, too terrified to flee, until I heard, more softly still, the words *Hush, Caesar.*

I slowly turned to peer inside the stable and from the corner of my eye saw a dim halo of light near the floor of

the stall farthest from the door. I crept forward until I saw
Francesca, outlined by the indeterminate glow of a shuttered lantern.

She knelt with one arm draped over Caesar's massive
back, gazing pensively into the stall. She and the dog were
surrounded by debris—boards, flagstones, scraps of burlap sacking. Her hands were filthy; her hair spilled in
auburn waves down her back and hung in tendrils over
her damp forehead. Despite her red-rimmed eyes, she
seemed composed.

Caesar's ears twitched, but he didn't reiterate his warning as I came closer. Francesca seemed wholly self-
absorbed. I stepped over a loose board and around a tilted
flagstone, leaned forward to peer into the stall, and felt my
pulse quicken.

The light from the shuttered lantern danced across an
elaborately carved stone slab. The slab's rosette-filled bor-
der framed a bas relief of a mounted Roman soldier riding
victoriously over a fallen barbarian. The high-stepping
horse seemed to prance in the flickering light, the soldier's
lance to plunge nearer his enemy's throat.

A panel beneath the bas relief contained a Latin in-
scription. I knew enough of the ancient tongue to attempt
a rough translation. "Marcus Petronius," I read aloud,
"son of Lucius, of the Menenian tribe; from Vicenza; a
soldier of the Fourteenth Legion; he lies here." I looked at
Francesca uncertainly.

"Papa found the gravestone many years ago, when he
was fixing the drainage in here for old Mr. Hodge." Francesca's deep-throated murmur twined with the drum of
the pouring rain. "Pietro was my father's proper name,
and Petronius is Pietro, in Latin. Papa's village was in the
Berici Mountains above Vicenza, where Petronius was
born. And both men were soldiers far from home. When

my father found Petronius's grave, it was as if he'd found a brother."

I sank to the floor and put my hand on Caesar's warm neck. "Did he tell Mr. Hodge about it?"

"How could he?" Francesca asked. "Mr. Hodge would've told the world. Then the experts would've come round, poking and prying and digging up Petronius's bones."

"And your father wanted Petronius to rest in peace," I said.

Francesca nodded slowly. "That's why Petronius let my father find him. Fools like your Mr. Gladwell looked high and low, but Petronius waited for someone like Papa, someone who would protect him, guard him, make sure no one disturbed his resting place." Francesca lifted the lantern and held it closer to the bas relief, to illuminate a carved medallion on the soldier's breastplate.

"Your *phalera*," I murmured. "It's a copy of Petronius's."

"Papa gave me the bronze *phalera* when Burt and I became engaged." Francesca placed the lantern on the floor. "I was supposed to marry Burt and become Petronius's guardian."

"But Burt fell in love with Annie," I said, "and the job went to her."

"I refused to give up my *phalera*," said Francesca, "so Papa made another—the one Rainey found at the vicarage." She hesitated, then went on steadily. "I thought Annunzia might have stolen the pamphlet to keep Adrian nearby."

The faint light of understanding began to shimmer. "You thought Annie would show the grave to Adrian, if the harvest failed. You thought she might make enough money from the find to carry the farm through to next year."

"I don't think it anymore." Francesca brushed a tendril of hair back from her damp forehead. "Hearing Mrs. Kitchen made me see that I've been angry with Annunzia for far too long. It's no good, holding grudges. It makes you blind and stupid."

"Just like Mrs. Kitchen," I put in.

Francesca managed a rueful smile. "After I came out here and had a think, I realized that Annunzia loved Papa as much as I did. She'd never betray his secret."

"She's worried that you might," I said gently.

Francesca's rueful smile faded. "Yes," she said, her dark eyes clouding over. "It's no good, keeping secrets from your husband."

And that, I realized, with heart-wrenching clarity, was why both sisters were worried about Adrian Culver. Francesca was falling in love with an archaeologist, an expert in Romano-British culture. If she married Adrian, she'd be faced with an impossible question of loyalty. Would she lie to her husband about Petronius's grave, or would she betray her father's secret?

"Francesca," I said, "Adrian loves you. If you explained things to him, I'm sure he'd respect—"

"He might," she said heavily. "Then again, he might not." She reached up and began to pin her hair back in place. "Let's cover it up. Will and Rob will be wondering where their mother's got to."

It took us no more than ten minutes to conceal the gravestone beneath layers of sacking, boards, and flagstones. We tamped dirt between the flags, covered them with straw, and gave Caesar leave to romp around the stall. Francesca blew out the shuttered lantern and hung it on a hook near the door. I let her lead the way back to the Mercedes.

Adrian was waiting for us in the farmyard, not sitting

inside the Mercedes but pacing beside it, soaked and shivering. The only time he'd availed himself of the car's shelter had been to answer the telephone.

"The Pyms gave Bill and the boys a lift back to the cottage," Adrian reported, through chattering teeth.

Francesca spent most of the return journey scolding Adrian for being too stupid to get in out of the rain. I wasn't surprised when she asked to be dropped off with him at the schoolhouse, but I was astonished when he pulled her into his arms on the doorstep.

Francesca's long hair tumbled once more down her back, and the rain soaked through her shirtdress, but she clung to Adrian as though she never intended to let him go. Chastely averting my eyes, I left her to it. There'd be gossip about them now, I thought, smiling contentedly, and this time it was likely to be true.

25.

Rain pattered on the slate roof, gushed through the copper downspouts, and splashed in its own puddles on the flagstone walk. It danced on the leaves of the lilac bushes and ran in branching rivulets down the living room's bow window. The long dry spell was over.

I sat cross-legged on the window seat beside Francesca and watched a raindrop skitter down a diamond pane. I was finding it difficult to concentrate on the trivial task I'd concocted to pass the time. Francesca asked me for the ball of twine and I passed it to her.

"You think ten each will be enough?" I asked, eyeing the stack of parenting magazines in Francesca's lap.

Francesca wound the twine around the stack. "Ten'll be plenty. Price 'em at five pence apiece and they'll fly off the table."

I handed her the scissors. "I don't know who'll buy them, even at five pence. Will and Rob seem to be the only children under thirty in Finch."

Francesca snipped the twine on her bundle and tied it off in a neat bow. "You never know. Folks with children may come from other villages. And my sister-in-law's got enough little ones to start a cricket club. You just put these out on a table during the festival and see what happens." She bent to place the bundle in the cardboard box beside the playpen.

I'd given Francesca every opportunity to tell me what, if anything, had passed between her and Adrian after I'd dropped them off at the schoolhouse the night before, but she'd been maddeningly discreet.

She'd returned to the cottage long after Bill and I had gone to bed, performed her morning duties with her usual efficiency, and kept her mouth determinedly shut. I'd so far resisted the urge to hold the scissors to her throat and force her to talk, but my patience was wearing thin. I owed it to the boys, I told myself, to find out if their nanny would be around much longer.

I picked a magazine at random and leafed through it casually. "You've taught me more in one week than the so-called experts taught me in nine months."

"I've taught you nothing you didn't know already," said Francesca. "All you needed was to relax a bit and realize what you knew. Young mothers need to take a break now and again. Used to be you could leave the kiddies with Grandma or an auntie, but it's not so simple nowadays."

"The boys' grandmas are dead," I said, "and I'd rather toss my babies into a tank filled with piranhas than leave them with Bill's aunts. But I take your point." I closed the magazine. "It's been a queer sort of break, though. Most people would spend a weekend at the seaside. I ran around, trying to find a burglar. And I didn't even manage to do that."

"You're not giving up, are you?" asked Francesca.

I shrugged. "I don't know what else to do. Sally Pyne didn't do it. Katrina Graham didn't do it. Adrian certainly didn't do it, nor did your sister. I don't know who else would have wanted to steal the pamphlet."

"Something'll turn up to point you in the right direction." Francesca smiled serenely and turned to gaze out of the window. "Sometimes the answer comes along when you've stopped looking."

I compared the calm, self-possessed figure on the window seat to the haggard, frantic woman I'd encountered in the stable. Was she talking about the burglary, or had she solved a far more interesting mystery?

"You know," I said, wrapping a length of twine around my finger, "if you decide that you have to move on, for any reason, we'll be fine."

Francesca's smile widened. "I won't be going anywhere soon, Lori."

I looked up in confusion. "Did you tell Adrian about Petronius's grave?"

Francesca chuckled. "I didn't have to. He'd already guessed that there'd been a villa on the hill. The topography fits the profile, he said, and where there's a villa, there's almost always a grave."

"Has he agreed to keep your secret?" I asked.

"Can't get funding for every dig in Britain, he told me." Francesca's dark eyes were twinkling. " 'Specially if you don't apply for it."

Francesca glowed with the unmistakable inner radiance of a woman who'd found her heart's desire. I couldn't for the life of me figure out why she'd choose to go on working as a nanny when she could be sailing off into the sunset with the man she loved.

"Then why in God's name are you staying here?" I demanded.

Francesca toyed with a snip of twine. "I need time to

make amends with Annunzia. And I'm old-fashioned. I believe in long engagements."

I thought I heard the sound of trumpets in the pouring rain. I looked out of the window, smiling broadly, just in time to see a delivery van pull into my driveway.

Stan's pamphlet had arrived. I tipped the damp delivery-man and opened the padded envelope in the living room. A note from Stan made it very clear that the collector in Labrador wanted his precious sample back as soon as possible and in pristine condition. I seriously considered returning it untouched, but decided against it. Stan had gone to a lot of trouble to obtain it, as a favor to me. The least I could do was take a look.

The pamphlet was entitled *Holding Fast*. It had buff-colored wrappers and sixteen leaves, measured five by seven inches, and was hand sewn. It had been printed in 1874. Unfortunately, as Stan had warned, it had nothing to do with archaeology. I felt defeated.

"Pathetic, isn't it?" I said, after showing the pamphlet to Francesca. "It's all I have to show for my efforts this week."

Francesca attempted to cheer me up. "Why don't you take it over to the vicarage?" she suggested. "Mrs. Bunting'd like to see it, I'm sure. It might even help her with that parish history she's been writing."

I glanced out at the rain-washed driveway. I had little doubt that Lilian would enjoy seeing another Gladwell pamphlet, even if it wasn't the duplicate she'd hoped for. I had even less doubt that she'd like to hear a more complete account of the confrontation at Hodge Farm than the one I'd given to her over the telephone after breakfast.

I slipped the pamphlet inside the padded envelope and reached for the phone. If the Buntings were at home, I'd head for the vicarage.

* * *

Bundled bulkily in a brown duffel coat, Jasper Taxman raised his crowbar to greet me as the Mini splashed across the slick cobbles. Peggy Kitchen had evidently ordered Mr. Taxman to dismantle the platform he'd built for the rally that never was, and Mr. Taxman had, as usual, obeyed. The rain streamed from his coat as he pried another board loose and tossed it aside.

Lilian welcomed me with a batch of lemon bars still warm from the oven and a pot of herbal tea to chase away the chill. I welcomed the opportunity to conduct a silent taste test. Her lemon bars were tangy, I decided, but mine were sweeter. I recalled the heap of sugar Dick Peacock had shoveled into his medicinal tea and concluded that if he judged the final contest, I was a shoe-in for the blue ribbon.

It was surprisingly easy to clear Annie of the burglary without mentioning Petronius's grave. I told Lilian that Annie and Francesca disagreed on many things, but both shared a strong aversion to archaeology.

"It's a superstition they picked up from their father," I said, knowing Francesca would forgive me. "If Annie had taken the pamphlet, she wouldn't have hidden it. She'd have brought it straight to Adrian, just to get rid of him."

We heard the front door open and close, then the rustle of an umbrella being shaken. A few moments later the vicar came into the library, carrying his wet shoes in one hand. He placed the shoes on the hearth to dry, then settled into his armchair to hold his stockinged feet to the fire and sip a cup of tea.

"I've just returned from the Emporium," he announced. "There's something wrong with Mrs. Kitchen. I've never seen her looking so subdued."

"Maybe she feels let down," I offered. "Her whole campaign to oust Adrian from the schoolhouse was a waste of time."

"A storm in a teacup," the vicar agreed. "Thank heavens she'll soon be gone. I must say that I feel sorry for the residents of Little Stubbing. They don't realize that their peaceful days are numbered."

"Before I forget . . ." I took *Holding Fast* from the padded envelope and handed it to Lilian. "This is the pamphlet I mentioned on the phone, the one Dr. Finderman sent on from the collector in Labrador."

"How interesting," said the vicar, leaning forward in his chair. "It's remarkably similar to the pamphlet that was stolen, isn't it, my dear?" The vicar paused before repeating, a bit more loudly, "My dear?"

"Yes, Teddy," said Lilian distractedly. "Remarkably similar." She crossed from the couch to her worktable and began searching through her papers. I noted with amusement that she'd added the collected works of Peggy Kitchen—the harvest-gold flyers trumpeting the festival, the petition, and the rally—to the rest of the historical documents.

The vicar rose from his armchair and went to stand behind his wife, who was examining the pamphlet with a magnifying glass. "What is it, Lilian?"

"It may be nothing," she said. "But I would value Lori's professional opinion."

I crossed quickly to the table as Lilian pushed aside everything but Peggy's flyers and *Holding Fast*. She switched on her work lamp, then stood back.

"Am I imagining things?" she asked. "Or am I seeing yet another striking resemblance?"

I opened *Holding Fast* to the title page and compared it to the flyers. "They're all printed in Caslon—that's a style of type introduced in England in the early eighteenth century. It's been popular ever since. But I don't see . . ." I hesitated, then reached for the magnifying glass.

I bent low for a closer examination. "It's not just the same typeface," I said. "It's the same font—the same set of type. Look . . ." I pointed from the *H* in *Harvest* to the *H* in *Holding*. "The crossbar's got the same hairline fracture. The *F*s are identical as well. See?" I tapped the words *Festival* and *Fast*. "Same faded serif, where the type's worn down. And there's a matching nick in two of the lowercase *T*s."

I passed the magnifying glass to the vicar. Either Lilian had sniffed out the biggest coincidence in the history of printing, or Peggy Kitchen and Cornelius Gladwell had used the same font for their printing projects. Jasper Taxman had mentioned that Peggy had no photocopier, but it hadn't occurred to me to ask if she used a Victorian printing press instead.

"What happened to Cornelius Gladwell's personal possessions?" I asked, turning to Lilian.

"I believe they were auctioned off." She rifled through a file box. "Yes, here it is," she said, pulling out an index card covered with handwritten notes. "They were auctioned off by Harmer's Auction House in 1901."

"Harmer?" said the vicar, laying aside the magnifying glass. "Isn't that the name of the fellow who used to own the Emporium?"

"Yes," said Lilian. "His father owned the shop before him and conducted auctions as a sideline."

"He must have kept the Gladwell printing press for himself," said the vicar. "It's probably in Mrs. Kitchen's back room right now." He chuckled. "Just imagine, keeping the old thing running all this time . . ."

Lilian returned the card to the file box and glanced at her wristwatch. "Why don't we pay a visit to Mrs.

Kitchen's back room, Teddy? There's plenty of time before evensong, and I'd like to find out if Mr. Harmer's father bought anything else belonging to Mr. Gladwell."

"Like his papers?" I asked, following her train of thought. "Do you really think that the other nine copies of *Disappointments in Delving* might be in Peggy's back room?"

"It would explain why Dr. Finderman hasn't been able to locate them," Lilian said reasonably. She switched off the work lamp and headed for the hallway. "Apart from that, I have a small score to settle with Dr. Culver. He's been very polite about it, but I'm quite certain that he thinks Teddy and I invented the Gladwell pamphlet in order to pacify Mrs. Kitchen. It would please me greatly to prove him wrong."

Moments later, we were bundled in raincoats and heading down Saint George's Lane for the Emporium. I would never have admitted it to the Buntings, but I was thrilled at the prospect of getting a peek inside Peggy's back room.

We'd gone no more than ten yards from the vicarage when we ran into Miranda Morrow hastening up the lane toward Briar Cottage. Mr. Wetherhead limped along behind her, planting his cane with care on the rain-slicked road and glancing over his shoulder. When he saw me, he turned scarlet and quickly lowered his gaze.

"Well met," said Miranda. Raindrops spangled her ankle-length black cloak and slithered down Mr. Wetherhead's aluminum cane. "George and I were just about to ring you."

"Why?" I said.

Miranda's eyes danced as she replied, "We've had a daylight encounter with Brother Florin."

"You've seen him again?" I exclaimed.

"I'm sorry to say that we have." Mr. Wetherhead seemed

very much annoyed. "If I'd known about the burglary, I might not have made such a stupid mistake. But it seems I let my imagination run away with me."

"Brother Florin?" said the vicar. "Who is Brother Florin?"

Miranda cocked a beckoning finger. "Come along, Mr. Bunting, and I'll show you." Without another word she led us to the edge of the square and pointed toward Kitchen's Emporium.

"There he is," she said. "Large as life—and I don't mean afterlife."

"Oh my God," I murmured as Jasper Taxman fastened the hood on his duffel coat.

26.

"Don't try to skate around it," Mr. Wetherhead said heatedly as Mr. Taxman listened calmly to our accusations. "I'd know the shape of that coat anywhere. It's exactly like Paddington Bear's."

"Sorry, darling, but the hood's quite unmistakable," Miranda added.

"You burgled our home?" said Lilian wonderingly.

"I don't understand," said the vicar. "Why would you, of all people, steal the Gladwell pamphlet?"

Mr. Taxman shouldered his crowbar and peered up at the sky. The rain splashed the lenses of his brown-rimmed glasses and trickled down his impassive face like falling tears. "Come in," he said, nodding toward the door of the Emporium.

The jangling sleigh bells gave our arrival a deceptive air of normalcy. Heads turned as we entered the shop, and at least one conversation trailed into silence. Sally Pyne left off chatting with Mr. Barlow, and Emma looked up from scratching Buster's ears, but I scarcely noticed them. I couldn't take my eyes off Peggy Kitchen.

The vicar had described her as subdued, but to me she seemed virtually extinguished. Her madly glittering eyes were dull, her skin was gray with weariness, and she climbed clumsily from her stool behind the cash register, like an elderly woman uncertain of her strength. I looked uneasily at Jasper Taxman. Had he done this to her? Did she know of his betrayal?

She took in our varied expressions and said to Mr. Taxman, "Is something wrong, Jasper?"

"Yes," he replied, with his usual economy of words. He brushed his palms together, then placed them firmly on the countertop and faced Peggy Kitchen. "I stole the Gladwell pamphlet," he said quietly. "I am the burglar."

No one moved. No one spoke. No one seemed to know how to react to such a preposterous declaration. It was as if the vicar had announced, quite casually, that he was the Messiah. Peggy leaned in to peer intently at Mr. Taxman, as though trying to read his lips, and Buster ran to cower between Mr. Barlow's legs, but the rest of us simply stood and stared.

Mr. Taxman turned to face us. "Leave your coats and umbrellas on the counter. I don't want Mrs. Kitchen's stock to suffer water damage." He reached for Peggy Kitchen's hand, led her out from behind the counter, and drew her through the small brown door that led to Xanadu.

"Is he serious?" Emma murmured, coming to my side. "Did he really take the pamphlet?"

"Stick around," I told her. "I'll let you know as soon as I find out."

I trailed behind the others as they entered the back room, but I paused just inside the doorway, feeling like a thief in King Tut's tomb. The back room stretched before me, row upon row of gray metal shelves reaching to the ceiling, dimly lit by dangling bulbs, and burdened with wealth hitherto unimagined.

There were rake handles, broom handles, mop handles, ax handles, buckets and pulleys and trowels. There were belt buckles, shoelaces, sunglasses, candlesticks, flea collars, diapers, and hats. Some shelves were filled with shoe boxes, others with aluminum teapots, all were crammed until they should have bent or broken. There were coils of rope, bags of peat moss, bolts of fabric, tins of paraffin— there was even a ship in a bottle.

The main aisle was so narrow that Peggy had to negotiate it sideways, the floor so crowded that Mr. Wetherhead had to hunt for spaces in which to plant his cane. Xanadu was magnificent, a hoard beyond description.

I heard a collective gasp ahead of me and hurried to catch up with the others. I dodged protruding butterfly nets, ducked under fishing poles, pushed aside the dangling arms of a Day-Glo slicker, and stopped short, dazzled by an incongruous, incredible sight.

I'd reached the back of the room, an open space as neat and tidy as a dentist's office. Lilian and the vicar stood to one side, Miranda and Mr. Wetherhead to the other, peering curiously at a six-foot-tall hand-operated printing press that must have weighed close to a thousand pounds. It was made of cast iron, with gracefully curved claw-footed legs and a walnut-clad lever above the tympan. The yoke's decorative scrollwork bore traces of gilt paint.

"It's an Albion!" I exclaimed. "Is it Cornelius Gladwell's?"

Jasper Taxman finished seating Peggy in a worn swivel chair and turned an inquiring eye in my direction.

"I know a man who owns one," I explained. "My old boss curates the rare book collection at my alma mater.

He's got an Albion in his basement. How many fonts do you have?"

"One," said Mr. Taxman. "The gentleman who acquired the press sold the others. He saw no need to have more than one."

A type case rested on a workbench along the rear wall, a honeycomb of squared-off recesses filled with Caslon upper- and lowercase type, punctuation marks, and furniture for spacing. Beside it, on the bench's level surface, lay a pair of galleys, a composing stick, a wood-handled bodkin, tubes of black ink, and reams of harvest-gold paper. An ink-stained apron hung from the Albion's walnut-clad cast-iron lever.

Mr. Taxman fetched a folding chair for Mr. Wetherhead, then took up a position between Peggy and the Albion. The rest of us gathered in a half circle around him. As we shuffled into our impromptu formation, I heard the faint click of a door latch and the telltale tapping of Buster's claws on the floorboards. We would soon have company, I thought.

"Yes, Ms. Shepherd," Jasper Taxman began, in answer to my question, "Mr. Harmer's father purchased the Albion from the estate of the Reverend Cornelius Gladwell. He used it to print advertisements for his auctions. Mr. Harmer showed me how to use it when I first came to Finch."

"You were always in the shop," Peggy said faintly.

Mr. Taxman looked down at her upturned face. "I wanted to be where you were," he said. "Since you and your mother were billeted with Mr. Harmer, I volunteered to work at his shop."

"Billeted?" inquired the vicar.

"Finch provided sanctuary for a number of evacuees

during the war," Mr. Taxman explained. "Mrs. Kitchen and her mother came from Birmingham, Mr. Barlow and I came from Bristol, and—"

"And I was sent all the way up here from Plymouth." Sally Pyne emerged from the shadowy aisle, with Mr. Barlow and Buster at her heels. "We were evacuated during the blitz, Vicar."

Mr. Taxman didn't flinch at the intrusion. He simply motioned for the newcomers to join the circle. He must have known that it was pointless to exclude them. Whether Mr. Taxman liked it or not, what was said in the back room would soon be broadcast to the farthest reaches of Finch.

Mr. Barlow spoke up. "You used to be back here all the time, Jasper, poking around Mr. Harmer's shelves. I used to think you were wheedling extra rations."

Sally snorted. "I could've told you he was sweet on Peggy. Trotted after her like a lapdog—like Buster follows you."

The acerbic comment didn't fluster Mr. Taxman. "I spent most of my waking hours back here," he agreed smoothly. "It wasn't as well stocked then as it is now."

"There was a war on," Mr. Barlow reminded him.

Mr. Taxman nodded. "As you say, Bill, it was wartime and most of the shelves were bare. Had it been otherwise, I might have overlooked the box of papers Mr. Harmer's father acquired when he purchased the Albion."

We watched with an air of expectancy, like children at a magic show, as Mr. Taxman opened the doors of a cupboard beneath the workbench and withdrew from it a wooden box the size of a picnic hamper. He placed the box atop the workbench and lifted the hinged lid. When he turned to face us, he was holding a slim pamphlet bound in buff-colored wrappers.

"Mr. Gladwell's pamphlets," he said, "helped pass the time on winter days when few customers came to the shop." He handed the pamphlet to Lilian. "I found this one particularly intriguing."

"*Disappointments in Delving.*" Lilian read the title aloud, then turned, almost reluctantly, to the colophon. "The first of ten numbered copies." She looked sadly at Mr. Taxman. "You took this from my husband's desk the day Dr. Culver arrived in Finch."

Mr. Taxman lowered his eyes but said nothing.

"How did you know where to find it?" I asked.

"Annie Hodge came into the shop last Sunday, on her way home from the vicarage. She'd just picked up her pay packet." Mr. Taxman turned to Peggy Kitchen. "Mrs. Hodge came to me, because she knew you wouldn't let her cash a check."

"Always had it in for Piero's family," Sally muttered.

Mr. Taxman ignored the interruption and continued speaking directly to Peggy. "Mrs. Hodge heard you on the square, berating Dr. Culver and his assistants. She said you were wasting your breath because the vicar would soon have Dr. Culver out of the schoolhouse. When I asked what she meant, she said that Mr. Bunting had on his desk a booklet that would force Dr. Culver to abandon his proposed excavation of Scrag End field."

The vicar emitted a forlorn sigh. "You knew, of course, the contents of the booklet."

"I had nine copies of *Delving* in my possession," said Mr. Taxman, gesturing toward the wooden box. "It was reasonable to assume that the tenth had been left in the vicarage. I determined, therefore . . ."

The high point of Mr. Taxman's account of the burglary was his close encounter with Christine Peacock, who'd nearly run him down in her mad flight back to the pub with Grog. He hadn't noticed Sally or Katrina in the meadow. As he described the difficulties of reconnoitering the overgrown garden in the dark, Mr. Wetherhead clucked his tongue in self-disgust.

"That's why you were bobbing and weaving?" he said. "Because of the weeds?"

"There were holes, as well," Mr. Taxman pointed out, "and some extremely vicious thistles. After I'd circled the vicarage twice," he continued, "to assure myself that the Buntings had retired, I ducked into the concealing shrubbery and entered the library through the French doors."

"I thought you'd disappeared," Mr. Wetherhead said glumly.

"There, there," said Miranda, patting his shoulder. "It was a very misty night."

Mr. Taxman resumed. "I took the pamphlet from your desk, Vicar, and brought it to my cottage. The following day, I placed it in the box with the others." He smoothed his tie, then looked around the half circle of expectant faces, like a schoolteacher awaiting questions.

"Why, Jasper?" Peggy Kitchen's voice trembled not with indignation but with bafflement. "Why did you want me to think the festival was ruined?"

"I had to prove to you that Finch still needs you," said Mr. Taxman. "I hoped your battle with Dr. Culver would reawaken your fighting spirit."

Sally Pyne gave a loud guffaw. "Reawaken her fighting spirit?" she scoffed. "Peggy's fighting spirit hasn't had a rest since the day she threw stones at poor Piero."

Mr. Taxman turned a cold eye on Sally. "You may have seen her anger on that day, but you never saw her tears. No one saw her hide back here and weep for her dead father. No one but me." Mr. Taxman flicked a dismissive finger at Sally Pyne and Mr. Barlow. "You thought young Peggy Kitchen had no heart, but I knew better."

Peggy peered up at him, wide-eyed. "I never knew you were watching over me, Jasper."

"I wanted always to watch over you," said Mr. Taxman. "When the war ended and your mother took you away, I thought I'd never see you again. Then Mrs. Farnham wrote to tell me that you'd bought Mr. Harmer's shop, and I knew I'd been given a second chance." He smoothed his brown tie with a trembling hand. "And just when everything seemed to be falling into place, you told me you'd be leaving town as soon as you completed the festival. I thought, if all else failed, I might at least postpone the festival by keeping Dr. Culver here. And the longer it was postponed, the longer I'd have you here with me. I'm too old to uproot my life again. I don't want to move to Little Stubbing. And, as I said, Finch needs you, Mrs. Kitchen. I stole the vicar's pamphlet to prove to you that your work here isn't finished. If you leave, Finch will be incapable of defending itself from outsiders like Dr. Culver."

Peggy bowed her head. "But I'm an outsider, Jasper. Annie and Burt Hodge told me so."

"Hodges got their own back on you, did they?" asked Sally.

"All they did was tell me the truth." Peggy's shoulders slumped. "They made me think of the way I treated Piero, all those many years ago, and the way I've treated his children ever since. I'm none too proud of myself, Jasper. I never knew how much Piero and me had in common. I was too busy being angry to find out."

"You and Piero Sciaparelli?" Sally shook her head in disbelief. "What on earth could a hellion like you have in common with that good, kind man?"

"We both came to Finch to find . . . What did you call it, Jasper? Sanctuary?" Peggy removed her pointy glasses and pinched the bridge of her nose. "Yes. Sanctuary. Finch gave us shelter from the storm." The glasses dangled limply from her fingers as she stared into thin air. "I've tried my best to repay my debt to Finch. I've tried to give the village a bit of life and bring back the old traditions, but all I've really done is interfere. Annie and Burt spoke true, Jasper. Finch doesn't need me."

"You're wrong, Peggy." The words sprang to my lips so unexpectedly that for a moment I thought someone else had spoken. It was strange indeed to feel pity for Peggy Kitchen, stranger still to realize, in a blazing flash of intuition, that Finch needed its hellion far more than it needed anyone else assembled in the back room, including me.

"You're not the only outsider in Finch," I declared. "I came here seeking sanctuary, too. I wanted a peaceful place to raise my sons."

"We, too, sought peace here," said the vicar, putting an arm around his wife, "when I could no longer cope with the demands of my London parish."

"Finch is the perfect spot to write a book," Miranda put in. "Absolutely *no* distractions."

"And we're absolutely useless to the village." I stared from face to face defiantly. "Left to our own devices, we'd enjoy the peace and quiet, but we'd give nothing in exchange. We'd huddle in our houses, hardly speaking to each other, and let the village take care of itself."

"Lori's right," said Lilian. "It's tempting to bury myself in my research."

"Not half so tempting as it is to sink into my armchair," admitted the vicar.

"Peggy won't let *any* of us sink into our armchairs," I

snapped angrily. "She's the one who started the garden fetes and sheepdog trials and morris dancing, and she hounded us until we all joined in. Peggy's trying to turn Finch back into a true village." I crossed to Peggy's side and swung around to face the others. "Do any of you think you could take her place? I know I couldn't."

There was a long silence as the others shuffled, shame-faced, avoiding one another's eyes.

Sally was the first to step forward. "I've been meaning to ask, Peggy, if I could help with the refreshments during the festival. My new line of low-calorie pastries went down very well at Rainey's birthday party."

Mr. Barlow nodded thoughtfully. "I could rig out a few more of those chariots," he said. "We could have races for the kiddies."

"I have a . . ." Mr. Wetherhead quailed as all eyes focused on him, but he gripped his cane tightly and went on. ". . . a train collection. Lori thought it might be nice to let folks have a look at it during the Harvest Festival, but I'd be glad of your opinion, Mrs. Kitchen."

"If you're in need of a fortune-teller," Miranda piped up, "look no further."

The vicar added his voice to the chorus. "I'm so looking forward to the beast blessing," he said, with more charity than honesty. "I can think of nothing more inspirational than to welcome Buster, Grog, and Caesar to Saint George's."

It took Peggy a full minute to find her voice, but when she did, it had a familiar ring. "Don't be stupid, Vicar. Caesar's an RC, just like the Hodges." She brushed the back of her hand impatiently across her eyes and put her glasses on. "But perhaps Annie and Burt would be kind enough to enter Caesar in the dog show. I'll invite them

personally. Come along, Jasper. There's so much to do."
She held a hand out to Mr. Taxman. "And only a bloody
fool would think that I could do it without you."

Mr. Taxman's sunken chest expanded until his buttons
nearly burst. He drew himself up to his full, though average, height, then sank to one knee and pressed his lips to
Peggy's proffered hand. Until that moment, I hadn't truly
believed him capable of a *crime passionnel,* but his gallant
gesture chased all doubts away. Jasper Taxman might be
an unlikely hero, a nondescript knight in dull brown ar-
mor, but I'd learned long ago that handsome princes
came in all shapes and sizes.

Peggy rose to her feet. Her mad eyes sparkled with a
new and lovely light as she turned sideways to maneuver
down the aisle. "I'll be by first thing tomorrow morning to
have a look at these trains of yours, Mr. Wetherhead. And
you know about fortune-telling, do you, Mrs. Morrow?
It'll cost a packet to buy a gypsy tent, but it might be
worth it. What do you think, Jasper? Can we raise enough
money by August to pay for a tent *and* goat-cart races?
I'm sure Sally won't mind donating the food."

Sally's squawk of protest shook the gray metal shelves,
but Peggy forged ahead. I had no doubt that she'd whip
her volunteers into shape, and by August they'd be almost
glad she had.

I sipped my tea and settled the blue journal on my lap.
Bill was reading stories to Rob and Will in the living room,
and Francesca was at the schoolhouse, helping Adrian
prepare a lecture on the many uses of sweet-chestnut
flour. The rain continued to fall steadily, spattering the
windowpanes and drumming on the roof. The study was
comfortably warm and dry, but I'd lit a fire in the hearth,
for the pure pleasure of watching the flames dance.

"It's funny, Dimity. I wasn't all that crazy about Finch in its natural state, but I think I'm going to miss the old wreck, now that Peggy's decided to fix it up."

Perhaps you shouldn't have told her about the man in Labrador.

"It just slipped out. When Lilian said that there were more than a hundred Gladwell pamphlets in the wooden box, I couldn't help remembering Stan's joke about the Lamborghini. Lilian mentioned it to Jasper Taxman, and one thing led to another. . . ."

Peggy had asked me to stick around while she placed her long-distance call to Labrador, but she hadn't needed my help to negotiate the sale of the pamphlets. She could have given Stan a few tips on playing hardball. When I'd left the shop, she and Mr. Taxman had been laying out plans to resod the village green, relay the cobbles on the square, and steam-clean the limestone facades on all of the buildings.

"By the time she's done spending money on Finch," I said, "she'll be lucky to have enough left over to pay for a marriage license."

How is Jasper holding up?

"Splendidly," I said. "He called her Peggy the other day, and asked her politely never to mention Little Stubbing again. He's getting to be a regular tyrant."

It's the first time I've ever heard of a knight fighting battles for a dragon.

"Peggy's a handful," I agreed. "But maybe you need someone like Peggy to move the rest of us along."

You seem to have made that clear to Sally Pyne and the others.

"I suppose I did," I said ruefully, "but I had no right to lecture them. I haven't exactly gone out of my way to get involved in my community."

You've been awfully busy with the twins.

"Yes, and what have I been teaching them?" I asked. "How to stay at home and ignore your neighbors? It's not good enough, Dimity."

It's easy to live in a place. It takes hard work to belong. I assume you're ready for some hard work?

"Not just me," I told her. "Finch is a family affair. Bill's putting on his dancing shoes if I have to hold a gun to his head."

You're more like Peggy Kitchen every day.

I laughed.

And what will you be doing while Bill dances?

I counted on my fingers. "Selling off my parenting magazines to raise money for the church roof fund, helping Mr. Barlow with the chariot races, entering the twins in the Cutest Baby contest, judging the Floral Arrangements Around a Stuffed Animal competition, and baking a blue-ribbon batch of lemon bars." I looked down at the journal. "Well? Do I sound like a true villager?"

A true villager wouldn't go within ten yards of a Cutest Baby contest. I've known riots to break out after the judging.

"But I'm absolutely positive the boys will win," I insisted.

Now you sound like a true villager. There was a pause, and a soft, sighing breeze made the flames sway and flicker. *How I wish I could be there with you.*

"You know what, Dimity?" I took another drink of tea and stared reflectively at the fire. "I think that can be arranged."

Epilogue

Finch glowed like old gold on green velvet. The late-summer sun flowed like honey across the freshly scrubbed stonework and glinted from each blade of grass on the lush, emerald lawn. I sat at my Union Jack–bedecked table in front of Bill's office, with my bundles of parenting magazines and my small tin of coins, and marveled at the changes Peggy had wrought. The empress had made a small fortune from the sale of the Gladwell pamphlets, and she'd invested every penny of it in Finch. Thanks to her, the green was finally living up to its name and the cobbles fringing the square were so smooth and straight that even Mr. Farnham could totter across them unaided.

Emma sat beside me, in a wicker armchair I'd brought from my back garden, and watched while I laboriously totted up my accounts. The sales figures were pathetic—there simply wasn't much demand for parenting magazines in a village full of retirees.

Annie Hodge had purchased three bundles, and Rainey's mother four more, but they'd done so at the behest of Peggy Kitchen, who'd made it her business to see that every facet of the festival had its share of success, however modest. I was grateful for the pity purchases, but they wouldn't do much to swell the church roof fund. My takings would scarcely cover the cost of a cupful of slate nails, unless Derek got them wholesale.

Emma looked closely at the columns of numbers I'd penciled in my ledger, then reached over to shake the tin. "I hope no one does an audit," she commented, "because if I didn't know you were scrupulously honest, I'd swear you were cooking your books."

"This is one book I have no intention of cooking." I lifted the ledger from the table and gave Emma a glimpse of the smooth blue-leather binding. "Like the disguise?"

Emma nearly fell off of her chair. "Is that . . . ?"

Good afternoon, Emma. Aunt Dimity's handwriting showed clearly through the faint pencil marks. *My compliments on the vicarage garden. I enjoyed the lecture tour immensely.*

"Th-thank you." Emma looked furtively around the square and spoke out of the corner of her mouth. "It'll be much better next year. It's still pretty scruffy around the edges."

Emma was, as usual, being too humble. In the past few weeks she'd transformed the vicarage garden from an untamed jungle into an enchanted bower. With Rainey's help, she'd transplanted brightly colored plants from her own greenhouses—blue geraniums, white spirea, pink cranesbill, and mounds of yellow potentilla—into beds bounded by narrow, curving grass paths.

You've created a floral stained-glass window. Very appropriate to the setting. And you were right about the Rosa hemisphaerica. *What a splendid discovery! I hope your tours were appreciated.*

"I think they were," said Emma. "I've raised fifteen

pounds for the roof fund, and I've been around the vicarage so often I feel dizzy."

"Dizzy enough to tell us what Derek's done to the war memorial?" I inquired slyly.

Emma shook her head. "Sorry. My lips are sealed. Peggy would have a fit if word leaked out before closing ceremonies."

"Not even a hint?" I wheedled.

"I've replaced the willows with holly bushes," Emma said, then closed her mouth decisively.

She hadn't told me anything I couldn't see for myself. I glanced over at the circle of neatly trimmed holly bushes, burning to see what lay beneath the swath of black silk that had shrouded the war memorial for the past week. Rumor had it that Derek had carved a new name on the dignified stone cairn, but Peggy had kept such a close watch on the memorial that no one had been able to give an eyewitness report.

"Be that way," I grumbled. "I can wait until closing ceremonies, just like everyone—"

"Mr. Peacock!" Peggy's indignant voice thundered from next door, as it had so many times that afternoon. "If you don't control that hound of yours, I'll have his ears on a plate!"

"Sorry, Mrs. Kitchen." Dick tugged a recalcitrant Grog away from the blue-painted concrete pillars in front of the tea shop.

Sally Pyne looked up from her table. She and Peggy had formed an alliance, of sorts. Sally had agreed to give away the Empire Tearoom's bounty on festival day if Peggy would defend the tearoom's pseudo-Ionic columns from the depredations of Finch's canine contingent.

Peggy hasn't spotted Buster yet, has she?

"Not yet," I murmured.

Let's hope Burt Hodge keeps Caesar on his lead. A dog with his capacity could put quite a damper on the festivities.

"Dimity!" I exclaimed.

Emma nudged me with her elbow. "Careful," she said, but her warning came too late.

Peggy Kitchen had overheard my cry. She left her post at the tearoom and strode over to my table. "Dimity?" she said. "That's the name of the woman who used to own your cottage, isn't it?"

"Yes," I replied. "Emma and I were . . . discussing names for Annie Hodge's baby. I like the sound of Dimity, don't you?"

Peggy favored me with the superior smile of the well informed. "Annie told me the results of her last sonogram. The baby is a boy—a fine, healthy boy. She and Burt intend to call him Piero, after his grandfather. I only hope the child will be able to live up to his name." She peered into my tin, then headed for the schoolhouse, calling over her shoulder, "Not having a very successful day, are you, Lori?"

Dimity's handwriting flew across the page. *There's nothing shameful about second place.*

I looked at the red ribbon lying beside the tin and gritted my teeth. Dick Peacock had awarded the blue ribbon to Lilian's lemon bars, declaring that their tartness made a nice change from the sweetness of the meads he'd been sampling all afternoon. In my opinion, the man had been dead drunk when he'd judged the competition.

The vicar, unlike myself, had had a wholly satisfying day. Adrian's students, under Emma's supervision, had decorated Saint George's aisles with sheaves of wheat, corn, and barley, filled the windowsills with bright-red apples and sprays of red barberries, and wreathed the pillars

with wild hop vines and stringed ivy. I'd helped Emma
dress the font with moss and white asters, and spread the
floor with fresh-cut rushes, in hopes of easing the burden
on the cleanup crew after the beast blessing.

The vicar was way ahead of us, however. He thought
Saint George's looked heavenly in its autumn finery, and
he wasn't about to let any creature, great or small, spoil
the effect. He promptly decreed that the blessing of the
beasts would take place at an open-air altar in the churchyard, and appointed Mr. Taxman the task of keeping the
graveled paths clear of their offerings.

The vicar had raised a cheer during the morning service by publishing the banns of marriage between Peggy
Kitchen and Jasper Taxman. Mr. Taxman had acknowledged the villagers' good wishes with a jaunty lift of his
shovel.

*You were very wise not to enter Rob and Will in the Cutest
Baby contest.* Dimity was still attempting to console me for
the ignominious red ribbon.

"I had no choice," I said. "There was only one prize,
and the boys would have forced a tie." I'd also withdrawn
Reginald from the Floral Arrangement Around a Stuffed
Animal competition to avoid the appearance of partiality.
I hadn't been able to award the blue ribbon to Rainey's
tiger, either, because Rainey had knocked her arrangement onto the schoolhouse floor before the judging had
gotten under way. It was a pity, because everyone who'd
seen Edmund Terrance peeking out from his jungle of
black-eyed Susans and tiger lilies had agreed that he was
the paws-down favorite.

Rainey had lost two of the chariot races to nine-year-
old Paolo Sciaparelli, who'd become her best friend in
Finch. The two of them had spent the rest of the day swip-
ing Constantine creams from Sally's table, derailing Mr.

Wetherhead's trains, and poking their heads under the fortune-teller's tent.

It was hard to say whether Miranda Morrow's contribution to the festival had been well received or not. There was no denying that she'd thrown herself into her role. She'd supplied her own crystal ball and dressed outlandishly in hoop earrings, gold bangles, a fringed paisley shawl, and a stunningly embroidered peasant dress. People had chuckled good-naturedly at her costume, but they'd emerged from her tent looking more thoughtful than amused.

Mr. Wetherhead's trains, on the other hand, had been an unqualified hit. Villagers had lined Saint George's Lane, waiting to get a glimpse of his choo-choos. Bill and Derek had spent the past week helping him to display his collection to its best advantage and had, in the process, gone train-crazy. They used Rob and Will as an excuse to hang around the schoolmaster's house for hours on end, but Emma and I knew which pair of little boys fought over the engineer's cap and which behaved like gentlemen.

"I saw you taking pictures during the morris dancing," Emma said. "Does Bill know you brought the camera?"

I looked at the stage Jasper Taxman had built at the south end of the green, opposite the war memorial, and grinned evilly at the memory of Bill thudding to and fro, bells jangling, hanky fluttering, and ribbons flying.

"I'm planning to surprise him," I said. "You know those Christmas cards, the ones you can have personalized with a family photograph?"

Emma gasped. "You wouldn't."

"I might," I said, "if he calls me Commando Lori one more time."

A roar went up from the crowd of students in front of the pub as Dick uncorked another jug of mead. Christine made no move to stop him. She was too elated to worry about poisoning a crop of budding archaeologists. Martin had come home the night before, to help his parents set up for the festival.

I'm so glad Martin Peacock kept his promise. I've never seen Christine look so happy.

"Speaking of happy . . ." I'd spotted Francesca and Adrian emerging from Saint George's Lane, arm in arm. "I don't know why he doesn't move to Finch. He's here almost every day as it is."

Emma's eyes lit with mischief. "Peggy says they've been canoodling in the churchyard."

"It's probably true," I said, noting the bloom on Francesca's cheeks. "Dimity's an expert at picking champion canoodlers."

Thank you, Lori.

The rented public address system crackled suddenly, and Jasper Taxman's voice came through the static. "Closing ceremonies will commence in five minutes. Would everyone please gather on the green for closing ceremonies. . . ."

Rainey and Paolo rounded people up, like a pair of sheepdogs chivvying a flock. Rainey's parents, along with baby Jack, were neatly tucked in with Paolo's multitudinous brothers and sisters, and Miranda Morrow was brought forth from her tent. Mr. Barlow and Buster, the Peacocks and Grog, Mr. Farnham, the Pyms, and Sally Pyne were coaxed toward chairs Martin Peacock had placed before the stage, while Katrina, Simon, and the rest of the college students flopped unceremoniously on the lawn. To judge by the amount of mead they'd downed, I doubted that many of them would rise again before morning.

Adrian and Francesca joined Burt and Annie Hodge

over by the war memorial, and the vicar sat with Lilian. Bill and Derek peeled off from the throng and headed toward my table, each pushing a stroller. Finally, Mr. Wetherhead came out of Saint George's Lane, followed by a coterie of ardent admirers. The little man seemed slightly intimidated by the amount of attention his hobby had drawn, but not altogether displeased. I sincerely hoped that his mother was rolling in her grave.

"Closing ceremonies will not take place on the stage," Jasper Taxman advised, via the loudspeakers. "Closing ceremonies will take place at the war memorial. Will everyone please turn round. . . ."

There was a flurry of activity while people rearranged their chairs, students scooted into new positions, and the little knot of people who'd gathered near the memorial made room for Peggy Kitchen.

"Thank you," Peggy roared, and the crowd fell silent. "Thank you all for coming to Finch's Harvest Festival. I hope you've had a good time, and that you'll come again next year.

"I'd also like to thank those of you who made this day possible. There's too many to name one by one, but you know who you are, so please give yourselves a big round of applause."

The villagers' polite clapping mingled with the students' heartier cheers and a chorus of enthusiastic barks.

"As many of you know," Peggy continued, "it's Finch's tradition to honor not only those who died for their country, but those who served and lived. They loved their homes enough to go out and do something to protect them. We could all learn a lesson from them.

"A place needs its people. Mrs. Harris'll tell you that a plant needs strong roots to survive. Well, so does a village.

Every single person who lives in our village has to dig into it and plant strong roots, and tend those roots each and every day, or the village'll wither away.

"Sometimes we need a chap like Dr. Culver to dig into our past, to remind us we're part of a family that stretches back as far as anyone can see. Finch has come down to us like a gift from the past. It's up to us to make sure it's fit to pass on to the future.

"You and I, all of us—we have to dig into ourselves, to find the time and energy to keep our village alive and strong. Finch honored its sons and daughters with a memorial because they did something to preserve the place they loved, instead of sitting on their hands and leaving the hard work to someone else.

"Maybe our struggles aren't as monumental as theirs were, but they're every bit as important. They're the everyday battles of ordinary life, the simple slogging that keeps the village young."

Peggy stepped through the encircling holly bushes and stood silhouetted against the black silk covering the stone cross. The sunlight glinted off her pointy glasses, and a soft breeze ruffled her flowered dress. The crowd had gone quite still. Even Rainey stood, gazing solemnly over the recumbent students, her freckled face sticky with Constantine cream, her braids askew. Peggy had brought the whirlwind to a standstill.

Peggy took a deep breath, clutched a handful of black silk, and yanked. As the cloth fell away, a shocked murmur rippled through the crowd. The Celtic cross had not been cleaned. It remained grubby and inglorious, a testament to years of neglect, a mute but potent symbol of what happened when people sat on their hands and left the hard work to someone else.

Peggy cleared her throat. "If ever you need reminding that the little bit you do can make a difference, just rest your eyes on the memorial, and you'll know."

The assembled throng stood as the jury-rigged speakers poured forth the tinny strains of "God Save the Queen." The Harvest Festival was over.

Visitors made their way to the car park, in the field just beyond the humpbacked bridge, leaving the villagers to begin the task of cleaning up. The bustling activity swirled around four motionless figures near the war memorial. Adrian and Burt stood a little ways off, but Francesca and Annie stood within the circle of holly bushes, their arms around each other, gazing at the row of names carved into the grimy stone. I wondered why they lingered when there was so much to do.

I was about to pack up my bundles and cart them off to the Mercedes, when Rob grasped my collar and tugged. I looked down at him, then past him, at the blue journal.

Take me to the memorial, Lori.

"Bill," I said, "let's take Rob and Will to see the memorial."

I stood, with Rob cradled against my shoulder and the blue journal open in my hand. We crossed the square amid the sound of chattering voices and the public address system's vagrant squeals, but as we stepped into the circle of holly, the noises seemed to fall away. Will gave a gurgling sigh and Francesca turned her dark eyes to me.

"Did you know?" she asked softly.

I looked at her blankly. "Know what?"

"About this . . ." Francesca pointed to the only place on the cross where the stone, freshly carved, glowed golden in the late-afternoon sun.

Piero Alessandro Sciaparelli. The name stood out, baroque and musical, strikingly different from the homely

English names carved above it, but it belonged there nonetheless. Piero had served the country of his birth and the country he'd adopted. He'd been willing to die for one, and live fully for the other. Finch's sons and daughters, I knew, would welcome him.

"I had nothing to do with it," I said. "But I think I know who did."

Francesca nodded slowly, then turned to scan the square. "C'mon, Annie. Mrs. Kitchen needs us."

Bill and I followed them into the square, and the noise closed in around us. Thumps, groans, laughter, babies squealing, women shouting, dogs barking—the joyous, raucous sounds of my village, coming back to life.

Lilian's Lemon Bars

Preheat oven to 350° F.   *Makes 20 bars*

¹/₃ cup butter or margarine
1 cup sugar
1 cup all-purpose flour
2 eggs
2 tablespoons all-purpose
   flour

2 teaspoons finely
   shredded lemon peel
3 tablespoons lemon juice
¹/₄ teaspoon baking powder
   powdered sugar
   (optional)

Beat margarine with an electric mixer on medium to high speed for 30 seconds. Add ¹/₄ cup of the sugar. Beat until combined. Beat in the 1 cup flour until crumbly. Press into the bottom of an un-greased 8 x 8 x 2-inch baking pan. Bake in a 350° oven for 15 to 18 minutes or just until golden.

Meanwhile, combine eggs, the remaining sugar, the 2 table-spoons flour, lemon peel, juice, and baking powder. Beat for 2 minutes or until thoroughly combined. Pour over hot baked layer.

Bake in a 350° oven about 20 minutes more or till lightly browned around the edges and center is set. Cool on a wire rack. If desired, sift powdered sugar over the top. Cut into bars. Win blue ribbon.